TRANSIENT

The Transient Trilogy, Book #1

M.K. Parsons

Printed in the United States of America

ISBN 978-0-9964135-0-3

First Edition

Cover Art and jacket design © 2015 by M.K. Parsons
Cover Image by Dmitriy Denysov@123RF.COM
Cover Image by Christopher Campbell

M.K. Parsons
Columbus, Ohio
www.mkparsons.com

For the watchers of the stars.

PROLOGUE

Morris' knife lay, lonely, beside his head, nearly submerged in the puddle of blood. The weapon waited for him to pick it up and return it to its sheath where it belonged, but Morris wouldn't do it. He was dead.

I stared at him, paralyzed. He was the last Protector. There was no one else—only me. A seventeen-year old girl, orphaned as long as I could remember, living underground with a bunch of other kids. Hardly the defender Morris believed me to be.

Roxy, you are so much more than you think you are, he had always said.

Sophie and I found the body in an alley behind an abandoned store near the bunker. Morris had been stabbed.

"He was teasing me today. He told me I'd be the death of him," I told Sophie, though I knew she wouldn't answer me. "He was the closest thing I had to a father."

Sophie's lip quivered and her eyes strained with tears, but she didn't say a word.

We left in a hurry, since I could sense others were near. I was never wrong.

The vacant expression on his white face became a familiar horror in my dreams in the week that followed. When the thought wasn't surreal, unbelievable, it was a chill that wrapped itself around me. It clamped a vice grip on my throat, pressurizing my head until I thought I would explode like a million shards of glass.

I didn't want to live in a world that didn't have Morris in it.

"It's not fair that the only decent man in all of New York City gets murdered," I fumed as Sophie watched me with wide, gray eyes. Maybe part of me hoped she would tell me what to do. "We needed him."

"*I am Sephora of the Transient. I was born to save the past. It is and was and shall be again my duty. We fly the winding loop of time that we may give ourselves for the redemption of our ancestors.*"

That was Sophie's mantra. It made no sense to me, but it was all she would say, in a whisper, in her strange accent and mannerisms. She had said it the night I found her, shivering in the dark of Manhattan's quarantined sector. She had been staring after some dark form that disappeared into the shadows as I turned the corner. I noticed tears in her eyes.

I'd rescued strays from starvation and hypothermia before. I didn't want them to end up in the daily collection of beggars who were fed to the portal at the Crystal Citadel. But Sophie was different. Though she didn't speak a word beyond her mantra, I sensed lightness, as if she could barely keep her feet on the ground. I read intelligence, sharp and focused, in her emotions. I saw them as a painted cloud of impressions that hovered around her.

I saw the same around anybody else. I used to think everyone had this ability, but Morris told me I was the only one, and that my gift had been given to me for the benefit of my people.

Whether it was a gift or a curse, I hadn't decided yet.

"How did you survive out there?" I had asked Sophie the night I found her. The streets were dangerous, ever since Leona had proclaimed herself the *Regal Manager* in 2058, and thrown all her resisters in the portal or shot them down like hunted animals. That was sixteen years ago.

Sophie watched me with focused resolve every day of that week she lived with us in the bunker. She stared at me as I sharpened my knife. As I checked the monitors in the control room. As I yelled at the Domestic Service Robots. She watched me with eyes that reminded me of the ones I saw in the mirror.

"I've always wanted a little sister," I told her the morning of the day she disappeared, observing how her features resembled mine in the way a sibling's might. "But I'm an orphan. So are all the bunker kids."

Our parents had been crushed by Leona. Sophie must have been an orphan as well. What parent would leave her defenseless?

I'd heard the stories about my city, how it had once been a place of peace, where the world gathered to discuss ideas and forge alliances. It was known as a gateway of freedom, when immigrants poured into the city and filtered out into the wild and empty space they called America—the land of the free.

I had never known my city free.

That world was nothing like the overgrown ruins of the Broadway I traveled now, searching for my lost little sister.

If anyone had asked me during the years I was growing up in the bunker, I would have said I was living a nightmare. But the nightmare really started the night I realized Sophie had left the bunker by herself.

And it would only get worse.

ONE

Electricity sparked as I tiptoed on the edge of the computerized street, trying to stay off the sensors. I saw the imprinted log of Sophie's steps, feeling sick when I realized she was headed in the direction of the citadel.

Why was she going against my rules? I told her she was only safe in the bunker. I suspected her pledge of allegiance had her out here. It would be the death of her, and maybe me.

Regardless, I promised Morris I would protect them. I supposed it was as good a day to die as any.

His image flooded my mind like the North Star kept us on track in the night. He had warned me of the dangers outside the bunker. He said there was only one reason worth the risk.

Love.

I rounded the corner and stared up at the dazzling display of reflection and light rising above the streets like a jeweled serpent ready to strike. Feeling vulnerable in the light, I backed toward the wall. I'd never seen the Crystal Citadel in person before. Security feeds or news accounts didn't register the dimensions. I felt tiny. Powerless.

The structure, though immense and foreboding, possessed an

air of delicacy. Elegant iron posts rose up out of the foundation, supporting thousands of glittering crystal windows in tiers of floors, arched in a continuous pattern over the whole of the face of the palace. The windows were like urbane eyes, inspecting the happenings of the city expected to conform to organized style.

I panicked. How could I get past the Peace Implementer outposts on either side of every entrance into the citadel grounds?

Roxy, the time will come when you have to find a way in, and know how to get around. You can't hide in this bunker forever. The day will come when you must leave. You can do it.

Morris had taught me the layout of the citadel. He seemed to know that I would inevitably be here. I could almost sense his thoughts, and I knew he wanted me to do this. I swallowed hard.

"Are you going into the citadel dressed like that?"

A woman stared at me in disgust. She wore a gold wig, a tricorn hat and a brown crepe dress piled high underneath with black crinolines. I almost laughed at her. But she blended in, and I stood out like an ancient, sparking light bulb in my black pants, jacket and army boots.

I pushed back into the shadow of a building until she passed, afraid she would report me to the nearest guard outpost. I was exposed, and I had no idea how to get Sophie out alive.

"I failed before I even started, Morris," I whispered. "I let you down."

Again his words returned to me. *Having courage doesn't mean you aren't scared, Roxy. It means you do what needs to be done, terrified or not.*

I peeked out and saw a HoverBot collecting supplies for the palace. It stopped in front of a grocery near where I cowered in the alley. While the grocer dutifully contributed the required homage, I slipped inside from the back. There was hardly room with all the supplies already stowed, but I managed to stay hidden until the overloaded bot finished its cycle and floated back to the side service entry of the palace.

It must have been dinnertime, or Leona was entertaining,

because the kitchens were a flurry of activity. It was a good thing, because I would have been discovered otherwise. The bot was pushed into the corner and deactivated.

I waited for a few minutes before noticing a kitchen servant's outfit hanging on a peg directly above me. The clothing I quickly donned consisted of a silk gold-and-black-striped blouse, black fashion corset and grey skirt. When I added the black newsboy cap, I felt ridiculous, but everyone else in the kitchen was dressed the same. It seemed stripes were reserved for servants.

I marched to the door as if I belonged there, and hiked down the immense corridor that led to the entry hall. I would have stopped and stared if I could risk it. I was unprepared for the grandeur.

Rich blue and white linen tapestries, edged with purple velvet and held by enormous silver rings, hung with majesty over the arched golden doorway. Five pairs of marble pillars lined the circular room, so thick it would take at least four people holding hands to surround just one of them. They shot up like age-old trees from floor to ceiling, so far above it was hard to judge the perspective. Couches of gold marked the perimeter. A mosaic of gems sparkled under my feet.

Anger boiled. This was how Leona spent the homage money she stole from everyone—from the wealthiest to the poorest. Those with some to spare and those struggling to feed their children each day.

She kept track of taxes and credits with BioTrack devices. Everyone was required to have them implanted in their neck. She passed the trackers off as health monitors and convenience devices, but to be found without a BTD meant the portal. No one avoided her watchful eye.

No one except us.

My fingers itched to grab the laser pistol I'd stowed in the skirt. I'd enjoy watching those tapestries burn. But Sophie needed saving, so I settled for slicing open the back of one of the couches with my knife as I passed by.

I crept down the grand hallway to the throne room. It glowed, spurting out noise of adoring subjects worshiping their queen. I wanted no part of it, but I didn't have a choice. It was an inconvenience to care. If I had any idea how to stop, I would.

I slipped into the back of the room. Marble contrasted the crystal and iron. Blue and white banners hung behind the stage nearly floor to ceiling behind an elaborate throne. The people created a parade of clowns in black, white and brown, members of the royal circus Leona dressed up like her puppets.

I chafed that I'd finally been forced to set foot in that place, putting all the bunker kids in danger. But I shouldn't have lost Sophie. It was my fault, and I had to save my little bird from the cat.

It was immediately obvious I had a made a major mistake. The clowns were giving me a wide berth and objecting to my presence. A citadel soldier stepped forward to deliver them by grabbing my arm.

"What do you think you're doing? Kitchen servants aren't allowed in the main hall." He hauled me to the edge of the throne room. I scrambled for a quick plan that would get me out of the citadel alive and unportaled.

"Hold still." The guard held his WristCom to the place in my neck where my BioTrack device should be. I prayed the invisible tattoo with an encoded false identity would work. We'd never had reason to test them before.

"Do you have some bizarre desire to die in the portal tonight, Evelyn Miller?"

I scanned the exits and my options. But the soldier and I realized the room had gone eerily quiet. The crowd of people parted, bowing toward the open path that led from the doorway we were standing in—all the way to the glittering throne.

"And what have we here?"

I clenched my jaw as I recognized the sing-song, childlike voice of Regal Manager Leona. The sweetness of her tone was a paradox.

7

"Your Highness," the soldier said, less intimidating with his voice faltering. "I was just removing her."

"And what were you going to do with our little intruder?" She didn't look at him as she spoke. Her eyes fixed on me, and the corner of her mouth turned up. I heard it clearly from her mind—she recognized me. How could she know me when I had lived underground for the past sixteen years?

I wanted to tear the flesh off the soldier's arm and claw my way out of the huddle of people. They watched in sick fascination, like I was a mouse caught in a trap, keening and squalling.

The tyrant of my city stood close enough to reach out and grab my chin with her cold fingers. I saw blood-red nail polish on her manicured nails. Dark lip stain lined her mouth. Her dress matched her nails, the neckline low in the front, the black embellished collar high behind her neck. The train of her dress stretched far behind her like a bowing subject.

Every other person in the room looked like a garish version of a Victorian from long ago, but she was as elegant and stunning as the queen she believed herself to be. I felt plain and silly standing so close to her, with burnished curls trailing down her bodice, and her crystal jewelry sparkling against her skin.

"Roxanne."

I sucked in air and tried to breathe while white spots dotted my vision.

"You wonder how I know you."

She had not let go of my face. I tried to pull away, but her grip only got tighter. She captured my eyes with her intense gaze, and I felt pain. My head filled with pressure, increasing the longer she held on. At the last moment, when I was sure my head was going to burst, she finally let go.

"You look like your mother. She and I were dearest of friends. Did you know that, Roxanne?"

Morris had said the same, hadn't he? But my mother had been dead for as long as I could remember. I didn't want to talk about her, and I didn't want to consider what Leona was saying. I wanted to knock her back and give her something to match her red ensemble. My knife whispered possibilities. But I waited.

"What has pushed my little mouse out of her hole?"

She caressed my cheek. I jerked away, lifting my chin and refusing to answer.

"You came for the young one, didn't you?"

My bravado failed, and I started trembling. She stared at me through eyes of iron—blistering iron seeking to brand me with the knowledge she had of Sophie. I felt another buzz of pain I associated with her focused, hot stare.

"Such a pretty little thing. It's a shame."

"What did you do to her?" I found my voice when I remembered my mission. "Give her to me, or you'll regret it."

"Oh, dear one," she said. "I can't just let children walk into the citadel. What kind of city would we have if everyone could do as they please?"

I bit down hard on my lip. She wouldn't admit what she had done, but I could see it in the chill of her eyes. A tight knot gathered in my throat and made it hard to breathe.

"You sent her to the portal?"

She gasped. "Of course not. What kind of person do you think I am? She was detained."

I knew what kind of person she was. "Where is she?"

She leaned toward me. The soldier held me so I couldn't squirm away, and she put her lips close to my ear.

"Poor little thing. Weak, like your mother."

I cried out and struggled to get free. I would make her pay. I would run her through with my knife before I'd let her hurt someone else.

"I know you didn't come alone."

Real fear flooded, washing away any remaining courage. I *had* come alone, but I knew she was convinced I had not. Had someone followed me?

"Your accomplice has been taken into custody. Would you like to see him?"

She waved her hand and the familiar image of Morris flooded the entire front wall of the throne room. I inhaled a jagged breath and would have fallen back if the soldier wasn't standing right behind me. The still sensitive wound on my soul ripped open. I directed my rage at Leona.

"That can't be," I whispered fiercely, my throat constricting. "You're a liar."

Surprise. She was surprised at my reaction. I tried to breathe. Morris—for the absence of a better word, my father—had been brought back to life, only to be murdered again. My knees buckled, but I made myself stay upright. I forced myself to watch his beloved features. He cried out in pain as one of the soldiers pressed a branding iron to his chest, and I cried out with him.

"On your command, Regal Manager."

She glared at me. "Do it."

I heard a strangled moan. It must have been my own as I saw the portal for the first time. Even just viewing it on the screen, it was impossible brightness, a deafening and oppressive scream of power that struck terror into every mind in the room. I choked back a sob and forced myself to watch when they pushed him in. He disappeared and the feed went black.

"I'm not unfair. But failure to comply must be dealt with. Your Morris has been harboring fugitives and he knew the risks. Now, lamb, I must decide your fate. I want you to be fully aware of what is in store for your people if you continue to hide and break the laws of this city." She folded her hands behind her back and turned away from me.

"Take her to the chair."

The guards moved to grab me. I tried to run but one of them caught me with a laser stun. I lay on the floor, helpless, struggling even with the simple task of breathing. While the guards closed in around me, I heard her voice as if from far away.

"I'll end your little rebellion before it starts."

In the hall, feeling returned to my limbs. I was not interested in finding out what sort of torture device the chair was, so I squirmed and bit until the soldier yelled and let me go.

I had time to grab my knife. All I had to do was hold it out and press my thumb to the heat setting. The blade sliced through his skin like it was butter. I ran while his attention was taken by holding together the gaping edges of his wound.

Without a tracker, it was easy to lose citadel soldiers. I hid behind tapestries and in closets as I slowly made my way to the servant's exit, which I figured would be the easiest way out. But I couldn't leave until I knew what happened to Sophie. I checked every room I passed, but I didn't find her.

Finally I came across a small door which contrasted with the grandeur of the rest of the palace. It was closed but had a security feed above, showing the inside of the room. I saw an antique armchair with hand-carved flourishes and a twisted assortment of wires.

And I saw Sophie.

Her head had fallen forward and her long dark hair covered part of her face, but she was wearing the same clothes she'd been wearing that morning. I knew because they were my clothes. I'd let her borrow my extra set while hers were in the laundry. My heart pounded in my ears as terror swallowed me whole. I willed her to make some movement, but it was an empty hope. My mind already knew her mind was silent.

I wanted to sink into the floor and never get up again. How could cheerful Sophie be no more?

Just like Morris. Just like my parents. Just like everyone else I cared about—she was gone.

I heard a shout at the end of the long hallway and knew I had no time left to mourn. I slipped into the shadows.

I'm sorry, Little Bird. I didn't keep you safe.

TWO

It's only blood.

A month had passed since I came back from the citadel without Sophie. The days had been long—establishing my authority in the bunker and keeping everyone alive. Not because I wanted the job, but because Morris wanted me to have it. He claimed it was my mother's wish. I was angry at him for leaving me alone.

Twice.

I twirled my hunting knife in the air, relished the weight and balance, and admired the black eight-inch blade. I sighed and glanced at the pair crouched on the street in front of me. A brother and sister, probably around my age. They also stared at my blade.

"Fine," I said with a shrug, returning the weapon to the nylon sheath on my belt. "See you around. Or not."

"Wait!" The boy held up his hand as he held his sister's shoulder with the other. "She'll faint. They had to put her to sleep to get that tracker in her neck."

I observed the girl. She was pretty. Blonde hair, huge eyes and face as white as a specter. Her government-approved costume seemed new. The purple sash indicated her status, since common

12

people were required to wear neutral colors. Only Leona could wear color, but she allowed prominent families banners of purple or silver, so these were rich kids. They probably lived within walking distance of the citadel.

It made me nervous. Why would they come to me for help? Most of the people who asked to join the bunker were homeless or without options. When I helped them—I never turned anyone away, and neither had Morris—I was saving their life. Leona detested poverty and sent nightly squadrons to round up the vagrants. The strong ones ended up her slaves. The weak, young or elderly went to the portal.

She said it kept our city strong.

"You contacted me, you know," I said impatiently. "Something about the love of your life being forced to marry another guy?"

His eyes went dark. I felt the spark of his emotions and heard the static of his mind as if it were audibly buzzing and crackling. Unfocused. Dissident. Angry.

"I have better things to do than sit out here in the middle of Broadway and wait for Imposers to show up." As I said the words, I gave a hard look in either direction of the overgrown street. I decided they had ten more seconds, and I used the time to listen hard. My mind searched the silence.

"Imposers?"

I sensed the guy was stalling, but I answered anyway. "They call themselves Peace Implementers, but since they are the opposite, I call them Imposers."

"Do it." The girl must have found her resolution. Her eyes remained on her brother. I heard their unspoken cohesion. They were tired of the way things were. They wanted freedom.

A frustrating pursuit when the portal was the prize for daring to consider it.

The girl locked eyes on her brother's and pulled aside her lace collar. She moved her curls to reveal the sensitive surface of her neck.

I grabbed her. Her breath caught in her throat and she made a strangled sound.

I'd learned it was best to be quick for their sake and mine, since I received the brunt of their emotional toll. I clenched my jaw and cut a quick one-inch line down her milky skin with the blade. I knew exactly where it would be, just above where I could feel her tonsil on the left side. I prepared my mind for the buzz of her pain.

I could tell she tried not to scream, but a cry cut through the still air. I glanced in every direction.

This time I knew someone was there.

As quickly as I dared, I probed the cut until I felt the knife touch something not muscle or tissue. I caught the tiny clear cylinder on the point of my knife and lifted it out. I pulled out the chain around my neck and unscrewed the metal closure with my right hand. I dropped the tracker in place. As it clinked against the other BioTrack devices, its bluish light went out.

"When they touch another BTD they think they're in storage and go dormant," I explained when I saw their curious expressions. "One of their many flaws."

"Won't they know it's been removed?" The boy asked the question as he hesitantly stretched his own neck toward me. I followed the same procedure for his tracker.

"The signals are known to go in and out. There are millions of signals in the city. It's never been a problem before. The thing I'm worried about is the nanos in your brain. They will have to be killed."

"Killed?" The girl trembled. She couldn't be more than sixteen. Her hair was in the approved style and her figure suggested she was wearing a corset under her layers of costume. It irritated me. The people of New York City were told what to wear. They had no freedom to say what they wanted or marry whom they wished. Couples couldn't even have children without filling out paperwork and submitting to testing. They had to prove their fitness and guarantee the correct gender if the Regal Manager had a preference.

We didn't just have a dictator controlling every part of our lives. We had a *crazy* dictator. Leona ran the city from her palace of crystal and portal by forcing everyone to follow her obsessions, like her preoccupation with the late nineteenth century. All of her subjects were compelled to join her in her play-acting.

"How many of those do you have?" The boy pointed at the tracker chain. As he spoke, I noticed his ridiculous fake mustache catching on the corner of his mouth. I leaned forward and ripped it off. What was trendy in the citadel would make him a clown where we were going.

"More than a hundred." I kept my answer vague.

I wound and replaced the chain under my jacket and held out my hand for them to observe. I made a small cut in my palm. As blood began to trickle down my hand, I pressed it against their bleeding wounds. I tried to be intimidating as I spoke.

"Now we're the same. Betray me, and you betray your own blood. You should understand—I don't respond well to betrayal."

The girl's face paled more with every second that went by. When she saw the blood dripping down my wrist, she fainted in her brother's arms. I looked back at him.

"I'm Roxy."

"Henry. She's Victoria. Tori."

I sheathed my knife and heaved Tori over my shoulder, batting the petticoats out of my face and bunching them together. I supposed it might be easier for Henry to carry her, but I wanted him to know I was strong.

"Let's go. We have a medic that can patch you up and laser off your scars."

"Where are we going?"

I eyed him. His question had been accompanied by a spike of nervous energy.

"East Village. Lafayette Street," I said as I started to move. I was still aware of someone nearby, watching us.

"Isn't that area quarantined?"

I scanned the alleyway in front of us. *Eyes sharp. Ears tuned. Mind listening.*

The fifty-year-old street lights dimmed for a moment. They

were solar powered like the rest of the city, but the tech was from a time when solar cell energy was newer.

When our parents were young, a powerful solar flare aimed directly at earth caused a global blackout. Old technology became useless. Several years passed with a world in survival mode, but a semblance of order had slowly been restored with the discovery of a new form of solar power that not only exceeded the old electrical power, it made the old ways seem like the Dark Ages.

But nothing lasted forever, and this area had been abandoned. The lights would go out eventually.

"It is a quarantined sector. Zombie flu. Starts with a fever and headache, then you go out of your mind and start eating people."

Henry gulped as if he'd just set foot in the smallpox floor of the med clinic. "I don't want to get zombie flu."

"Then it's a good thing I made the whole thing up."

He was confused. "But I've seen the news feeds. Whole communities of people lined up and shot because they were infected. I couldn't watch it."

I fumed. "Leona took the public fear caused by my fictional disease and used it as an excuse to get rid of certain people. I created the rumor to protect our bunker; she used it to kill her enemies. Which is why we need to get off this street, because I'm at the top of her kill list."

We moved in silence, staying in the shadows of the buildings. That was my mantra. *Always stay in the shadows*. None of the kids living below in the bunker would forget if I could help it.

We came upon the old section of townhouses almost completely lost to the clutter of what used to be Lafayette Street.

"Here we are." I dumped Tori on the bench.

"It looks like it's going to crumble to dust any minute. Those marble columns can't have any stability left in them."

"They haven't fallen yet." I read his anxiety, which bothered me, but I couldn't decide why. I looked up at the pillars, nearly worn away and covered by vegetation.

At one time the elite of New York resided here, but the city never remained the same for long. The columns along with the building had been chipped away until all that was left was a remnant. A souvenir of a time forgotten.

Which was fortunate for us.

Henry seemed more afraid of the bunker than standing in the open street. "How did this bunker come to be?"

I scanned my surroundings, ready for anything. "Our people rebelled when Leona took over the city. They ransacked the new citadel in the uprising fifteen years ago. Before the revolt, our parents built this bunker to protect us. Most of us were babies. The few adults left after the slaughter took measures to halt the erosion and increase the internal strength. Even though it looks like an old crumbling building, this whole block is a smart window."

He nodded and his eyes brightened. "Meant to fool the eye and turn attention away. Well done."

I tried to see my home through his eyes. The underground bunker spanned the length and width of an entire city block; it held over two hundred people below, but it was completely invisible to the offhanded glance.

"I figure we are in more danger of being thrown in the portal than having this collapse on us."

His fear spiked at the mention of the portal.

"Hey, Greer," I kicked the shin of the boy resting on the crumbling sidewalk, his cap over his face. He peered out and smiled at me. His dark skin blended with the night in perfect cohesion.

"Glad you made it home, Captain." He stood up.

"Get these two to Doc." I gestured to them, but a sudden sensation behind me made me grab my knife.

"It's a Peace Implementer!" Tori had started to come around. She stood and backed up, tripping over loose stones. Greer grabbed for her, but not before she reopened her wound and bled all over both of them.

"Get inside."

Greer pushed aside the moss behind him and let the scanner

read his handprint. The nondescript tinted window next to it rotated to reveal a white circular tunnel sitting just below street level at the mouth of a small abandoned theater. It was five feet high and illuminated by solar fluorescents only bright enough to allow us to see where we were going. A sealed steel door at the end of the tunnel opened to the bunker itself. As soon as Greer pulled them inside, the tunnel vanished behind the smart window.

Only seconds later, an arm went around my neck.

"Well, what do we have here? Have I actually stumbled on the leader of the filthy rebel cause?"

He held me tightly against him. I felt the sturdy material of his uniform. The cold steel of the bayonet topping his laser rifle pressed against my back. It argued with the warmth of his arm next to my face.

My skin prickled with anticipation and my fingers tensed as adrenaline flooded my senses.

"Can you imagine the awards the Regal Manager will shower on me when I drag your rebel carcass into her throne room?" His voice was smooth as silk next to my ear. I felt the heat of his breath, smelled the taste of his last meal. I could hear every emotion rolling around in his mind.

Prepare to die, Poser.

THREE

I grabbed the arm that held me and used it as a lever to roll the Imposer's taller, heavier body over me and onto the ground in a fluid motion. He fell hard, grunting and laughing at the same time.

I crossed my arms over my chest and scoffed. "Whose carcass?"

"One of these days, Roxy," he said as he stood up and brushed off his uniform. "I'll catch you off guard."

"Not going to happen. I can smell you a mile away. You reek of citadel." I shrugged.

"Your mind-reading probably helps a little, too." Levi grinned and started to reach a hand toward me, but he must have thought better of it. He let it drop back to his side. "So how's the prettiest insurgent in the Divided States?"

I avoided his appreciative gaze. I hated the way he made me feel vulnerable with a look. Well, hated it as much as I loved it. But loving it terrified me, so I sniffed and rubbed my nose in a way I hoped was a little boyish. His patrol cap had fallen next to my feet, so I picked it up and threw it at him.

"Depends," I said as I sat on the rusted bench and gave the area another scan with my mind. "What are the whispers from the citadel?"

"Well," Levi said as he sat next to me. "Word is Her Majesty is having her hair dyed. A beguiling shade of red. One might even call it scarlet."

He leaned toward me with a teasing smile, so I moved back and sneered. "Any day the word is about hair dye is a good day for me. Do you think she finally forgot I was in her citadel?"

"Unfortunately, I doubt she'll ever forget. She put two new search teams in the quarantine areas. I managed to steer her north. Zombie flu is said to have decimated Washington Heights."

I nodded, though I didn't understand why someone in his position was willing to help us. "Thanks, Levi. I never asked you to put yourself in danger for us. And thank you for helping me get out of the palace that night."

"I wish we could have saved Morris and Sophie." Levi sighed and looked down.

"Me, too. But I owe you one for saving me."

He smiled. "I'm a sucker for rebels who seem bent on getting themselves thrown in the portal. Maybe it's the challenge of keeping you alive."

"You're lucky I let you live, Poser."

"Actually," he said. "I'm a Peace Implementer. You could be portaled for calling me anything else."

"You mean like Buzzard, Possum, Devilfish, Mudsill, or Doughface? We call you those names, too."

"You've done it now." He caught my arm lightly behind my back. "I'll have to portal you twice. A kiss for your life."

I scoffed. "Try it and I'll hit you so hard you'll wish you'd been portaled instead."

"Fine. I'll settle for a tour of the bunker."

I pulled away from him. "The day you let me dig out your tracker and add it to my collection is the day you get to see my bunker, Koenig."

He chuckled, but I could read his discomfort. "I saw you had some new recruits. I assume you enjoyed ripping open their flesh."

I reached for my knife. "I'd like it more if it was your flesh."

He held up his hands and gave me an uneasy chuckle. "One of these days. I'm not so sure it's a good idea yet."

We were quiet, and it was awkward. Since the day he started coming around—I'd beat him up pretty badly before I realized he was there to help—ever since, I'd been asking for his tracker. So far he had always said no. I could see why he would hesitate. He spent his days at the citadel, and he might be worried our tech was not advanced enough to keep his secret. But it bothered me that he didn't trust us.

Didn't trust me.

I sighed and tried to stretch the tension out of my neck. When I closed my eyes, I heard the murmurs. The voices that permeated the air did a strange dance with the whispers inside my head. I kept my eyes closed, knowing I would see them if I looked.

"What?"

I waited for Levi to see them.

"Ah, specters. You aren't afraid of them, are you, Rox?"

I elbowed him hard. "Don't call me Rox."

"I think it's amazing that ghosts walk by us day or night, hundreds of years in the past. Just think of the science at work. The universe keeps changing and becoming more complex. More beautiful." He smiled his easy-going smile that fooled a person into thinking Levi didn't have a lot of concerns in life.

I knew him well enough, or at least I could read him well enough to know that he was deep water underneath that smooth surface. He didn't talk about it, but I could see conflict always simmering just below his calm demeanor.

"I guess it's amazing if you don't consider how it means the universe is coming apart at the seams," I replied darkly.

"You always see the downside."

I peeked at the backs of the unknowing visitors of the past. This time it was two women in nineteenth century clothes, their bodies transparent and huddled together in secret conversation.

21

Glowing mist framed their outline as it projected onto the screen of our time.

According to the science news feed, the high number of specters we were seeing was due to the heavy electromagnetic field that had settled over the Atlantic coast in the past twenty years, interfering with our perception of time. I couldn't help but notice that time had gotten unreliable right about the time Leona took over the portal chamber.

I glanced at Levi, who had gone quiet. We had tried to discuss the state of the city, the crumbled countries of America and the disease-ridden warring factions left on the other continents. It was how I'd figured out how incredibly smart Levi was. I'd never met anyone smarter. But it had become uncomfortably obvious that although he was on my side, he didn't see everything the way I did.

"I brought you something," Levi said. He pulled out a small paper bag from his coat pocket. I caught a whiff and grabbed for it, but he held it out of my reach. "It wasn't smashed when I bought it from the vendor in the gardens a few minutes ago. You only have yourself to blame for that."

I punched him hard on his arm and grabbed the bag. As he watched in fascinated disgust, I stuffed the bread in my mouth, my taste buds bursting with joy from the explosion of the sweet flavors of caramel and cocoa baked into buttery warm bread.

We didn't have treats below. The most decadent thing our gardens offered was a peachy-pear tree. We had some honeybees, but what little honey they produced didn't go far with over two hundred people. And with only two milk cows and so many kids, butter was also scarce.

"For singing in the night, Roxy—at least savor it a little." He stuck his finger into the mess to retrieve a taste. I smacked his hand.

"You seem especially vicious. Didn't get to slash open enough victims today?" He watched me lick every last sweet taste from my fingers. "And your manners are all aces, by the way."

"Your face is all aces, mudsill."

He stood up. "Oddly, it works for you. You're still hot."

I scoffed with extra repulsion so he wouldn't notice the heat I could feel on my cheeks.

"I better get back," he said with an unwilling sigh. "But first— you know what I have to ask."

"No, Levi, I will not bond with you. I have 239 people below, and I don't have time to look out for you."

He scoffed. "You let kids down there *bond* as you call it—or break the law, as the Regal Manager says—as young as fifteen. You're already two years past that, and I'm three years past you." He gave me a reproachful stare. "Am I that ugly?"

"Yes," I lied. Actually, Levi was anything but ugly with his curly dark hair, warm brown eyes and tall, sturdy physique. I took a quick peek.

He leaned closer, his hands on either side of the bench behind me, a pleading expression in his eyes as smooth and rich as chocolate. I felt a rush of pleasant fear and dove under his arm, lunging for the scanner.

"I'm not bonding with you or anyone else. Ever. Get back to the citadel and find yourself a prize at one of your over-the-top parties."

He made a face and dusted off his hat by hitting it against the bricks. As he pulled it over his curls, he took several quick steps toward me and gave me a loud kiss on the cheek. "Only one girl for me."

He was promptly rewarded with a hard kick in the shin.

"Get out of here, idiot."

"Someday I'll get through to you."

He turned to go, but after he had taken a few steps while I shamelessly watched, he looked back. I quickly looked away, sensing his uncertain emotions and wanting nothing to do with whatever he was going to say.

"Speaking of over-the-top parties …"

I braced myself.

"There's a banquet next week at the palace. Leona has invited everyone, from the vagrants to the governors. I don't suppose you'd want to do your citizen's duty and come with me?"

"Why would I want to do that?"

He shrugged and pretended to study some indeterminate object at the end of the dark street. "To spy on your enemy? To see how easy it is to get away with? To dance with me?"

I wrinkled my nose. "You want me to walk into the same palace where I watched Morris and Sophie get murdered and barely escaped with my life? Really, Levi? I thought you were on my side."

"I wouldn't let anyone hurt you." His voice was quiet and I sensed he was insulted. I shook my head.

He nodded and turned abruptly, disappearing into the shadows and leaving me alone on the empty street that now felt cold and unsafe.

The idea of taffeta and silk twirling and wine flowing in Leona's overdone spectacle in honor of herself repulsed me. I wanted no part of it. But—minus the sea of brown automatons and the psycho leader who wanted to kill me and all the kids I was protecting—I wouldn't have minded dancing with Levi.

Don't let him make you weak.

I had the future of the Resistance to think about. My choices had been made for me when I was a baby. The *Daughter of Hope* didn't get to make normal teenage decisions.

Despite my resignation to the role my mother had envisioned for me as leader of the Resistance, I didn't know how to live up to a title like that. My mother was the true hope and she was long gone. I felt the weight of the responsibility like a cement block on my chest, holding me down, keeping me captive. I had no options. I had to figure out a way to save them, but I had no idea how to pull it off, and no parent left to ask.

Meanwhile, that portal loomed in the distance, sending its menacing hum to every sector of the city. The sound was a constant reminder from Leona's citadel.

Conform or die.

Neither was an option for me.

FOUR

I cringed at the heavy clank of the steel door. No part of me wanted to wake up the babies.

I was glad for the quiet inside the bunker. When everyone was in quarters and most were sleeping, the jumble of feelings I shouldered all day long lifted, and I could almost hear my own mind again.

"How do things look?" I turned to the left toward the bunker's control room, flooded with the lights of twenty transparent screens working constantly to bring us news of the city around us. I leaned into the room and hoped Lon had good news for me.

Lon, my senior engineer, who was the ripe old age of eighteen, gave me a reserved smile. He was plain, but not unattractive. He wore black-rimmed glasses, had longish sandy brown hair and a quiet demeanor. His only fault was being far too serious. The last time I had made him aware of it, he'd said I had no room to talk.

Levi had agreed.

"Things are peaceful. Relatively." He turned his head to each side as if gauging and hoping he was right.

"So we should brace for disaster?"

He didn't smile, and I sensed his worry.

"Just a joke. Levi said it was a boring day. Good boring. Hair dye boring."

He shrugged as if to say he was not interested in the private jokes I shared with Levi.

"I do have some news," he said.

I stepped fully inside the room, pulled an old metal stool out from under the console and sat on it. He waved his hand in front of the SmartScreen projected from the computer well in the center of the room. He quickly sorted through documents and news links as the old tech labored to keep up with him.

I frowned. Who used projection wells anymore? The gradient of clarity pixelated in and out and the surfaces of all the transparent screens along the wall were scratched and cloudy. I needed to upgrade our equipment to the mind-interfacing computers available in the city.

Outside New York, tech was hard to come by. Leona held the monopoly in the world, because her computer engineers had been the ones to get the internet running again after the Blackout. I couldn't be sure what interfaces were safe and what would enslave us to Leona's regime. Old tech was safer. Hence my hesitation to upgrade.

"These went out today." Lon brought up an elaborate invitation and boosted the power so I could read it from my position.

I curled my lip in distaste.

My Beloved Subjects
You are cordially invited to my home
The Crystal Citadel
Old Bryant Park, New York City
An entire week of feasting and dancing
No one turned away

June 1-7, 2074

Attendance is mandatory without valid absentee forms, due one week prior to feast. Appropriate identification, attire and manners are required. Violators will be prosecuted.

"How generous," I sneered at the projection of the Regal Manager's gently smiling face. "I'm afraid we'll have to decline."

Lon twisted his mouth and stared hard at the projection. I read his tension and braced for whatever argument he was about to have with me.

"It's not hard to sense you don't agree," I said with impatience.

"Not going means hacking into Leona's encrypted system and changing everyone's identification. Again. Those firewalls are hell to crack through."

"You have something better to do?" I was used to Lon reminding me how hard I made his job.

"That's 239 neck tats I have to rescan."

"Do it when they come in for a meal and get the stragglers after."

He gave a short laugh of disbelief. "You say that like it's easy."

"You say it like it's hard."

"It *is* hard." He tossed his scratched regulator on the console and crossed his arms over his chest. He blinked hard behind his glasses, as if he had been up for three days straight. "Why don't we go?"

It was my turn to laugh. "Are you serious? All 239 of us will just waltz down to the palace and have a party with Leona?"

"Obviously I don't mean children or new mothers," he replied with irritating calm. "But everyone else could use a night away from this bunker. Some of them haven't seen the light of day in fifteen years."

"That's not true. We have a solar window in the gardens. With the Invisibility Wrap, we have sunlight and fresh air. Rain. The sun is what powers all our equipment."

"I know about the solar window, Roxy. I keep it working. But it's not the same, and you know what I mean. Maybe there wouldn't be so much of the bickering and drama you hate if they were allowed out once in a while."

I heaved a dramatic sigh that I hoped was irksome to him. "It's not just one night. It's seven. Seven long evenings for any one of us to slip up and ruin everything. Every last rebel—thrown in the portal with the citadel garbage. I didn't ask to be, but I'm responsible. Our parents gave their lives keeping us safe, and history proves we are safer if we stay put."

We stared each other down for a few seconds. I sensed his resignation, but I knew he was making a point.

"Leona shouldn't win that easily," I said in a softer voice.

"Sooner or later we have to face her. We're stuck in limbo here. Don't you just want to get on with it, Roxy?"

He didn't wait for me to answer. He dropped his gaze and started pulling up the government firewalls. I knew he had a night of citadel security measures to withstand. He'd be attacked by electric pulses and disorientation programs before he managed to break through. I felt guilty, but I didn't know what to say. I wasn't good enough with the sophistication of citadel code to take his place. I turned to leave.

His quiet words followed me out into the hallway. "You know we can't stay down here forever, right?"

I went to my quarters. Uncertainty followed close, a dark shadow plaguing my mind.

Who are you to think you can lead them?

I was nobody. I was a kid like everyone else in the bunker. The only difference was my mother. She had been extraordinary. But she was long gone, and I was nothing like her.

You're living a lie. You're going to get everyone killed because you have no idea what you're doing.

My eyes fell to the animated photo of my mother I'd stuck to the small mirror over the sink. She was standing in front of the Statue of Liberty, her hair blowing across her face as she held me, pointing upward. It was from the days before Leona had polished off the patina so the old icon would "match her personality better."

Her face was obscure, and just as she started to look toward the camera the animation ended. I'd tried and failed to find a better picture of Mom on the internet databases from just after the Blackout. It seemed like someone had gone through them and erased all evidence she had ever lived. The picture, as well as the chain and compass that stored the BioTrack devices, were the only tangible evidence that Arabella Eisen had existed.

I wish I could change the past. What if I could go back and right the wrongs that sent us to this dead end?

But I couldn't. We were cornered like mice, and Leona was going to squash us.

We lived in the single advanced society of the world. We had complex computer systems running every part of our lives, computers that interacted with our minds, robots that saw to our needs. But we traded our freedom for it. We all lived with the doom of that portal chamber hovering. Everyone had to ask themselves if today was the day they'd make the mistake that would turn out the lights on their future.

We can't stay safe forever.

FIVE

Alarms. They screamed in my head, tearing my dreams to shreds.

I reached blindly for my com. I meant to answer like a respectable leader of a community but I only whined Lon's name.

"Sorry, Roxy, I'm on it. The singles' quarter is lit up, but I don't see intruders or heat signatures on the cams."

"I'll be there in a sec," I mumbled. The com dropped to the floor, and I fell back against my flat, musty-smelling pillow. I wanted to stay in my room. I didn't want to be responsible. If I got out of bed I'd have to check alarms and referee arguments and sidestep children all day long.

Not to mention keep them all safe.

With great unwillingness I stood up. I caught sight of myself in the little mirror and made a face.

There was a part of me that wanted to be pretty. Or at least I wanted to *want* to be attractive on some level. But if I took the time to brush out my hair and put color on my lips, I'd have to make the effort to be happy as well.

I went for my black leggings and jacket, strapped on my

weapons belt, pulled on my boots and adjusted my ponytail.

It was better this way.

I left my quarters and headed down the long and narrow hallway toward the control room. The halls were not dim and quiet as they had been when I entered the night before. Now there were people. Everywhere.

I focused on my destination. I didn't want to look at them and see them tripping over each other or arguing. I didn't want to look at the babies and toddlers who had wandered away from the family area and down the hall toward my room, screaming at decibels that were sure to ruin our hearing in such a cramped space.

I didn't want to see them because I knew they were vulnerable, and I knew there was no one left but me who had been trained to protect them.

Despite their obnoxious messes and endless bickering, everyone I passed in the hall gave me a look of respect that I sensed rather than saw, since I wasn't looking. They tried to clear a path, though I still stepped over a baby or two.

Don't look at me like that. I'm not a deliverer. If I'm your best hope, you should give up now.

I ducked into the control room, where Henry and Tori were standing with Lon.

"False alarm. The new kids on the block were trying to find the canteen but instead they found the hidden release bar to the basement steps."

I shrugged. "At least it wasn't Henderson again. Or the toddler from hell."

His name was really Charlie, but I'd had enough run-ins with him to suspect he was a demon. A demon with the superpower of chaos.

"Who's Henderson?" Henry asked. He walked the length of the room and eyed the tech with curiosity.

"Domestic Service Robot." Lon was back in front of the well working on new identities. I fully expected him to work without stopping for a couple days and nights just to spite me.

"You have DSRs? Where did you get them?"

I tapped the console. "We stole them. How else would we get anything? Why were you out of the infirmary? Doc shouldn't be done with you yet."

Henry shrugged. "We couldn't find the doctor last night, so Greer showed us our bunks and said we'd find him today. Nice guy. I think he has a little crush on Tori."

She made a face and smiled at me. It reminded me that she was pretty and I was trying my best to be ugly, so I scowled at her.

"You could lead a unit of Imposers to our door with those brain implants. I let you come here because you said you believed in the cause. And you thank me by jeopardizing an operation that has kept us safe for fifteen years?"

Lon gave me an even stare. "It's not their fault. And you know the nanos get confused by our tech."

"So are you taking responsibility?" I flung the harsh words back at him. He shrugged.

"I'm saying it happened. Let it go and find Doc."

"Easy enough," I retorted, pointing at the DSR standing near the storage door with hands folded in front of him and a pleasant, vacant smile on his lips.

"Arty!"

He came to life, moving in an unnatural manner that was mildly clumsy, yet precise. He cast his lifeless blue eyes in my general direction. "Good morning, Captain Eisen. How may I serve you?"

I bit back a sarcastic reply. He would apologize and there was nothing more infuriating than a contrite robot.

"Locate Miles Solomon."

He went into his processing trance. I imagined drool dripping from his chin as I waited.

"Miles Solomon is located in the infirmary."

"Imagine that," I said. "The doc is in the infirmary."

I walked out of the arched doorway and took a left, motioning for them to follow. I wanted them to feel my annoyance, but Henry was too busy talking to notice.

"Your servants are outdated. We have some at our estate that are mistaken for people. They have programs for emotions and brains that can learn and process at amazing rates."

"I didn't even want these," I answered. "I was looking for the old-fashioned plastic kind that does all the work and doesn't talk. I had to settle for these two heaps of junk."

"We try to stay away from Arty. His language can get colorful. His previous owners must have been very free with their words." The passing bunker member smiled as she spoke to the newcomers. I shot her a look and she hurried on, adjusting the weight of the baby on her hip.

"This bunker is well-organized," Henry continued. "I didn't expect it to be so big. All underground, but filled with natural light. Gardens growing; even an animal shelter. Did you build this?"

"How old do you think I am? This place was built when I was a baby."

"By whom?"

"Enough questions. For all I know you two are spies straight from Leona's fancy cesspool."

He nodded as if he understood my doubt. "We are tired of not being able to think for ourselves. It's time someone stood up to her, and maybe you're the one that will be able to pull it off."

I listened hard, past his words and into his motivations and emotions.

Betrayal. Disillusionment. Lost love.

It was hard to read anything from Tori beyond trepidation. I had no reason to question their allegiance. I turned around. "Open infirmary."

The door opened with a weary, pitiful sound. I met the gaze of the only medical authority in our compound. His father—killed in the Resistance Riots like many of our parents—had been a healer in his division. Miles had studied all of his father's books and papers with as much focus as I had studied my mother's.

Sometimes experience grew from necessity.

"Where were you last night when these brains needed debugging?"

"Good morning to you too, Roxy."

He smiled. His good looks aggravated me. I was alone in my opinion, for he was popular with the single girls. He had a steady stream of female patients with vague medical complaints to prove it.

I suspected he might take advantage of their adoration in ways I didn't approve. My rules about relationships were simple and without exceptions. No bonding without promising me they'd stay exclusively with each other. No break-ups were allowed in my bunker. If a guy and girl wanted to get together, they had to pack up all their stuff in the singles' quarter and move to the family bunks. There was no return.

Morris had instituted the rules, but he was more diplomatic than I, and they had respected him more.

Reinforcing his guidelines was the only way I knew to keep the drama to a minimum. I wished I could convince them all to follow my example and show some self-control, but the biology of hormones had left me alone on my soapbox.

They liked to compare me to Leona and her stringent marriage laws. She prearranged or blocked almost all the formal marriages that took place in the city. People caught together without her permission got portaled.

Miles started attaching biofeedback sensors to Henry's forehead. The tiny machines grabbed on to his skin and flashed blood-red as they began the process of cleaning his brain. They would remove most of the software that had been uploaded to his mind when he was only days old. The program monitored brain waves and sent generalized reports of thoughts to a mainframe that was supervised by citadel personnel.

"Does it hurt?" Tori gulped as she watched. Henry smiled and reached for her hand.

"No, it tickles. Like an electric pulse."

Miles caught my eyes with his. His emotions told me he had

bad news. I'd known something was wrong since the moment I walked into the infirmary with him, but I had avoided it as long as I could.

"I was called to the family bunks last night. It's why I wasn't available. Meora's in labor."

"Still?"

He tried to appear positive, but his mind was not as hopeful. I thought of the red-headed, freckled sixteen-year-old. She was small and she'd always been delicate. I could remember Morris sitting up nights with her when she was younger, helping her breathe with lungs that did not want to cooperate. He had showed me how to help her take slow, deep breaths until the spasms subsided. I'd shown Noah when he and Meora moved to the family bunks.

Her pregnancy had been one trial after another. Miles and I had made countless ventures into the abandoned neighborhood, looking for medicinal herbs growing wild or drugstores that still contained some stores of medicine from before the quarantine. Anything to help her survive.

Should I have stopped them from bonding? They had been close friends since childhood. Who was I to tell them they couldn't be together after everything they had lost? Noah cared for Meora in a way that reminded me of the way Morris had looked out for us. If anyone deserved to have a family, it was Noah and Meora.

"If you go there, you stay there." In the end, it was all I said to them. That had been ten months ago.

Miles' voice brought me back to the present. "I don't know what to do for her. She isn't progressing like the girls usually do. I'm worried."

"Do you need me to do anything?" Even as I said the words, I knew I didn't want to go into that delivery room. I glared, willing him not to ask it of me.

"Not unless you want to go steal an extractor."

He was kidding, of course. An extractor was a two ton medical device that transported the baby out of the womb and safely into the warming tube in emergencies. But any hospital that had an extractor would also be overrun with Posers. Hospital and doctor care was ridiculously expensive. Only the wealthy could afford it. I would stick out in a hospital like a flashing red light. I might as well wave at the security cams and wear a sign asking Leona to portal me.

"Maybe Levi could sneak her into a facility." I rejected the words as quickly as I said them. "No. It would only get her killed."

"She may die anyway," Miles said quietly. I knew he wouldn't voice it if it wasn't a possibility. I felt the terror of responsibility for another person's death.

Two peoples' deaths.

Miles put a hand on my arm and squeezed. I made my getaway and headed for the door. I needed to get out of the bunker and think. When I passed the control room, Lon stuck his head out.

"Levi sent an encryption. He wants to see you at the usual spot."

I eyed Lon. Was he judging me for my increased interaction with Levi? Did he think I was risking the lives of everyone because I had a crush on a cute enemy soldier? I tried to search his emotions, but there was only Lon's calm and methodical demeanor.

It didn't keep me from feeling guilty.

"He's never been suspicious. And I don't like him. I just think he's useful."

Lon gave me an even stare. He didn't seem surprised I was defending my questionable relationship.

"I never said he was suspicious or that you liked him, Roxy. He is useful."

But his eyes and his spirit hinted at more. I didn't want to think about what he wasn't saying. I didn't have to, because someone started yelling in the family area. Either something was broken or there was drama.

I put in my wistful vote for broken.

I turned down the long corridor that led to the family sector.

All the small, enclosed quarters for families were situated with their doors facing a common area that was used for school or play.

I stepped over a discarded apple core and puddles of spilled milk.

I knew it was going to be drama. I just knew it.

"Arty!" I hit the com pad on the wall outside the family quarter. It was sticky. "Mess!"

I heard a few vulgar words through the com.

When I went into the commons, I had to dodge a book and several items of clothing.

"Take your junk and go to the portal, mudsill!"

Katie Rose.

At least she was consistent. No less than once a month she threw Edison out of their cabin. Sometimes she threw out their two-year-old, Jack, as well. So far the baby was safe, but she was only a month old.

"Are we going to have this conversation again?" I narrowed my eyes and folded my arms across my chest.

She burst into tears.

I hated tears.

"Captain, you don't understand how he treats me! How would you feel if your Imposer boyfriend flirted with every girl he met, and right in front of you?"

I fumed. "He's not *my* Imposer."

"And Edison is mean," she continued with a loud sniff. "He yells at Jacky and baby Astra."

"I have never yelled at the baby." Edison looked as annoyed as I felt. He was tall and muscled for his age. I felt intimidated by his good looks, which meant it wasn't a leap to think he had the attention of any girl in the bunker.

"I don't know how I'm supposed to live with him," Katie said with a frustrated groan. "I was sixteen when we bonded. I had no idea it would be like this."

"You're eighteen now. Old enough to stop acting like a baby."

She was older than me, for crying out loud. My fists tightened and my frustration boiled over.

"The rules haven't changed. You're staying, he's staying. Do you know what kind of place we'd have if I let you people break up?" I heaved an exaggerated shrug. "I don't think any of us are mature enough for bonding. It's illegal and you could be portaled for it. Outside this bunker, teenagers disappear every day just for thinking about crossing the line you blew across."

I wanted to grab her and all the rest of them by the shoulders and shake some sense into their brains. Katie Rose only sulked. At least she didn't argue.

"Morris should have put a brick wall down the center. Girls on one side and boys on the other. It's like having fire and dynamite in the same close quarters. It's never going to work."

I wasn't getting through. They wouldn't even look at me. A few of them exchanged glances as if I was the tyrant that had taken over New York City.

I was *nothing* like her.

"I'll just move to the singles' for a few days." Edison towered over me. How was I supposed to tell guys over six feet tall what to do? And why did they listen to me?

I heard their bitterness in my head, mingling with my doubts about my abilities and my resentment at Morris for leaving me. The emotions crowded into my brain and made it hurt. I wanted them all to go away and take their petty problems with them.

All the emotions flooded, and I lost it. "You are not single! Go back in there with the person you chose and WORK IT OUT!"

I gave him a shove and threw some of his things at his chest. He wasn't happy about it, but he went. The door went about its task of closing.

I turned around to the mess. The whimpering babies. The whispers. Forget Leona and her palace of tapestries and mosaics. Forget her Poser army and her portal. The scariest thing was being stuck in the ground with this frail, clueless young band, and trying to keep them alive when it seemed like everything in the world wanted them dead.

I fled, stomping down the hall toward my room. Arty and Henderson turned the corner, lumbering toward the mess I had told them to clean up. I didn't have time to stop before the collision.

Cleaning tools and robot arms and legs went flying. From his precarious position on the floor, Henderson offered a vacant smile and apology. Arty started swearing.

I admit it was pretty stupid to punch a robot. His left cheek was always a little dented after that. It didn't affect his wide-eyed smile.

Or his foul mouth.

SIX

Why do I have to lead them, Morris? What makes me so special?

It was the question I had asked him regularly from the day he told me I would be the next leader of the bunker. I kept asking because I wasn't satisfied with the only answer he would give me.

We are all part of a larger story. If you don't do your part, the whole thing could unravel.

I crept along East Fourth Street, doing my best to stay off the SmartPavement. If I were going farther, I would have used the old subway tunnels. The city stopped using them when the lightning fast maglev trains opened. They flew on laser-marked channels above the city. I found solace in the tunnels. No one else was ever down there since BioTrackers prevented people from getting through the blocked entrances. I'd found advertisements as old as 2018 down there. It was as if I was back in a simpler time, where Leona did not yet exist and the legendary country of America had yet to fall.

The SmartStreets were made of magnetite. It repelled magnetic cars and made them levitate above the ground. Since vehicles never touched the surface, and since defacing a public street was grounds for the portal, the roads were always in excellent condition. They were smooth and transparent, relaying news and weather, monitoring anyone walking on them. The citadel didn't pay attention to the quarantined sectors. There were no BioTrackers to measure, so they considered the area abandoned, but I never took chances.

I thought about what was happening in the bunker. Meora was still barely three centimeters dilated though she'd been in labor for over twenty-four hours. Miles said the best hope for her was a removal, but he'd never done one. Even his father wouldn't have attempted such an archaic procedure. The most basic medical tech available, even in the divisions throughout the old country of America, had rendered blood surgeries needless at least twenty years before.

There had to be a better solution. I berated myself for not seeing it. I felt helpless; completely at the whim of hormonal teenagers living shoulder to shoulder.

I stood under the crumbling arch in old Washington Square Park. The marble had fallen away in many places, but the inscription remained.

Let us raise a standard to which the wise and honest can repair.

The quote whispered as it always did. This had been written for me. This was my purpose. I had been born for one reason—to repair the broken standard. I shut my eyes and waged the same argument I did any other night.

I'm not wise or honest. I'm a fraud. I have no idea what I'm doing.

The park was dark and still. The fountain had ceased its endless flow of water and all the paths and benches had long been covered in a blanket of vegetation.

There were some that wanted to petition to have the park repaired after the quarantine lifted. I hoped Leona's contrary attitude would prove to be my ally in this case. Victory was life retaking what once belonged to it, snaking up over iron bars and cement walkways and being untamed once more. Free.

"Hey, Beautiful." A voice from behind the brush made me jump, and my hand went for my knife.

"Hold up! I'll willingly be your prisoner, no need for violence."

Levi stepped out and grabbed my hand, his adorable smile lifting the corners of his mouth. I was surprised to see him out of uniform. I was used to seeing his long black coat with gold buttons and gold edging around the seams. Now he wore clothes that seemed to come out of a time machine.

When was the last time anybody wore a pair of new jeans? It wasn't just the high quality of the vintage jeans and the leather jacket that struck me. It was the way Levi wore them. He owned them in the manner he moved, giving the impression they had been tailored specifically for him. But why would he do something so reckless? Leona had portaled people for wearing the wrong shade of purple.

That was something I'd noticed about Levi. Overall, he was very careful. He was serious and determined, though he softened it with genuine friendliness and concern for others. These times when he did things so bold made no sense to me. And it made me uneasy. I was used to being able to tell when someone was lying, and nothing was dishonest in his emotions.

He gave me a questioning look. I was glad he couldn't see my thoughts. What would I do without the privacy of my mind where I could freely make Levi observations? Things would get sticky if he knew how I really felt about him. How *much* I felt about him.

"No, you can't be my prisoner. I have too many people to keep alive as it is," I said, injecting as much disdain into my tone as possible.

"Have you ever stopped to consider that maybe *I* could take care of *you*?"

I narrowed my eyes in warning. But he took a step closer. "I'm a Peace Implementer. It's what I do."

"You toss people in the portal or tie them to electrocution

chairs."

His lighthearted teasing seemed to short out. He looked away as I tapped my fingers absently on the rusted iron fence.

"What did you want?"

"Do I have to want something for us to see each other?" He was offended. "I'd like to think after everything we've been through I might be able to talk to you sometimes just because we're friends."

I avoided his eyes and didn't remind him of the reasons we couldn't really be friends. The image of Sophie's lifeless body as she lay dead in the chair would never vanish from my memory. It was Levi or someone like him who had pulled the lever that tortured and killed her.

"So this is a social call?" I heard the bitterness in my tone.

"Roxy, stop." His tone was edgy, as if in warning. I wondered what would happen if I pushed him. Would he reveal a dark nature hidden beneath the one I could see and feel? What if I was forced to fight or kill the one person in the world I wasn't sure I could live without?

"When are you going to trust me?"

It was as if he had read my thoughts. I shrugged. He sighed and folded his arms across his chest, leaning back against the fence.

"Doesn't it count for anything that I've risked my life for you? Do you know what would happen if I was discovered?"

"I didn't ask you for anything. And I don't have time to socialize."

I didn't add that I had done nothing that day other than argue with a robot over whether it was appropriate to call an escaped toddler a "filthy jackass."

"Tonight I've decided it's your turn to risk life and limb on my behalf." His tone lightened considerably; though I felt the effort it took for him to push aside his hurt. He reached for my hand and pulled me toward the bushes.

I was getting ready to kick him in the shin and run, but he let me go and went into the brush, returning with something on wheels, black and very shiny. I had never seen one in person. I tried to remember what they were called.

"It's a motorcycle." He smiled and ran his hand across the long leather seat.

"That has to be fifty years old."

"Fifty-seven. I restored it. It's for the history museum, but it won't hurt to take it for one test drive."

I backed away. "You have to be joking."

He straddled it and pulled a sleek helmet on. I was handed another one. His smirk held a challenge.

"Are you too scared, Roxy?"

I huffed and grabbed the helmet. While I shoved it on my head, I swung my leg up and mounted behind him, grabbing the sides of his jacket.

"You do realize this thing runs on the ground."

Levi laughed. "That's what makes it exciting."

"You better make sure I don't die."

He craned his neck to give me a reassuring smile as he turned the beast on. He revved the engine a few times before he kicked back the stand, released the clutch and twisted the right handle forward. The front tire bounced into the air and suddenly we were flying down the path and the stone steps.

At first I could only imagine us crashing and sprawling on the pavement, blood smearing all over Leona's precious SmartStreet. After all, there was a reason the LinkSystem controlled every vehicle in the city.

I held him a little tighter. We were going to be the first people in at least twenty years to die in a traffic accident.

He seemed to know what he was doing. I started to relax—a little—and wondered if this was what freedom felt like. Throwing off oppressive tyrant leadership and figuring out what it meant to be alive. We were taking risks to find out who we were.

It was over too soon. He returned to the park and let me off. I turned for home, but his words stopped me.

"I have a plan."

It was going to be something I wouldn't like. I folded my arms and turned, assuming a wary pose.

"You're cute when you do that." He got off the bike and took a step closer.

It made me uneasy. And warm. And a little tingly, if I was being honest.

"Spare me, Koenig. Just spit it out."

A soft glint rested on his dark eyes. I tried to ignore the annoying way they shone in the moonlight glow.

"Come with me to the banquet."

I sighed. "We've already had this discussion. I don't date Posers."

He reached out and fingered a strand of my hair that had come loose from my ponytail when I wore the helmet. I felt his admiration, and my stupid brain chose that moment to remind me how little effort I'd put into my appearance that morning. I took out my frustration on him.

"So you drag me out here and risk my life on an antique just to ask me a question that I already answered?" I pushed him.

I was relieved when he was further back. Something always seemed to be pulling us together. If I had to describe it, I might use the word magnetism, even though it sounded cheesy. There was a vivid, invisible hum that connected us with an unknown cord. It was something both of us felt and neither mentioned.

I had never been a fan of attachments. Maybe if we were back in the America where people picked their own mates for reasons of love, not because the Regal Manager thought it would aid her personal agenda. Maybe if she didn't have a portal to a black hole humming loud enough for the whole city to hear, warning of the price to defy her wishes. Maybe if I didn't have a girl in the bunker about to be gutted like an animal for giving in to the same sort of pull that Levi had on me.

Maybe.

"I want you to come with me. But I do have a reason other than wanting to see you in a Leona-approved ball gown. I found out I'll have portal duty the first evening."

I looked up with immediate interest. "You'll have the key code?"

He smiled. "One of them. As you know, Leona has the other one at all times, and she monitors what goes on in there. But I talked to Lon—he thought he might be able to scramble the signal for a few minutes. That means we'd only have the problem of the guards."

"I could take them myself," I shrugged, my excitement growing.

"I know you could."

I paced the length of the path. "We could get a scan. We'd know what we're up against. We might even find a way to disarm it."

He nodded, touching my sleeve. "Do you think you can face it?"

His question held a dare. I turned it over in my mind. Now that Morris was gone, only Levi knew how much that portal terrified me. He knew what had happened to my mother, and we'd discussed the horrible way Morris had died a second death.

"I have to," I said in a small voice. "It doesn't matter whether I can or not. I have to do it."

"I could do it for you." His eyes searched mine. His emotions were empathetic. He wanted me to let him protect me.

"You couldn't do it alone."

He sighed in silent agreement and ran his fingers down the length of my arm. With a final squeeze of my fingertips, he was gone.

Then the night was foreboding. I imagined the meandering paths of vegetation out of control, winding their way around me. It was hard to breathe.

SEVEN

I expected quiet when I returned to the bunker. Well, maybe I only hoped.

I heard the cries before I was through the safe door. People stood in the hallway murmuring and staring at me as if I should fix it. Lon came out of the control center.

"It's worse. Doc is as scared as Meora at this point."

"Miles warned me this might happen. He wondered if taking out the trackers and nanos could have consequences in sensitive people," I said in a dazed voice. "He said the hormones involved in pregnancy and birth might set off a reaction. He'd been watching the new mothers closely."

Fear pulsed like electricity. All the overwhelming emotions in the underground space joined together and zapped me like a bolt of lightning. I clenched my jaw and pushed the button to open the door. If I could raise the dead, Morris would be there assuring me and everyone that it was going to be okay. For a moment I could almost hear his voice, but the screaming from the little room drowned him out.

It was a gut-wrenching shriek. Meora must have had no control over it, because she was strong, quiet and super-smart. She was in charge of the gardens and her knack for botany had taken our food sources to a new level. What would we have done without her? Everyone loved Meora.

Especially Noah. He gave me a wild stare, his eyes begging me to do something. I gulped. If Miles didn't know what to do, what did they expect from me?

I couldn't say anything. Miles shook his head at me, wiping sweat from his brow and studying the area I was trying to avoid looking at. Without looking, I could still see pools of red in the corners of my vision, and I smelled the metallic odor that permeated the enclosed space. I never had the occasion to consider what happened at a birth. I had been content to think that a girl pushed and out came a baby.

"She's been at this too long. She's out of strength." Miles' emotions told me he was blaming himself for her condition. "The baby is just there—stuck."

I knew the feeling. Not of birth—I hoped I never knew that feeling—but I knew what it felt like to be stagnant. Afraid to move forward, unable to go back.

Another contraction seized her and Meora writhed, clutching Noah's hand so hard he had to clench his jaw against the pain. Her cries were agony to my soul as I shared her emotions.

"Give her something," I said, looking away and bracing against the torture Meora and I endured together. I reached for the wall.

"I have," Miles said in a dull tone. "I gave her everything. It's worn off."

"I'll get more."

By the time you get back, she'll be gone."

I sunk to my knees, my body stiffening in sympathetic reaction to Meora's contraction. Miles turned toward me, but I waved him away with an irritated groan.

"I don't accept this. It's 2074. We should be able to have this baby safely. What are you going to do to save them, Doc?"

My voice was strained, my head ached and my vision blurred,

49

but I made myself win the stare down with Miles. He didn't get the option of failure. She wasn't going to die.

He finally looked away from me. His eyes darted to Meora's pale, sweaty face. He was terrified, but reconciled.

"I'll do the removal."

I felt hope. Maybe he had been avoiding the easy answer. I grabbed his hand as he reached for the scalpel with trembling fingers.

"You can do this."

He motioned to Liza, who was assisting him as she often did in emergencies. She probably possessed the most mature brain in the bunker, and now her peaceful determination spread through the room as an antidote to the fear. She doused a clean cloth with ether and held it over Meora's face as she whispered comforting words close to her ear. Meora's breathing slowed, and her movement stopped. My own torture dissipated, and I sank back against the wall in relief.

It was surreal. Here we were, just kids, dealing with birth and death and choices beyond our years of experience. Was it worth it? Was freedom worth the sacrifice we might give up? I wondered if Noah thought so.

Was there an alternative? Out in the streets of Manhattan our chances were no better. How could we know the value of freedom, anyway? None of us had ever tasted it.

Whether it was right or not, after he made the decision to act, Miles was sure and steady. He ran the sharp blade against the lower part of Meora's abdomen. Liza mopped away the blood as he quickly made another incision inside her. I looked away. There was so much blood. It was everywhere. It was in my nose, stuck in my brain. How could anyone lose that much blood and survive?

I squeezed my eyes shut and waited. The room was quiet except for the whispered exchange between Miles and Liza. I heard a sucking sound and Noah's sharp intake of breath, but it was the sudden overwhelming emotion of love I sensed that made me open my eyes.

Miles lifted a bit of flesh from the blood bath below. He handed the baby to Liza and turned his attention back to Meora. Liza set the baby on the table and listened for a heartbeat and breathing. She frowned and suctioned the baby. It seemed like hours went by while she alternately suctioned and listened with the old stethoscope. Finally, with tears in her eyes, she looked up at Miles.

"I don't know what else to do."

He looked at the baby—a boy—and then back at Meora, who continued to bleed. I knew he was torn between two lives. He reached for the baby and tried to massage his back. I knew by reading his emotional gauge that his instinct told him nothing would save the little one.

"He's gone, Noah," I said for him, cringing at the sorrow that came at me like a tidal wave.

Miles sadly turned his attention back to Meora as Liza gently wiped the baby's face and wrapped him in a blanket. She placed the tiny bundle in Noah's arms before she turned to help Miles.

Noah looked at the baby and winced, his gaze darting to the low ceiling. "I didn't even want him. I didn't want my son and now he's dead."

There was nothing I could say. It was the way of things in our bunker. In our city.

"What about Meora?" Noah focused on her white face. Miles shook his head as he worked.

"I don't know. We'll have to wait and see. She's going to need rest."

Noah looked from her face to his child's, then to mine. He came and pushed the bundle into my arms.

Nothing in me wanted to take that baby. I wanted to run off to some dark corner of the city and wait out this tragedy until all the emotions had leveled out. My throat burned with cries that pleaded to be free.

This job belonged to Morris. He was the one who dealt with the dead. But he was gone.

I took the baby. Liza came and covered the peaceful little face with another cloth. It was hard to believe the baby was dead. He was warm. Soft. Everything you'd think a newborn would be.

"You can come with me if you want," I said to Noah. He considered it, but shook his head.

"I need to be here. There's nothing I can do for him now."

I turned to leave, but his voice stopped me.

"I was named after my grandfather. I don't know where he is or if he's still alive. I never met him because he was in Ohio when the country fell. But my dad always said he was brave and smart, and he helped build the walls that made that region secure. It probably doesn't matter now, but I'd like the baby to be called Noah as well."

"It matters," I said before I returned into the night, carrying the baby in one arm and a shovel in the other. Beneath Washington Park there was a host of dead that spanned centuries. Tonight this little one would join them.

I felt release in the digging. There were easier ways to bury a body, but it seemed like the only tribute I could give. When I was done and the earth covered his unmarked grave, time would forget he existed. It was the least I could do to put some effort into the task, and in that way honor the life that had been taken before it could start.

Part of me wondered if it he was better off this way. Maybe we all would be.

When the task was accomplished, I crawled into the shadow of a tree and allowed the tears.

EIGHT

Meora made it. Her color gradually returned and she got stronger. I felt her grieving no matter where I went in the bunker. I also knew she was angry I had taken the baby before she could say goodbye. I avoided talking to her about it. I didn't know what to say. At the time I had just wanted to get it over with. I hadn't thought about how she would feel. It was hard to put myself in her place, because I had no intention of ever having a baby, let alone losing one.

It was just more evidence that I shouldn't be in charge.

A few days after Meora returned to limited work in the garden, Noah found me in the control room. Panic was written all over his mind.

"What happened?"

"Meora—it's like she went crazy. She started mumbling about the citadel and Leona. She said she was going to get her baby. I told her the baby was gone, but she wouldn't even look at me." He took a step toward me. "Let me go get her."

I weighed the options. Noah could handle himself on the streets. But I didn't want to lose anyone else.

"Let me try first," I said to Noah.

I traded my basic laser rifle for a bigger one in the stockpile below the bunker. I turned to him before I left.

"Try not to worry. I'll find her, and Doc will fix her."

He hesitated. "Bring her home."

Giving Noah a brave face was one thing. Going out there and finding her was another. I followed tracks on the pavement, concerned that they seemed to be headed in the direction of the citadel. Were we really going to do this again?

Finally I caught sight of her running down the center of Broadway.

"Meora!"

She turned, but an Imposer cruiser floated between us and stopped.

I felt heat on my face. This couldn't happen. I could not lose someone else. I refused to stand and watch as Meora was dragged away to the portal—just like Sophie, just like Morris, just like my mom.

It began to rain as if the tensely wound thread that was our atmosphere had been snapped by my swirling emotions. The hero was supposed to know what to do. If that was true, I was definitely not the hero. And I didn't want to think about what that meant for everyone who was depending on me.

"Hold back your hair." The Poser held her still as he scanned her neck with his WristCom. Information appeared mid-air above his arm. I held my breath.

"Annalise Iverson," he said, skimming the details embedded in her neck tat. "What are you doing out after curfew?"

Her eyes darted wildly as she tried to pull loose from his grip. "I lost him!"

An alarm flashed on his readings. He frowned and reached for his restraint cuffs. "My readings show you have high levels of childbearing hormones, Miss Iverson. Are you aware of the punishment for disregarding the Regal Manager's procreation laws?"

Meora only moaned. "My baby! I can't find my baby!"

With regret, I took aim with my laser rifle. The young soldier would be my first kill.

As my finger pulled back the trigger, Levi stepped into view on my scope. I let the rifle drop.

"Good catch, Wallis. I'm headed into the citadel; I'll take her with me." Levi took Meora's arm and tried to ease her out of the other guard's grip.

"You know, the rest of us would like some credit once in a while."

Levi scoffed. "For her? She's crazy and sporting some funky hormones. She'll be seen by psych or sent to the portal like the others. Leona doesn't care about them. Why would that give you credit?"

Levi opened the door of his maglev unit and guided her into the seat. "Believe me; I'm doing you a favor if she happens to be a rich kid. Remember what happened to the last guy who reported a faulty hormone reading on one of them?"

Wallis narrowed his eyes, but I felt his uncertainty. "She's not wearing a wealthy sash."

Levi shrugged. "She's crazy."

Levi gave the other soldier a condescending smirk before he got into the car with Meora. I wondered exactly how high Levi went in the chain of command. I'd never seen him subservient to anyone.

It started to rain as I walked home. I stood outside the bunker in the downpour for a long time, paralyzed with dread that settled in my head like a black spot in the center of a canvas.

This wasn't over.

Swirling madness. Uncalculated, unmeasured darkness. Objects bending, distorting, falling forever. My mother—falling. Always falling, never fallen.

I tried to shout, but my voice was distant and childish. I grasped for my knife or a rifle—anything to save her—but I only saw chubby baby hands where mine should be.

The pull of the portal reached invisible black hands to grab me and pull me into never ending death.

She didn't disappear. She hovered inches from the gateway, arms outstretched toward me. Her desperate eyes focused only on me. Why didn't she disappear or break apart? Would she keep dying for the rest of time?

The skin of her chest was seared like a brand. Why was she branded? Why the mark?

"Mama!" I screamed, but I only heard a baby cry.

I sat up quickly, finding myself in my small cabin in the bunker. It had been a dream.

I rolled off my stiff cot and went to the sink to splash water on my sweaty face. I caught a glimpse of myself. Dark circles. Furrowed brow.

What a mess.

I glanced at my bed, but I didn't want to go back to the dream. I headed to the corridor instead. A peachy pear might help me forget the dream.

The memory.

The corridor was dim and quiet. I heard a buzzing sound somewhere in the distance, perhaps the faulty light Lon had mentioned. The stillness made me uneasy. What if everyone had been taken while I slept? What if I was left alone?

I went toward the soft light of the control room. The night guard had fallen asleep with his cup of coffee in front of him on the console. Since coffee had to be stolen, I only allowed the night guards to drink it. I decided to save my lecture for the trip back to my bunk.

I tiptoed toward the arched doorway that led to the gardens. The only sound was the thump of my boots against the cement floor. As I turned the corner and stepped over the threshold, a raucous noise assaulted my ears. Heart pounding, I looked down and saw something small and vaguely lifelike fly against the wall and fall to the floor.

A toy.

I blew the air from my lungs and willed normal breathing to resume.

Dread remained in the pit of my stomach as I went into the echoing room, using the light of the solar plant pots to see my way. They retained the sunlight during the night, helping them to grow faster. It had been one of Meora's ideas.

I pushed the image of her face from my mind. I wondered what Levi would do with her and when she would come home. I had sent word to Lon to let Noah know she was safe. I hoped he was getting some rest.

I reached into the tree. After a moment of searching, I found the soft flesh of a perfectly ripened peachy pear. Just as I started to take a bite I heard the voice.

Roxanne.

I dropped the fruit, turning in a circle. Had someone followed me into the garden? My hand fumbled for my knife, but I knew it hadn't been a sound I heard.

I had heard a feeling. A silent whisper in my mind.

I had never heard words before. I didn't even think it was possible. In fact, I'd never given my ability much thought at all. It was just a characteristic, like blond hair or freckles or an extra toe. There was nothing I could do to change it, so I lived with it.

I heard a dripping sound. When I lifted my hand, I saw a crimson flow of blood. I had sliced open my hand with my knife and not felt it.

Roxanne.

"Who's there?" My voice cut through the silence, but the room was dark and empty as it had been since I came in. The voice that spoke into my mind seemed feminine. Wistful and sad.

A chill shook me. I turned and charged down the hall, glad for the sound of my boots clunking against the floor. Anything to distract from the eerie silence. I turned into the control room.

"Do you have anything on the monitors?"

The young intern sat up and looked at the monitors with wide eyes, probably sure I was going to yell at him for sleeping. I held out a hand to calm him down, but it was still bleeding and that only scared him more.

"I'm not mad. I just need to know if something's out there."

He checked each screen as I did the same over his shoulder. Broadway. Astor Place. Old Lafayette. East 4th.

There was nothing. I motioned toward the entrance corridor. "Unlock it. I'm going to make sure."

He nodded and I heard the pressurized lock disengage. I cringed, hoping the sound didn't wake the babies.

"Here," the kid said and handed me a cloth bandage from the first aid kit. I wound it around the cut and headed out into the night.

Rain still fell. It was humid, but coolness tried to permeate the thick night air. Nothing was unusual. I almost turned back.

Roxanne.

The spirit was close. She waited somewhere nearby. I saw her with my mind the same way I saw the huge columns behind me towering into the sky even though they were hidden from my sight.

My eyes caught on the theater across the old street. It was dark and empty, crumbling like every other building in the area, but suddenly it was all I could think about and all I could see. I shivered. A thousand shapes and shadows closed in around me, but still my eyes saw nothing. Not even the random glow of a specter in the distance.

My boots began walking toward the ruins without my permission. Each step crunched against the gravel of what was left of the sidewalk. The arched entryway seemed like the mouth of a monster gulping me as I climbed the stairs. My fingers passed over the gold plate that marked old Astor Library, built over two hundred years before.

I would not have been able to see anything in the spacious hall except that something was glowing—something just out of my vision and removed. The old columns strained under the weight of the ornate ceiling and rows upon rows of shelves that lined every alcove section around the perimeter of the great hall.

Each breath I took, each step echoed within still vastness. I surveyed the desolation as something reached for me. Watched me.

As if a switch had been thrown, she was before me. Less than a foot from my face, she cast sad eyes my way. She wore a heavy black dress covering her from neck to feet and a thin black veil covered her ethereal face. I saw the hint of eyes, nose and mouth.

Her skin was bluish and dead-looking. Her whole body was surrounded by a halo of muted light. She faded in and out, sometimes transparent, sometimes solid.

A specter?

I had never seen one so close. It horrified me. I wanted to run, but I could only stare at her, my eyes drawn to her expression and her mournful inward cries.

Specters never interacted with the living. Never. They went about their business, unaware of a future generation observing them. Yet this one stared straight into my eyes.

She slowly looked around her, her movement static and inconsistent. Her hand reached for her throat and unbuttoned the neck of her blouse. As she pulled apart the sides and revealed the hollow at her throat, I gasped.

She had the mark.

An electrified sensation passed through my brain and adrenaline surged. I would wake up now. I closed my eyes and shook my head to make it happen. I heard a sharp, charged sound and opened my eyes. The specter was gone.

I stood in absolute darkness, staring into nothing and feeling nothing. I was alone.

NINE

Had it been a dream? I stared at the ceiling of my quarters and wondered.

I sat up and rubbed my eyes, reliving the encounter again, trying to understand what it meant. After I saw the specter in the theater, I had paced the bunker, checking on everyone. I remembered the sounds of babies crying and the smell of the guard's coffee and doubted it had been a dream.

But I was unwilling to consider the ominous questions raised by the event in the old library.

"Roxy," Lon's voice crackled from my com on the table next to the bed. I pressed the button on the side of the ancient device that hardly worked at all most days. I wound it around my ear, resigned to join the day.

"What?"

"You're going to want to get to the canteen."

I sighed loudly, hoping it made him wince. Dragging my feet the whole way, I went to the large white room filled with tables and benches. The breakfast hour had passed, but plenty lingered, huddled in groups talking. Toddlers created havoc, ignored by their socializing parents.

Before I had a chance to yell at them all to clean up and move on, I was surrounded by several gushing girls.

"You're going to the ball?" They hung on my arm. "Please, PLEASE let us go!"

I caught Liza's gaze from where she sat, sipping tea. She smiled. "I have a ball gown from before I came here."

"You're conspiring against me, too, Liza?" I made a face at her. But I was curious what the gown looked like. Liza had been from one of the wealthiest families in the city, and there had been mayhem when she disappeared from her home and never returned. Regular patrols were still sent looking for her now, two years later, but Levi always steered them the opposite way, planting clues as far north as Old Bronx.

"I don't need a ball gown."

I was being stubborn, and we both knew it. Of course I needed a ball gown.

"I'm a little more interested in how you all found out about this." I crossed my arms over my chest.

The younger girls broke into giggles and looked to the back of the room. I narrowed my eyes.

I also realized I had known the entire time he was there.

I crossed the room and kicked Levi's leg. "Out."

My fierce whisper elicited laughter from the surrounding tables. He stood up and followed me, sharing smiles with his co-conspirators on his way out.

"What are you doing? Who let you in?"

"These lips shall never tell." He leaned his face toward mine with a smile that told me he didn't care if I was mad. That irritated me more, so I pushed him. His back hit the wall but his smile didn't fade.

"I know the rules. No outsiders. But I consider myself exempt, being your own personal spy."

"Oh, please," I jeered. "No one likes a spy. They always just end up dead."

61

He shrugged and stuck his hands in his pockets. It infuriated me that I couldn't make him sorry.

"What if you were followed? You have a tracker and nanos. It's not going to be funny when we're watching the babies get tossed in the portal." I jabbed his chest. He caught my finger.

"That's not going to happen."

"What makes you so sure? And why are you telling them I'm going to the palace? That was supposed to be secret. They're all going to be whining about how they never get to do anything."

"I thought you might need some assistance getting into the proper dress." He pulled on the seam of my gray wool crossover jacket that I had worn nearly every day he'd known me.

"You should have asked." I pulled away from him. "You need to go."

He stepped closer and gave me his best pout. "I'm here now. You might as well give me a tour."

I swung out my knife so quickly we could hear the blade cut through the air. "You're ready to give me your tracker?"

His smile faded. "I know what I'm doing and no one is going to find you because of me. Why don't you trust me?"

I motioned to his uniform. "Why should I?"

He sighed and leaned back against the wall. "Don't you know I'd never let anything happen to you if it was in my power to stop it? You can read minds, Roxy. You have to know I'm telling you the truth."

"I can't read minds. And if I can trust you, why won't you give me your tracker?"

"And then what? I just waltz back into the palace without one?"

"We'd give you a neck tat," I said, but honestly, I hadn't thought that far ahead. It was all about trust to me.

"If I thought it would help you, I'd tear out the tracker myself. There are reasons why I don't. That doesn't mean you can't trust me."

I shifted and avoided his eyes. "Fine. You can see the bunker.

But then leave and don't come back."

By the smirk on his face, I knew I was wasting my breath, and Lon would be adding his ID to the scanner by the end of the hour.

I dragged him along, pointing out the control room, sidestepping toys and a wet mess of questionable origin as I headed down the long hall opening to the common area in the family quarter. The noise level increased as we approached, but it didn't seem to bother him.

"The infirmary is just off the common room. This is where the children have school and the toddlers play."

Without coming to a stop I went through the common area and proceeded down the hall. He caught up to me and grabbed my hand to stop me. I tried to ignore the pulse that went through me at his warm touch.

"What's this?"

I frowned as he gestured to the door to my room. "That's my bunk."

"I don't get to see?"

I gave him a suspicious glare. He raised an eyebrow in challenge.

"Open!" I didn't take my eyes off his face. The door sputtered to life and actually managed to open, revealing a dim view of my bed, table and bathroom, as well as the patched, painted brick wall beyond.

"Close!"

The door groaned and eventually obeyed.

"There. Satisfied?"

"Hardly." He followed me back down the hall that gave access to the large central gardens and stables. I led him through the center of the busy area which led to the canteen and kitchen across from the single quarter.

"That's it," I said when we ended back at the commons, which had grown quieter when the older children started lessons. "Have a nice day. I'll scan you out."

"How does that work?" He reached across me and fingered one

of the control panels. I wondered if he regretted the action when he realized how smudged and sticky it was. He just grinned and wiped his finger on my sleeve.

"You're stalling."

"How do you know?"

I pointed a finger at the side of my head, reminding him of my ability to read his motivations.

"So, this whole bunker is covered in Invisibility Wrap?" He ignored me and looked up.

Of course it was Invisibility Wrap. I rolled my eyes. "Tinted window with a twist. Our parents took the tech that makes smart windows tint automatically and combined it with wrap so we could turn the whole block into an illusion."

"Where'd they find the wrap?"

I shrugged. "I assume they stole it from an abandoned building. I think Morris said someone was hiding it, and they came across it during patrols."

He nodded, surveying as he did. "It seems like things are getting a little worn down."

I glared until he held out his hands in a defensive gesture.

"We steal everything to survive, Koenig. We can't replace things like you citadel people. It's not worth risking our lives. And I have to find things from before the Resistance Riots. Less tracking tech to override. Hence my old EarCom instead of your fancy WristCom."

I tapped the burnished gold band on his wrist. It was covered with flourishes and intricate wings surrounding a transparent digital screen where all his credentials, information and contacts were stored. It made me aware of the chasm between our worlds. He had the very best tech available in the world. My simple EarCom was older than I was.

He was quiet. I felt an emotion from him I assumed was disappointment. It made sense. I felt the same way.

"This crap is so old. How are we supposed to survive like this?"

I felt his surprise at the crack in my composure, but he didn't comment. He looked down the corridor behind me. We stood there for a long moment, and the sounds of many people in a small space taunted me. I wouldn't be able to keep protecting them for much longer.

I heard Liza's voice as she started her history lesson. Levi's fingers trailed down my arm to my hand and he led me to the arch opening in the common area.

Nursing mothers sat in huddles gossiping as they cared for babies. Toddlers played. The older kids huddled around Liza to hear her story.

"You have a lot of little ones," Levi whispered.

As if I hadn't noticed. "Tell me about it."

"Ever thought about stealing birth control?"

I rammed my arm into his side and he coughed a laugh.

"You have any ideas on finding such contraband? Now that would be something useful you could do."

He smiled. "I'm just teasing. I actually think kids are great. I hope I get to be a father someday."

I stared at him in surprise and found I had no response. We both turned to watch Liza.

"We've discussed what happened in our city all the way back to the beginning of the century—when terrorists flew planes into the World Trade Center in 2001, and the people rallied against terrorism and fought for freedom. Now I want to tell you why we aren't free today."

The children stilled and listened. I could hear their curious confusion. They couldn't fathom freedom. It hurt me to think about it.

"Over thirty years ago, a black hole in the center of our galaxy became so strong that we began to notice its pull on the earth. Scientists knew that if it were to pull us out of orbit around the sun, we would all die. A smart scientist named Arabella Eisen used a powerful magnet with a huge mirror to deflect the pull of the black hole and cap its power. She was a hero!"

The children clapped in excitement. I felt their hope surge and wished more than anything Mom was still alive.

"Unfortunately, an evil woman was jealous and stole the portal. She wanted to use it to control people who didn't agree with her. With this power she took over the city and made it her kingdom."

"Leona!" one of the children called out in disgust. A few booed. Liza waited until they were quiet. I sensed a wave of hollow sadness from Levi. I didn't get it. He was the one that chose her side.

"The Regal Manager Leona killed your grandmas and grandpas by throwing them in the portal. Some escaped to build this special home for us to hide in, and a man named Morris was chosen to take care of us."

At this, the kids all started talking at once. They remembered Morris. They missed him. He had loved every one of them like they were his own children. Tears stung my eyes, but I fought them off when I felt Levi's eyes—and mind—on me.

"As you know, Morris gave his life to protect us. And he left Captain Roxy in charge."

"Tell the story of when Cap'n Roxy was a baby!"

Levi's emotions got louder. I eyed him curiously, wishing for a moment I knew exactly what he was thinking.

"When the Regal Manager threw Arabella into the portal, Mrs. Eisen had a little girl not yet two. Leona tried to kill her, but she escaped. Because of that miracle, we call her *Daughter of Hope*. It is her destiny to save us from Leona."

The kids cheered. I ducked out of the doorway so they wouldn't see me. Levi followed me down the hall and stopped me by gripping my arm. I faced him unwillingly.

"Thank you for showing me your home and your family. I'm glad they know how special you are."

I scoffed and pulled away. Kept walking. "The only thing special about me is a genius dead mom who wanted me to lead. That's not enough to qualify for a destiny."

I didn't want him to respond. Fortunately, at that moment, Lon met us outside the control room and asked Levi to brief him on citadel security in preparation for the banquet. As they talked, my eyes were trapped on Levi and I couldn't pull them off.

He had a friendly smile, which was a paradox, or at least an irony, considering the injustice and death represented by his uniform. I noticed how his hair was trimmed just enough to meet citadel standards, but still long enough to curl around his ear and wave at the nape of his neck. His features were defined within his olive complexion and dark eyes.

Those were the obvious traits, but what brought them to life was the light in his eyes, especially when he was looking at me. He wore an intense and almost sad expression, and the feelings that spilled from his mind and reached out to wrap their warmth all around me were an experience. Like taking a drug or drinking wine.

Two things I didn't allow my people to consider.

As comfortable as I felt with Levi, as close as we had gotten in the past months, it only became more obvious that there was a knot between us. Some kink we couldn't discuss, couldn't resolve. Unfinished business.

He was done talking to Lon, so I opened the safe door for him to leave. He turned, leaning close to my face.

"See you Sunday night. And don't wear your stretch pants."

TEN

Sunday found me in front of a mirror for a good part of the afternoon. I made sure to grimace and sigh as much as possible while Liza expertly turned me into the Regal Manager's dream subject come true.

"I hate makeup," I said as she contoured and blended.

My hair was tamed into ringlets and pinned in a loose chignon. She pushed a flowered silver comb into the mass of curls she had created. Her fingers swept over it longingly as if she was remembering something that made her sad. She forced herself to smile when she saw me watching her. I didn't remind her I could see past the smile.

She sprayed her artwork of hair with an old bottle of crystalline, which gave the illusion of dewdrops sparkling in the sunlight. I complained.

"This will protect you." She was unperturbed by my protest. "If you went without the things she expects, you would be discovered."

She was right, so I sat and let her finish. The worst part came when she put the smart corset around my waist and clicked the remote to initiate the sizing process. It grew tighter, measuring my curves as it calculated the best way to make me look ridiculous.

Finally she pulled the soft cream taffeta gown around the corset and buttoned the back. When she stepped back she gasped in delight.

"You look amazing."

Unwillingly, I looked for myself in the mirror while she added a fashionable leather outer-corset. Apart from the sneer on my face, I had to admit I looked the part. I touched the soft material of the bodice. The rosette edging that lined the décolletage met in a cinched waist before it flowed outward on either side to reveal my laced leggings and glittery boots.

Liza finished by adding a string of pearls that looked antique. She was satisfied.

I hoped to escape the bunker without being ogled, so I had told them earlier they could have a Sing. There wasn't much to do when your life was hiding. I didn't let them watch movies or old television shows. I was too afraid of what might be embedded in the Leona-approved entertainment. But what I could allow was music—at least the music they made themselves. So I had stolen instruments. We had everything from flutes to violins to drums. Even a piano, though I never would have pulled that off without Levi's help. I found lesson books and plenty of music, and the kids taught themselves to play. They'd become pretty good at it.

I felt a little wistful as I headed for the exit. I could hear them singing along to the music. Every voice joined in; melody and harmonies blended in a disciplined and untamed dance. I wished I was in my place with my cello and bow string.

The colors of our songs were often sad. We told our story over and over by the music we adopted and the music we created on our own. I felt the burden of its weight, but at the same time relief, like putting salve on a wound.

I breathed in their strength. I would need it where I was going.

When I reached street level, I motioned to Greer. He was dressed in an approved brown corduroy suit with a top hat and spectacles.

"Let's go."

He stared at me for a long moment.

"What?" I snarled at him.

"Whoo-ee, Captain!" He hit his knee with his hat. "You sure look like a girl tonight."

"Shut up."

"Yes, sir. Just saying, Captain. All aces."

As Greer continued to mutter about my appearance under his breath, I dreaded the moment Levi would see me. Not so much because I was afraid he would allow himself to be distracted from the task.

I was afraid he would distract *me* if he was too impressed.

The Crystal Citadel shone from blocks away. Leona had purple beams emanating from the top of the palace, joining the usual blinding ray that shot into the sky from the dome that housed the portal. Smart copters circled, and the streets were congested with hovering maglevs.

The citadel had been Leona's first project when she took power. She had demolished the public library, where she and Mom had first developed the portal. Leona took over all of Bryant Park and the surrounding blocks. For some reason she had chosen to make her palace out of iron, glass and crystal. I questioned her choices. They seemed weak.

"Some say she built it this way so the portal would make everything gleam for blocks around, reflecting the light," Greer said. "Probably to remind us of her power."

I focused my attention on him. "Tell me what you're going to do."

"Distract Leona and keep her busy when Lon signals he's about to take down portal security protocols. I'll keep it up until Levi signals that you are out of the chamber."

"Remember—low profile."

He nodded with a thread of impatience and headed away from me toward the throng of people waiting to get into the palace.

"No wine!" I called after him. He made a face he thought I couldn't see. One day maybe they would get the fact that everything they felt was displayed in the air like subtitles for me.

"Aye, sir. I'll keep a low profile. Just like you keeping your low profile," he mumbled as he walked away.

I was left alone in a sea of people; I felt like I was drowning. I was tempted to go home. But before I could flee, Levi was behind me, his breath on my ear and his warm hands on my bare shoulders.

"I used to like this girl named Roxy. But you could make me forget all about her."

I felt his tidal wave of emotions. Everything from familiarity and comradery to the more predictable feelings you might expect from a twenty-year-old guy seeing a girl in a pretty dress. I didn't want to know. I could not afford to feel what he was feeling.

"Don't," I said in desperation. "Don't say it. Don't even think it. You'll make me weak."

He was surprised, but he nodded. He escorted me up the marble stairway into the immense and impossibly bright palace where every soul in Leona's kingdom gathered to pay homage by sharing her excess.

Well, not every soul.

"What do you think?" Levi asked as we stepped inside the banquet hall. My breath caught in my throat.

The crystal ballroom, much like Leona's throne room only exaggerated, stretched on forever with ceilings so high my perception of space was disturbed. Around the outer walls stretched hundreds of tables covered by rich blue and white textiles and golden bowls filled with every imaginable kind of exotic food. Servants stood with heads down, ready to serve. The floor was a dazzling display of tiny squares of mosaic tiles in purple and crystal.

"Seems to me Leona has something to prove," I said.

A colossal fountain of gold in the center of the hall gushed purple liquid from a naked cherub perched on top, down the tiers to the pool of wine below where citizens freely dipped golden goblets and drank their fill.

Levi pointed to one of the many warning signs written in elaborate script.

THIEVERY OF THE GOBLETS WILL RESULT IN THE MAXIMUM PENALTY BY LAW.

"She'd portal someone for stealing a cup?" I curled my lip in disgust.

"That surprises you?"

"No. She'd probably portal someone for using the wrong brand of toilet strips."

He laughed.

A full orchestra played from a balcony on the back wall over the massive throne where Leona sat. I recognized it from her throne room; it must have been moved from its normal location. She smiled with affectionate air at those who waited in line to pass by and gawk at her diamond and sapphire studded gown and the tiny diamonds threaded throughout her elaborate hairstyle. She wrinkled her nose merrily, as if she wasn't the sort of queen that would get up and throw someone in the portal if only she could find an excuse.

Levi and I watched the center screen that covered the entire east wall of glass. Leona stood and held her arms open wide.

"My dear subjects, I am humbled you have come to share in my wealth. I encourage you to eat and drink your fill. Know my power and rest in the security I offer to all my people as an oasis in this dark world."

Sweeping applause followed her statement. I huffed in disgust. I expected Levi to do the same, but when I glanced at him he was looking at Leona with a guarded expression. I read his melancholy tone.

"Let's dance!" Leona called out in a voice I supposed she

thought was cute. The people swarmed the center of the room to begin formal dancing. Not exactly anyone's idea of fun.

"There," I gestured as Leona took a dramatic bow onscreen. "Inside her dress. You can see the chain where she keeps the portal monitor."

Levi patted the chest of his ceremonial uniform. "She's not the only one."

We made our way through the room. Levi introduced me as his friend Fiona, which matched my new neck tat details. I started to relax when I saw that no one suspected anything.

"Want some wine?" Levi stepped to the fountain and reached for two goblets. I glared at him.

"Might make the job easier."

I shook my head. He shrugged and put one golden goblet back before he filled the other one and sipped. I watched with reproach.

"Don't judge me, Roxy. I don't follow your rules. Let's dance."

I backed away from the dance floor, but he grabbed my hand and pulled me back. "You have to play the part tonight."

He took firm hold of my waist and hand. I was whisked into the crowd of dancing couples performing a brisk waltz. I could smell the sweet wine on his breath and I couldn't deny the strength in his arms as he moved, taking me with him.

"I hate dancing." I tried to keep up with the bold movements. I looked up and got dizzy when I saw the second glass dance floor above us, also brimming with dancers. "Someone should tell Leona it's not the nineteenth century anymore."

"It may not be your style, but it can still be fun. Enjoy yourself for once."

The music slowed. I tried not to think about how it was probably Levi's nearness and not the dancing that made it hard to breathe.

"This isn't my idea of fun."

"You don't have an idea of fun," he said. "You're going to give yourself away with that scowl."

"I have nothing to smile about."

73

His eyes found mine. Though humor lit them, there was a challenge buried in the depths. I was suddenly trying to stay afloat.

"Nothing?"

I wasn't sure the way he made my stomach attempt acrobatic feats unknown to man was anything I'd ever smile about.

"You have to relax. Believe that I am not going to hurt you," he said so quietly I had to strain to hear him. "We can do this, but you have to make up your mind to change your attitude. I can't do that for you."

I knew he was right, and I hated him for making me look weak. I tore my gaze out from under his and attempted to breathe again.

"I know." I forced a smile I imagined as brilliant. I leaned close to him and acted like all the other teenage girls gushing all over their dates. He skimmed both hands around my waist, to the consternation of everyone around us, including me.

"Leona doesn't go for this kind of dancing." I nodded to the official guards standing in front of the throne.

As usual, Levi seemed unconcerned at being caught.

"A friend asked what you look like," he said in a casual tone. I figured he was trying to distract me, but I played along.

"Why are you telling your friends about me?

"I just said I liked this girl I've been hanging out with."

I looked away, embarrassed and uncomfortable with the way my cheeks were heating up.

"I told him you are pretty without even trying to be. Don't get me wrong—I'm not complaining that you tried today."

I felt him studying my face as I avoided his eyes. "I didn't try at all. I sat on a stool and whined while Liza tried."

He ignored me. "You're strong but still soft underneath your boring clothes. But I like your eyes best. They are exactly the color of a storm right before it lets loose out over the Atlantic."

"That's so cliché." I tried to act bored.

"Then I guess your eyes are cliché." He made a face at me. "But I think they're art. Especially since the light of all your determination almost physically shines out of them. You wear your heart in those stars you call eyes, Roxy."

"I'll have to close my eyes more." I made sure he thought I was indifferent. It was a very good thing he couldn't see my thoughts.

I was relieved when I felt the tattoo on my neck vibrate, signaling the twenty-minute warning from Lon. I'd had my fill of Levi emotions, which were heightened every time he took another drink of wine. I sensed he was thinking about trying to kiss me and that wasn't going to happen. Ever.

"Showtime."

Levi pulled me off the dance floor with flair, holding me possessively and smiling at friends. I noticed a few girls send him alluring glances while they aimed eye daggers dripping with jealousy at me.

In that moment the music changed. Really changed. A single mournful chord from an electric guitar filled the hall with a striking and unfamiliar sound.

"In honor of our most superior queen, we are going to play a half-hour medley of music from the time period that gave us our beloved leader. Her Highness, the Regal Manager, be honored as we ... *rock the house*."

Greer.

"So much for low-profile," I said.

Greer continued the mournful melody. The static popped in our ears as the notes echoed through the hall. It was haunting. The music spoke to the heart of the collective unconscious, desperate for freedom. Chained by each minor chord, each dissident harmony represented our liberties torn away.

When the band hesitantly joined in, the chords became more focused. Harmonic and confident. Every eye and heart dared to look up and let the music lead them on a symbolic march. I gulped in surprise. An unfamiliar emotion was sweeping through the immense room in time to the driving beat sending out a beacon of motivation to weary conformists.

It almost felt like hope.

I had considered Leona's subjects her willing puppets, but the sudden vibration strumming across minds told me there was discontent. Had I been seeing my city all wrong? Were there more to save than just the bunker kids?

"Leona is going to have a meltdown." Levi watched her face displayed on the screen. Her eyes were wide and crazed with rage; her cheeks were pink. She wore a chilling smile.

I wasn't close enough in proximity to hear her emotions above everyone else's. "What do you think she'll do?"

"She won't say anything publicly. She can't without ruining her image. But Greer better disappear when he's done, because if she finds him, she won't need a reason."

His words troubled me.

"Are you ready for this?" he said solemnly.

I didn't answer him at first. I didn't think I could—fear was like a cord around my neck. But I fought it. I had to.

"Let's get it over with."

ELEVEN

We crept down the reflective hallway that led toward the center portico and the winding staircase up into the glowing dome. I had to force my feet to follow Levi's steps. At the top of the stairs I looked back and saw the height we had climbed.

Two guards stood at attention outside the double arched doorway. An ornate brass mechanism opened to reveal a star shape around a sensor pad. And Levi had the key.

I was ready to reach for my knife between the folds of my skirt where it rested against my right thigh. I sensed a sudden rush of apprehension from Levi that worried me. After observing his emotion, I realized it wasn't the guards he was afraid of. It was me.

He grabbed me around the waist and started laughing. Loudly. The kind of laughing people did when they drank too much wine. I was sure he was drunk and that he was going to ruin everything in the plan. I pushed against his chest, expecting he would move away when I protested, but he didn't. His iron grip was so tight it hurt when I tried to struggle away from him.

It was a trap. All I could think of was the buzz of that black hole waiting just beyond the door, ready to swallow me up for the rest of eternity. I felt physical pain at his betrayal as I shrieked and clawed at his face. I managed to slice his cheek with my fingernails and cause him to loosen his hold on me, but he only grabbed me again as I tried to escape.

He leered at the guards. They smiled back with an easy stance. I could sense their respect for Levi. They would do whatever he said.

"Hey." Levi's voice slurred. "I found a girl."

"Sure did." One of them ogled me, nodding his approval at Levi's find. I was disgusted when I saw the pathway to his thoughts.

"Why don't you two get lost for a few minutes?" Levi glanced up at the cams. I hoped Lon had not disabled them. He could alert Greer to rescue me. I continued to squirm, hoping Levi would get tired and lose his hold.

"Lon!" I managed to scream the word before Levi clamped a hand over my mouth. I had to fight for breath. The guards laughed uneasily, torn between duty and desire to please Levi, who was clearly their superior.

"What about the Regal Manager?" The other guard checked his WristCom, probably to avoid eye contact with Levi.

"How will she know? She's a little busy being worshipped. Let me by."

They looked at each other.

"I assume you don't want me to turn in a report on you."

Their concern spiked. They both shuffled away from the door and allowed Levi to access the lock mechanism. He held up his key card and waved it against the circular brass star scanner on the wall. It unfolded to reveal a weird glass eye that scanned Levi from head to foot. The door vanished and we were looking into the portal chamber.

Levi pulled me inside and threw me to the floor, turning to reseal the door behind him. An unnatural, hot light filled the space, buzzing with unseen energy radiating off everything. My breath was coming in short little gasps as I looked up and saw the mammoth containment capsule that opened to the portal. Just beyond those steel access panels the power of a distant, dying star was ready to capture me in its powerful hold.

I stood up and rushed against Levi, knocking him back. He quickly grabbed my shoulders and turned me around so my back was against the wall. He held my flailing arms at my sides.

"Shh," he whispered close to my ear. "It's okay."

I didn't believe him for a second. "I can read your guilt, you disgusting traitor."

He shook his head. "Roxy, it's me. I'm not trying to hurt you. I just needed them to believe it."

I stopped struggling and glared at him. I tried to read his mind more than I'd ever tried before. I felt a sharp pain in my head. I pressed my fingers against my temples and closed my eyes tightly.

His voice was gentle and pleading. "You know I'm telling you the truth."

I searched him one more time even though it only made the pain worse. He wasn't lying, but I still sensed a certain emotion that wanted to stay buried, just out of my reach. I released my breath.

"I don't know how long Lon can keep the system down. We should hurry."

I nodded and pulled out the small pen scanner Lon had given me. All I had to do was hold down the button and shine the infrared light across the surface of the doors. It would record everything beyond them.

I fumbled with it as I walked the long expanse of the room. The sound of my steps echoed, causing an eerie duet with the persistent static hum of the portal. It occurred to me that the portal room was similar in size and elegance to both the ballroom and the throne room, though the portal chamber was mostly empty and quiet. All of Leona's rooms seemed, by design, equal. The marble floor felt hard and cold under my impractical footwear. The pillars that lined each side of the room lent a stern warning that every step I took closer to those steel doors was a step closer to death. Levi watched the monitor over the door as I held the scanner toward the doors. A few seconds, and the scan would be uploading to the bunker network.

My eyes fell on the brander sitting on the console. It was turned up so I could see the fine lines of the marking it made—a solid star with a dot on the upper left and lower right, and an arc under the lower left and the upper right.

It was the mark my mother had in my dreams.

Something else occurred to me in that moment of paralyzed terror. It was also the mark the specter had shown me in the theater.

Faint noise outside the entry to the chamber made me drop the scanner. I stared in disbelief. My sole purpose for coming to the citadel broke into pieces as it smashed against the marble.

"Someone's coming," Levi said, motioning me to him. I picked up the pieces of the scanner and ran to him. He grabbed me around the waist. I gulped back my protest and allowed him to heave me over his shoulder.

"Act like you're unconscious," he whispered. The field disappeared with the door and he stepped out into the corridor.

It was too late. Leona elegantly ascended the stairway followed by a large group of Posers surrounding a prisoner. She stopped at the top of the stairs. I didn't know what was happening, but I could read her suspicion.

"Levi Koenig," she said sharply.

His voice was even and confident. "Regal Manager."

She stepped closer. "What do we have here?"

I buried my face in the cloth of his uniform as he answered her. "She tried to steal the goblets."

He dumped me against the wall and I slumped with my face turned toward it. There was a long pause.

"Very well. Prepare the chamber."

Levi's apprehension spiked. "You would portal her for stealing a cup?"

"I said prepare the chamber." Her voice got higher as it got louder. "Is that too much to ask? Shall I ask someone else?"

"No, Your Majesty," he answered, accenting her title in a way that almost sounded sarcastic. Was Levi not afraid of the most powerful woman in North America?

I peeked and saw the prisoner behind her, flanked between the guards.

It was Greer.

"My subjects," Leona called to the live feed outside the portal that broadcasted to the city. "It grieves me to make you witness this on such a happy night, but where would I be if I allowed my tender heart to overlook such blatant disregard for the rules of this kingdom?"

The hallway was quiet. I felt the intimidation of every guard standing around her. She turned to Greer, folding her hands demurely in front of her.

"Young man, if you will tell me where you hid the items you stole I will reduce your sentence. I am not a cruel woman, but I would not be a leader if I did not require your respect and obedience."

I watched Greer. He stared at Leona defiantly but said nothing. I felt the familiar panic of responsibility, the same feeling of helplessness I had when I saw Morris dragged away to the portal. When I found Sophie lifeless in the chair. I couldn't lose another one.

Greer frowned straight at me when he saw me move. His frown became a vicious glare. I knew what it meant. I could hear the words he would say if he could speak to me.

Don't you dare leave everyone unprotected on my account. Greer can take care of Greer.

Leona twisted her face so she would look distressed and compassionate. She motioned for the guards as she wiped tears from the corner of her eyes.

"Give him the brand," she whispered and handed her key to a Poser. She turned away as if she couldn't bear to watch. The field vanished and I felt the static again, crackling in the air around me, making the hairs on my arm stand straight up.

They dragged him toward the console and prepared the brander. The coils glowed blue. Greer's shirt was ripped open and he was held down on the floor. Skin and heat met with a searing hiss. Greer cried out, and I gasped, sharing his pain.

"One last chance." Leona didn't look back at him. A guard pushed a button to open the steel panels and a wild, bright fury sent the room spinning. A magnetic force seemed to beckon me toward the blinding ray. Even the marble pillars supporting the portico seemed to bend toward that light.

I was ready to throw myself at the guards and give Greer a chance of escaping. My fingers were reaching for my knife. Suddenly, Leona turned back.

"Wait. Throw him in a holding bay in the archives. He may change his mind overnight."

I felt relieved until I noticed that both Greer's and Levi's concern had grown. I sorted their emotions. Suspicion. Foreboding. Why would Leona extend grace? She only would if it somehow benefited her.

She must suspect there was more to Greer than the music stunt. Did she know he belonged to my people?

If she did, she would torture him. She would get the truth and kill him when she had what she wanted. Not only was Greer in danger, but every teenager and child in our bunker.

I slipped my knife into my hand and slowly sat up. But Greer was way ahead of me. He threw his elbow back and hit the guard in the nose. He slammed his foot into the gut of the other one.

"For Captain Eisen and the Resistance!" Greer shouted. He gave me a smile and sank back toward the portal. "For freedom!"

He vanished into the light.

Leona stepped forward, rage burning in her expression. I dropped back to the floor and covered my face, trying not to sob aloud.

While I attempted not to scream my protest, I heard Levi tell two of the Posers to take me to his room and lock me in a holding field. Leona directed unspoken disgust and disapproval his way, but she let it go and returned to her banquet without a word. The portal was disarmed and the door secured.

The guards dragged me to the elevation tunnel that rocketed upward and then to the right, stopping abruptly but smoothly enough that no one lost their footing. The door disappeared and I remained limp as they took me down a long hall. Their boots echoed elegantly across the polished floors and against the high, arched ceilings.

They stopped in front of an ostentatious doorway with thick trim covered in beautiful scrollwork. The material of the door looked like wood, but it sounded like iron as they opened it with their WristCom ID.

"So Leona treats you Posers pretty well," I smirked at one of them. "I thought you minions probably slept in the dungeon."

They didn't answer, but they exchanged a glance with each other. One of them pushed me into the room and used his WristCom to imprison me in a narrow, invisible field that buzzed with electricity and jolted me back when I tried to touch it.

"I wouldn't try to escape," one of them advised. They left, closing the heavy door behind them and leaving me alone in the dimly lit room.

The space stretched on forever. The walls were dark and rich, made of the same material as the door. Arched windows lined the outer wall, floor to ceiling, providing a spectacular view of the city as I had never seen it before.

I tried not to look at the mammoth maglev bed that fit the scale of the room, but not doing so was difficult, as it seemed to be the focal point. Intricately carved posts rose so high they nearly touched the ceiling, and opulent, masculine bedding covered the thick mattress.

Where in the world was I? How could this be a simple Poser's bedroom?

I waited there for what seemed like hours, my unease growing with every second that passed. Levi finally appeared, looking rather sheepish. There it was again, shelved behind his friendly manner. Guilt.

"I'm sorry, Roxy. This wasn't how this night was supposed to go."

"Whose room is this?" I tried to sound indifferent, but my voice came out small and weak. We both knew I was completely at his mercy.

His expression was dark as he glanced around the room. "Unfortunately, it's mine."

"Unfortunately?" I raised an eyebrow, doubtful. "I could fit about twenty of my rooms in this one. Double that if you factor the height. Why don't you like it?"

He shrugged. "I didn't ask for it."

"So all the Posers have rooms like this?"

He shifted and didn't answer.

"You might as well tell me. I can see everything you're feeling, anyway."

"No, not all the soldiers have rooms like this. Most of them live in military housing across the street."

"Why you?"

He walked to the window and stared out with a morose expression. "I'm ... in charge of the other Peace Implementers."

"What do you mean? Like a general?" I stared at him in confusion. He sighed and turned around to look at me.

"Why did you think I could help you, Roxy? You think a regular soldier could pull off the things I've done for you? Didn't you figure I had a little power?"

I didn't know how to respond. He seemed sad. Torn. I hadn't considered the position he was in. Maybe it should make me have more faith in him, but I only felt more suspicious. This all had to be an elaborate trap. Leona wouldn't have a dissenter in such a position. If Levi was in charge of her army, she would trust him with her life.

I tried not to let my voice betray my fear. "What now?"

He came to the holding field and disarmed it with his

WristCom, and then he stood next to me, searching my eyes, letting his gaze wander down my arm. Tentatively he reached his hand toward mine. I wanted to pull back. I tried to. But my hand wouldn't obey. It craved his touch. It wanted to feel his skin next to mine.

His fingers slid between mine. The hint of a smile played at his mouth.

"I think you kind of like my room." His eyes teased me. I forced a frown.

"It's gaudy. And drafty."

"No, you like it." Pressure increased on my hand. "This is the longest you've ever let me touch you."

"It's also the last time." I pulled my hand away. "I've seen enough of your world, Levi. I want to go home."

His smile faded, but he nodded in agreement. "Just a few minutes. I need them to believe I'm doing what I hinted I was doing."

My cheeks heated as understanding dawned. "That's another thing. Why did Leona let this go? I didn't think she would hesitate to portal anyone for breaking her procreation laws."

Sometimes she turns a blind eye." Levi was evasive again. "When it benefits her."

I wanted to ask more questions, but he moved to the window and looked out into the darkness. "I'm going to call for a maglev. It will be in the bay at the end of the hall in five minutes. Get on it, have it take you a couple blocks away, then take the subway tunnels home. I'll cover for you."

I nodded, unable to speak. I realized I had learned more today about Levi Koenig than I had in the past year put together.

And I didn't feel good about any of it.

TWELVE

When I got back to the bunker, some of the kids were still in the common area. The song was solemn and full of heart—their version of an old hymn. Did they somehow know about Greer?

I didn't want to, but I went to them. I stood in the archway and stared at the floor as I spoke.

"Greer's gone."

Most of them only stared at me sadly. Some turned their faces away and cried.

"You should know he died protecting us. He gave his life for you. We are still safe because he isn't."

I made myself look them in the eye. They were no strangers to loss. Morris had taught us losing people was a part of our lives we had to accept, but that we shouldn't let it hold us back from loving.

I learned that from my parents. He had given me a direct look as he said the words. *They weren't afraid of love. They faced it head-on, even though it cost them everything.*

I couldn't accept this sentiment from Morris' mysterious parents. I was convinced they were wrong. Love was a liability.

How could I come to any other conclusion?

I felt justified in my thinking when I went to say goodnight to Lon. He cleared his throat and looked away from me, which was always a bad sign.

"What?"

"It's Meora."

I thought back, remembering she had been safely returned by night in Levi's patrol maglev the day after she had disappeared. "What's wrong with her?"

"She's been summoned. To a Rehabilitation."

I didn't say it aloud, but I wondered how Meora was so calm. She sat in front of the large desk of the counselor, staring at her folded hands in her lap.

"Good afternoon, Miss Iverson. I'm so honored you could join me."

The view from Meora's feed in her contact lens shifted as she looked up at the official. I sneered at Lon, who gave me a passive glance.

"Ridiculous."

The fabric of her costume clung to her waist—tightly corseted—in a way that made me feel the need to take a deep breath. Her skirt, supported by hip hoops, flowed widely to either side, revealing sepia-toned stockings and pointed leather boots. Fake black curls piled atop her head, contrasting the smooth white polish of her makeup.

"My name is Mrs. Bowery. Of the Fifth Avenue Bowerys." She smiled grandly, as if Meora should be impressed. Meora managed a nod. The woman looked annoyed, but she kept the sugary smile pasted to her face.

"I will supervise your Rehabilitation," Bowery said. "May I ask you to please verify your name and identification number for security purposes?"

Meora repeated the false number I spoke into her EarCom from the tablet Lon held up for me to read.

"Annalise Iverson. 65125621510."

Bowery reached toward Meora's neck and scanned a confirmation.

"Now, dear, a Peace Implementer was, unfortunately, able to detect hormones in your bloodstream consistent with pregnancy and birth. In his report he claims you shouted the words 'My baby, my baby.'"

"Don't say anything," I instructed her. I watched Bowery rise to pour coffee and get a plate of pastries.

"I get so hungry this time of morning. Don't you?" She set the plate down in front of Meora. "Would you care for one?"

"No, thank you."

"I'm sure this is going to end up a silly misunderstanding when my readings of your blood sample are done, so I'll only ask once. Have you given birth to an unsanctioned child or been involved in an unsafe physical relationship outside of government approved marriage?"

"Just say no," I said. Meora hesitated, probably because she knew it was a lie and she was worried she'd be discovered, but she did as I asked. Lon furiously worked at the computer well to hack into the woman's medical scanner and change the results based on a blood sample Doc had taken from me.

"Dear, you don't have to be afraid to tell me the truth." Bowery smiled with nauseating sweetness. She rotated her hand, gesturing to herself. "I am a safe space."

"Ah, she got Bowery. Of the Fifth Avenue Bowerys." Levi mocked from behind me, making me jump. I turned around and glared, stepping hard on his toe. He frowned and mouthed "ow" to me. I rolled my eyes and turned back to the screen. I felt the same unsettled churning I'd been having whenever I thought about Levi since the night of the banquet.

"What are you doing here?" I said with accusation. I sensed darkness behind his easy smile that made me apprehensive.

"I saw Meora on the schedule this morning and came by to see if I could help," he said.

I pushed against him with my back, anxious to widen the distance between us.

"Just stay out of the way," I said before I unmuted my voice in Meora's EarCom.

"So tell me, Annalise," said Mrs. Bowery. "I know sometimes our Regal Manager's policies concerning relationships between young men and women can seem harsh when emotions and attraction are involved. Once again, it's okay to tell me the truth."

"Because she's a safe space," Levi whispered.

Meora's voice was confident. "I asked permission to allow Ethan Hutchins to court me with the intention of government-approved union."

"Hmm." Bowery scrolled through the screen that hovered mid-air over her WristCom. "I don't see any record of your request."

"There must be a mistake," Meora shrugged.

"Dear, you cannot be more than fifteen. Of course you realize our leader feels that is too young to be emotionally prepared for the ordeals of these kinds of relationships."

"I'm nineteen," Meora said, and Bowery seemed to accept the answer. As the woman turned her back on Meora to check the readings, Lon gave me the thumbs up. I watched Levi lean back against the console and fold his arms across his chest.

"You know, it just occurred to me that you don't approve of most of the romances going on down here." He smirked at me. "You and Leona aren't really all that different, are you?"

"We are NOTHING alike," I hissed, forgetting my voice was still in Meora's EarCom.

And I don't approve of ANY of them.

One of the toddlers came down the hallway at top speed, naked as the day he was born and on a mission of escape. His mom huffed along after him until he finally fell victim to his short legs and uneven girth and went careening into the wall. Howls filled the air until Lon reached over to shut the entrance doors and muffle the noise.

I gave Levi a barbed look.

"I feel like you're trying to make some kind of point." He was trying not to laugh. Bowery began speaking again, so we turned our attention back to the screen.

"The guard who apprehended you must have had some faulty equipment. It happens, though not often. I'm going to allow you to go with this word of advice: Don't think we are unaware of the undercurrent of youth in this city believing the Regal Manger is some sort of monster. Nothing could be further from the truth. Sometimes the things we think we want aren't good for us, and it's a sign of maturity to take this to heart. Your leader has your best interests in mind."

Bowery came around the desk and placed a lacy gloved hand on Meora's shoulder.

"I'm sure," she answered.

"Of course, you must also keep in mind what your punishment could have been if hormones were detected. I would have been forced to turn you over to the citadel, and I'm sure you are aware of the penalty for unlawful childbearing."

I glanced at Levi, but he wouldn't look at me. On occasion, Leona sent new mothers and illegitimate babies into the portal. I wanted to ask him if he still thought I was like her, but I sensed enough shame that it didn't seem right to add to it.

Noah met Meora in the tunnels and brought her home. She leaned against him as they walked back to the family quarter, hand-in-hand. Their feelings inside my mind were like thorns pricking my psyche, showing me all the things I couldn't have.

Someone to hold. Someone to hear me. Someone to share the burden of responsibility.

Levi ran a finger down my arm. "Can we talk?"

"Go home to your fancy bedroom." I tried to walk away, but he took my arm and directed me toward my room.

"I don't allow socializing in rooms." I tried to sound extra obstinate.

"As I said, I don't follow your rules. I have something to tell

90

you and you don't want anyone to overhear this."

Adrenaline rushed and made my throat tight. I called for my door to open and followed him in.

He looked around. His gaze fell on the picture of my mother and he reached for it with a sadness I couldn't interpret.

"Leona's looking for you," he said without looking at me.

I shrugged. "Leona's been looking for me for sixteen years. So what?"

"You're on the security footage from the ball."

Anger pulsed through me, and I pushed him. "See? Why don't you ever listen to me?"

He was ready for the abuse and stood strong. He held my arms and eased me back against the door.

"Take it easy. She's already seen your face anyway, Roxy. And I was in the footage with you. I told her it wasn't you."

I bit my lip and stared past him as he continued.

"But since Greer, she's been more determined than ever to end the rebellion before it starts. She vowed she would find the girl on the feed with Greer, even if the girl is Fiona who stole a goblet and spent an evening in my chamber. She wants to know more about Greer because she thinks it will lead to you. She put the picture of both of you on the city SmartBoards and has a warrant for your arrest."

I wanted to scream. I walked across the room and kicked the brick wall with my boot, which only made my foot hurt.

"I understand you're mad at me." Levi's voice was petulant and low. "I didn't expect Greer to do what he did or say what he said. I'm sorry."

He stepped behind me and took my hand to turn me around. He looked into my eyes as if he was trying to read my mind. I could see his feelings. Shame and concern.

Well, he wasn't the only one who was worried.

"What am I going to do?" I rubbed my face with my hands. "They'll all die because I was stupid."

He shook his head. "This isn't your fault. We'll deal with it together."

"How?" He couldn't fool me. I saw his uncertainty.

"You know I haven't got it figured out yet. Stay here and lay low until I come up with a plan." His words soothed as much as his fingers that reached to my face, barely brushing against my cheek.

I agreed, but only because I didn't have any other option.

Staying low was hell.

I was going insane. Arty and Henderson weren't going to make it through the week without being disassembled and put in storage for parts. Likewise, the toddler from hell had stolen my apple for the past three days, and I was pretty sure the sadistic smile on his face was proof he'd done it on purpose. I told his parents I wouldn't mind if he ended up in the portal.

I admit that may have been extreme.

I paced in my room. I pulled weeds in the garden. I had Lon show me every second of footage from the banquet so I could obsess over it. While we were at it, we hacked in and replaced the picture of me with one of Leona, altered to look like a court jester.

I admit that may have been a little childish.

I walked into the garden shed to find another couple attempting to break my rule. I tried to talk them out of it with scare tactics. I gave them a long lecture about the horrors I had witnessed during Meora's labor, described in detail her dead baby, told them that having their nanos removed had likely made them insane and anything disruptive like having children was going to make them die if they weren't portaled first.

I admit I may have been exaggerating.

They still ended up moving to the family quarter.

I wouldn't admit it, but my *extraordinarily deep funk*—as Lon described it—was mostly about not seeing Levi. It had been over a week since we'd even traded a text. It was the longest I'd gone without talking to him in a year. And in the absence, my brain started remembering all the things that bothered me, all the things that didn't add up with Levi. I thought back to the night I met him.

I'd been stealing a cow.

Where do you find a cow to steal in 2074 Manhattan? I found one wandering down Broadway during my nightly patrol, and I thought I'd just been lucky.

When I was trying to coax the beast back to the bunker and wondering how to get it inside without a crane, and then wondering how I might steal a crane—I saw him. He was hiding behind the corner of a boarded-up grocery, watching me.

As soon as I saw his uniform I let go of the cow and reached for my knife. He had a military laser rifle and obviously knew how to use it. He aimed it at me as soon as I went for my weapon.

Okay, what happened next varies on who is telling the story. At this point, he insists I yelled "Die, Poser scum!" and jumped on him and started hacking away with my knife.

That's not exactly what happened. But I did end up on his back with my arms wrapped around his neck, my legs wrapped around his torso and my knife situated at his throat. He may or may not have received a small cut or two in the preceding moments. Okay, maybe it was more. I thought he bled more freely than was necessary.

That's when he told me he was there to help me. Anyone with a knife to his jugular would say the same, but I knew he was telling the truth. So I moved the knife away from his neck about an inch so he could explain.

The thing is—he never really did explain anything. He said he brought me a cow from Leona's farm in Central Park because he guessed we had kids who needed milk.

I was not about to discuss the kids with a Poser. "How did you get it out without being seen?"

"I just said Leona wanted it."

I knew he was lying. Or at least he was leaving parts out.

It also occurred to me that his hair smelled all lemony and his shoulders were solid. And for some reason being close to him made me feel different. Almost sick, but in a way I kind of didn't mind.

After that, he started coming by regularly. He brought me treats or supplies, listened to my rants, had my back whenever there was trouble. I had no reason to distrust him.

In my thinking, I had no solid reason to trust him, either.

THIRTEEN

I was sure when things went bad, as they inevitably would, it would be because of a stupid mistake I made. And when the frantic buzzing summoned me to the control room, I knew I was right.

The look on Lon's face assured me we were in trouble. I felt his apology. He'd run into a problem he couldn't fix for me.

"It's Henry and Tori."

"Are they in danger?" I was prepared to go out and risk my life. It was my duty.

"No, we are. They were spies."

White hot rage went through me like lightning. I wanted to throw Lon's rickety old chair into the scratched up old computer well. How dare they come into my bunker and betray me and every last child under my protection?

"I tracked them when I found out they left. They're headed straight for the citadel, and they aren't trying to hide it."

I went to the arsenal and pulled extra ammunition and another gun. "They're together?"

He caught the rifle I threw to him and nodded.

"Try to get a message to Levi. I'm not sure you'll be able to; I haven't heard from him in a few days."

When we got to the street a few minutes later, he said the readings showed Henry had dropped Tori off at her home. I motioned him on. "Take care of Tori. I've got Henry."

All the way to the citadel I berated myself. I was rarely wrong about people's motivations. I'd felt their emotions, and they were real. Henry had been angry at Leona. Even if he could fake that, how could he know I was listening? Why would he direct feelings of hate and fear toward Leona if he was there to spy for her?

Unless he'd been forced. Unless she'd threatened him in some way, made him infiltrate our safe house.

My anger translated into determination. Whatever his motivation, I had to get to Henry before he got to Leona. Even if he was a victim, I couldn't let him put every child in the bunker in danger. I would do whatever was necessary. My fingers tightened around the handle of my blade.

"I have Tori." Lon spoke into my EarCom as I closed in on Henry. He was about two blocks ahead, looking over his shoulder. He was afraid.

"I have eyes on Henry," I said. "Lon, I don't know if I'm going to make it home tonight."

There was silence on the other end. When he spoke, Lon sounded like he always did, except for a slight tremor in his voice.

"I'll keep them safe until you get back, Captain."

I stuffed raw emotion down to the pit of my stomach and turned off the EarCom. I focused on the target. There was no time for weakness.

I caught up with him at East 39th, one block from the citadel. I jerked him back with the blade of my knife pressed into the side of his coat.

"Going somewhere?"

He had a tortured expression. "I'm just trying to keep Tori safe."

"Is Leona threatening your sister?"

He hesitated. "She's not my sister. I want to marry her. When I asked permission the agent told us our pedigree was not compatible."

He stared at the ground in disgust, his mind a wasteland of defeat. "She told us if we helped the government weed out the city's destructive gangs, she might reconsider. I had no option. Can you see that?"

"All I see is a coward who was willing to portal over two hundred kids, including babies, so he could find his own personal happiness. How touching."

He wouldn't look me in the eyes. "I don't expect you to understand."

"Did you ever consider just staying in the bunker?" It seemed obvious to me. He frowned.

"And be separated from Tori?"

"You don't think I would have let you move to the family quarter if you told me the truth and promised to stay together?"

His internal reaction was shock. "But that's not the same as being married."

I didn't bother to argue. I watched for Posers as I tried to figure out what to do with him.

"They're probably monitoring me by now," he said, but he was nervous. We both knew he didn't have a tracker.

"And you're going to tell them everything."

"I can't lose her. Nothing personal."

"It's very personal."

I weighed my options. I didn't want to kill him. I hated the thought of resorting to the kind of violence I was trying to fight against. But I couldn't let him go. I considered taking him back to the bunker, but I couldn't be sure he hadn't already told the citadel his tracker was stolen, and whether he'd given them a chance to track him by another means.

I scanned the area and saw a clinic. It jogged a memory of a conversation with Miles.

He had told me about new tech that wiped memories. I wasn't sure a general clinic would have it, considering most medical care was only for the rich and done remotely. There would be a few imaging transporters and consoles with heavy security. But it was my only option.

I pushed him into the building, relieved the foyer was empty. There were voices in the next room and a variety of emotions floating around the immediate area. I sheathed my knife and aimed my rifle at Henry while I sifted through an immaculate white medical bay console. I found medical glue and used it to bind his hands together. After a moment of hesitation, I used it on his mouth as well. I shoved him in the transportation bay and went in search of the memory wiper.

I pushed my EarCom. "Lon, I need Doc."

It was only a moment before I heard his voice. "What can I do, Roxy?"

"Tell me how to find a memory eraser in a clinic."

He paused long enough for me to wonder if he questioned my judgment. "Is it a remote clinic?"

"Yes."

"If they have one, it's going to be in the storage room. But it will be locked and monitored. I'll have Lon take down the security. Give him a minute to find your location."

I found a door marked "Storage" and waited for the sound of the lock disengaging. Once inside, I searched and eventually found a small box labeled Memory Deactivator. I grabbed it and ran.

As I launched across the foyer, I heard a shout and saw three security guards come toward me, pulling laser pistols from their holsters.

I managed to dodge three beams by dropping to the ground and rolling to the right. As I did I grabbed my own rifle and balanced it one-handed against my shoulder.

I ran toward the transporter where I had left Henry. I shot the pistol out of one guard's hands and hit another in the leg. The third guard sidestepped the beam meant for him and chased me. His rifle laser got me in the arm just before my last shot caught him square in the chest.

My stomach knotted as I opened the transporter and hauled Henry out.

It was the guard or my people. I had no choice.

My rationalization did nothing to make me feel better. For the first time in my life, I had killed another person. It wasn't what Morris had taught me. I should have found another way.

I set the device to take two years of Henry's memory. I hoped it was enough. He was in a deep sleep when I left him there.

As I stepped onto the street, thunder was beginning to grumble in the gray sky over the city. I didn't know what to do. Levi would be angry when he heard how my "staying low" was going.

It would only be seconds before Posers arrived. They would find the guards and Henry, and it wouldn't take anyone long to figure out who was responsible. I needed a place to hide.

The reflective windows from the palace caught my attention as they mimicked the threatening clouds that gathered overhead. Maybe my best option was to hide in plain sight.

I tried to stay with the crowd as I moved forward toward the citadel. Citizens headed that way in droves, so even my noncompliant clothing stayed hidden in the mass of bodies.

Something was happening in the gardens behind the palace. Trying to find me without a tracker would be next to impossible. I kept moving toward the citadel as I tried to think of a plan. As the rain began to drip on the SmartPavement, I climbed underneath an umbrella bush by the back steps of the palace. Maybe I could wait out the storm until daylight was gone, then sneak back to the bunker. I tore the bottom of my shirt to make a bandage for my bleeding arm and winced as I wrapped the burn.

There were cheers for the entertainment on the citadel green. I found it ironic to see captive, miserable people laugh and applaud. But as the rain poured over them, I saw the truth. They were only enjoying a diversion. Leona was good at distracting them, making them forget she was trying to control every thought in their head. For everything she offered, she demanded a higher price in return. Everyone had to obey or suffer a fate worse than their wretched existence.

The spectators dispersed in the rain, their smiles quickly fading. I clenched my fists. People were meant to be free. How could anyone not see that?

I was exhausted and bored out of my mind. I fell asleep waiting for an idea of how to escape the gardens surrounded by guard outposts and electrified iron fencing. I woke up hungry, surrounded by darkness. I wondered if Levi would walk by now that the gardens were empty. I watched the top of the stairs for his familiar face. Had Lon let him know I was missing?

I wasn't sure I wanted him to find me. He was hiding things from me and I didn't know why. I didn't know how he would react to hearing I had killed a guard. Maybe his allegiance had limits.

He came out later in the evening. I dared to creep out of my hiding spot to confirm it was him. Lightning flashed, allowing me to see his face. As thunder rolled in response, I peeked around the marble wall of the stairs.

"Levi!"

He didn't hear me at first, but after I said his name a couple times, he looked up from his WristCom and saw me.

He wasn't happy. He scanned the vicinity before he came to me. When he stopped beside the bush I crouched under, he pretended to be interested in a text.

"What in the world are you doing, Roxy?"

I heard his disappointment that I hadn't listened to him.

"Do you want me to explain or do you want to get me out of here?" I was sulky.

"How do I do that? Every inch of palace grounds is monitored."

"You've done it before."

He sighed. "And every time it gets harder."

His WristCom dropped to the paved walkway next to me. He kicked it under the bush and knelt to look for it. He crawled in, his hair wet and curly from the rain.

The pale light from his tech gave us a dim lamp. He noticed the blood soaking through my bandage.

"You're hurt."

His emotions were unfocused. I knew he was mad. I figured it was at me for getting hurt or being there, but I didn't ask. He was also worried. That didn't make me feel better.

I knew it was the worst time to mention it, but after a loud crack of thunder, I swallowed hard and made myself look him in the eye.

"I killed a Poser, Levi."

He had a cascade of dissonant feelings. Anger. Admiration. Concern. I wished I could climb inside his mind and make sense of them. I wanted to hear the words of his thoughts.

"Roxy," he said in barely more than a whisper. "How am I going to keep you safe now?"

"Henry betrayed me. I had to come after him or he'd have led Leona to our door."

"Did you find him?"

I nodded.

"Is he dead, too?"

I looked up sharply. "No. I stole a memory deactivator and erased two years of his life. I had to."

His jaw was tense. "Why didn't you know he was going to betray you?" He tapped the side of his head.

"I can't read minds," I said, defensive. "He was being coerced by Leona in exchange for her permission to marry Tori."

"His sister?"

"She wasn't his sister."

He sighed again. His hand slid up my injured arm and he held it. He felt warm. Too warm. The contact made the wound hurt so I pulled away from his touch.

"I don't know what to do, Roxy. I don't know how to get you

out without getting you killed."

I shrugged. "I'll think of something. You better get back to work or you'll get in trouble."

He narrowed his eyes. "You know I'm not going to leave you. But you've got to give me a minute to figure it out."

"Koenig?"

Both of our terror levels skyrocketed as we heard a voice outside the bushes. Levi gave me a strangled look of panic and climbed out.

"Hey, Mills. Just dropped my WristCom."

"Were you talking to someone?"

"Yeah, I uh …"

As Levi's voice trailed off, Mills stooped down and looked straight at me. My breath was ragged as my hand went for my rifle.

He seized my leg and pulled me out, grabbing my rifle and deactivating it. He held me down while I screamed and tried to squirm away. My knife and extra pistol were also confiscated.

"Do you know who this is, Levi?" Mills, older than Levi by at least ten years, secured my hands in smart cuffs. "I think it's that rebel leader the Regal Manager is trying to find."

I took the opportunity while he was distracted to pull hard on his arm and send him over me. He jumped up and reached for his rifle. I started running, but Levi grabbed my arm and held me by the cuffs. He adjusted them more tightly around my wrists.

I was afraid of him. But I knew he had no choice. If he let me run I would be at the mercy of the Posers and be shot down before I got to the street. Even if I wasn't safe, I was safer with Levi.

Mills reached for me, but Levi pulled me out of his reach. "I have her."

Mills wasn't going for it. "I had her first, Koenig. I'm not going to let some kid push me around even if you do have the Regal Manager wrapped around your snotty little finger."

He pushed Levi back and put a hold on my cuffs with his WristCom so I couldn't move more than a few inches from him. Interest lit his gaze and he closed that small distance, running his hands along my sides.

"You're a pretty one for sure."

He nuzzled my neck as I stared at Levi in panic.

Levi barely controlled his anger. His pistol appeared in his hand and he shot near the foot of the guard. Mills swore and jumped back.

"What do you think you're doing?"

"Just get her inside," Levi seethed. Inside, he was a bomb ready to explode.

Mills jerked me next to his body. "You can't have all the girls, Levi. No matter how special you are. You ever aim a gun at me again I'll make sure you see the inside of the portal."

FOURTEEN

"Look what we have here, in my throne room for the second time. Roxy Eisen, on her endless escapade to save her people from wicked Queen Leona."

I refused to lower my gaze or answer her. She might have me bound and defenseless, but she wouldn't take my dignity.

"Would I have any reason to harm you if you were following the rules?" She heaved a long sigh and tapped her fingernails on her armrest. "Look at you, Roxanne. You dress like a twelve-year-old boy at Military Camp. You snarl and demand your own way like a toddler. You think you should be queen instead of me."

"I follow the rules," I seethed. "Just not your rules."

"Do your people follow your rules, Roxanne? Do they respect what you say?"

I didn't answer. She seemed to think she had left me speechless, although I was silent only because I thought it useless to argue with a crazy person. She stood up and came close. Put her hand on my arm. A dull ache began there and quickly spread through me until I felt dizzy with pain. I faltered and stumbled back, but she didn't let go.

"You just want to be me," she continued, and so did the pain. "I can't have you taking my place. You're only a child. You have spirit, but no control. And that will be your undoing, Roxanne."

I saw Levi take an involuntary step toward me. He was trying to hide it, but he was a tangle of anger inside. I sensed he was torn, probably wondering if he should give up his cover and protect me. I didn't want him to do it. I figured I would be dead before nightfall, and he would have to see that the bunker kids were safe.

"Your rules are for your benefit," I said through clenched teeth. "My rules protect the people I promised to set free."

She watched me with eyes of cold steel. "You must know that if you insist on denying my authority, I have no choice but to make you an example to those who may be inspired by your disobedience."

I wasn't really afraid of her words until I felt Levi's reaction to them.

"How do you punish your people, Miss Eisen?"

I yell at them.

I fought the shame. It was no time for weakness.

Leona sighed with false melancholy. "For the offenses of inappropriate dress, encouraging unauthorized sexual contact between minors with subsequent illegitimate children; for thievery and tampering with government implanted technology, I sentence you to ten seconds in the chair, followed by imprisonment in the archives until you reveal the location of your hiding place."

I stared hard, trying not to think about what her words meant.

"You're wondering how I know all this. I have my spies everywhere, Roxanne. You should have known better than to think you could hide from me." She cast a gracious smile across the room, and for a moment I was sure she had shared a glance with Levi.

"I know I should send you to the portal," she continued. "I find my merciful nature is my greatest weakness. But I do look on you with affection. I hope you will turn over the children you are endangering. Then we can work together for peace."

I kept my jaw set and my eyes narrowed. She wouldn't see the fear.

"General Koenig," Leona said to Levi. "You may have the honor of carrying out her sentence. We will watch from here."

Mills started to protest but thought better of it. Tech servants began to prepare the viewing screen. Levi panicked. I watched his face turn white as a specter and wished I could tell him to stay the course.

He did his best to subdue the rage. "Regal Manager, I understand the need to punish the child. But to make everyone watch?"

Leona's expression froze over like a window in an ice storm. When she spoke, she seethed. "I thank you for your opinion, *General*, which I did not request. Pain will not motivate her to reevaluate her ways as well as humiliation will. We will watch for her benefit. In fact, you inspire me. Turn on the live feed for the entire city to watch!"

Levi took a ragged breath through his nose, his jaw like steel. They stood facing each other in a silent stare-down while I despaired for the bunker kids, because Levi was surely headed into the portal with me.

He was about to give himself away. I focused on his emotions with such intensity that the familiar ache began in my head. It was a burning deep in the center of my brain, like I had been plugged into an electrical outlet. As it grew in strength, I saw a line of energy stretch from my head across the room toward Levi, as if the energy was reaching and straining toward him. I didn't care about the pain. I just wanted that white light to reach him. Somehow I knew if it got to him, he would know what I wanted to say to him.

Do what she says. Please, Levi.

He looked at me in surprise. His eyes searched mine as if he had heard my plea. After a moment that seemed eons long, he came forward and took hold of my arm.

His grasp felt harsh.

I shook off the hurt. He was doing it for the bunker. It was what

106

I wanted. But part of me refused to be understanding. Levi had never been anything but gentle, no matter how many times I punched, kicked, poked or pinched him. I swallowed back the lump in my throat as he pushed me from the throne room into the corridor.

I'm sorry, Roxy. I'm so sorry.

I stopped walking and stared at him. I thought I had imagined it, but as I focused, I heard him again.

What are you thinking? Did you change your mind? Tell me what you want me to do, Roxy!

I couldn't move. I couldn't speak. I was dumbfounded at the silent sound of his voice inside my head.

I forced myself to start moving. He dragged me down the corridor, followed by two more guards. I put up a fight for the sake of the audience as I wondered if the newfound ability went both ways. I tried to focus on him as I had before and spoke to his thoughts.

Levi? Can you hear me? Look at me if you can hear me.

He turned wide, dark eyes to meet mine, his breath catching in his throat. Seconds passed like years.

I can hear you.

We had arrived at the room where Sophie died. The closeness of the space made me feel like I was suffocating. I sensed the fear that seemed to have burrowed into the walls and lingered, from victims who had suffered here. It gave me the instinct to run, but the Posers blocked the doorway. The bronze chair with hand-carved flourishes sat on a pedestal. Levi took my arms and pushed me back into the chair. When I felt the cold inductor coils that would deliver the shock, fear overwhelmed my senses and I fought him.

He forced the restraints over my arms, head and legs while he silently spoke.

I've seen people die in ten seconds.

It made me think about all the things I didn't know about Levi. All the things he had done that threatened our fragile trust.

I'm strong. I won't die.

He went to the console. His voice betrayed the frantic doubt that possessed his mind. "On your command, Regal Manager."

"Now."

While he continued a silent and continuous appeal for forgiveness, he flipped the lever and focused all his attention on the timer that would tick off the seconds of my sentence.

Pain shot through my body as I convulsed. The horror of being electrocuted mingled with Levi's shock in sharing the experience with me. The seconds dragged by like years as I fought to keep control of a body that wanted to rip apart and die. Finally the alarm sounded, and Levi switched it off.

On the monitor I saw Leona brush away an imaginary tear. "Thank you, General Koenig. Have Miss Eisen escorted to her holding bay and given appropriate clothing. She will remain there until she tells us where her people are."

The screen went dark. I groaned, fighting for consciousness. I vaguely felt Levi releasing the straps. He winced as if he was enduring a residual current passing from my skin as he pulled me into his very warm arms.

When I woke up, I was laying on a white floor in a bright room. I heard the buzz of an invisible field like the one that had held me in Levi's room the night of the banquet.

I tried to sit up. I was dressed in a thin chemise with a drawstring front. It fell to the tips of my bare toes. I also wore a brown leather corset and shackles on my wrists.

I surveyed the immense open room. I hadn't imagined the underground archives to be so spacious. Apparently Leona used the old archives as a dumping ground for every beautiful statue and work of art that had disappeared from the city above when Leona took power. This must be where she'd hid everything that made her feel threatened.

I supposed that included me.

I felt my arm where I had been wounded by the rifle blast, expecting it to have a new bandage. There was nothing there. I pulled up the sleeve.

The injury was gone. There was a slight pinkish tinge to the skin, as if a wound from weeks ago had healed.

I was confused. Why would they go to such lengths to heal me? Why waste this kind of medical tech on a criminal likely headed for the portal?

The wall dematerialized suddenly and a woman and two men dressed in white jumpsuits came toward me. The woman held a tray. One of the men deactivated the field around me as I sat up and glared at them.

"Good evening, Prisoner Eisen," one of them said with a cheerful voice. As if I had not just been tortured and thrown in the basement. As if they weren't there to torture me more to extract my secrets. I scowled at them.

"I'll have to take your word since there are no windows down here."

"Yes, yes. Kindly lift your shift."

I tried to back away, but one of the men caught me and held me down while the woman lifted my skirt and injected my thigh with a green vial. My leg burned along with my dignity.

"We are going to have a conversation. The Regal Manager needs to know where you are holding the children so we can get them to safety. You will give us that information now."

"No I won't," I said as the room started to spin.

The second man placed a metal ring around my neck that suspended in the air without touching me. He activated a switch on his remote, and I felt pain unlike anything I'd ever known. It wasn't the buzz of electricity. It was raw and strident pain that came from within me. I heard myself screaming, saw myself writhing, but as if I was seeing it from outside of me and I was unable to control myself. At the back of my mind I sensed the sadistic pleasure the torture gave them.

Before I lost consciousness, my mind called to Levi. I hoped wherever he was he had heard me.

FIFTEEN

They left the collar on. When I was alone, the device continually caused a sick, empty pain in the pit of my stomach. I supposed it was to make me think I was afraid. It also gave me vivid, terrifying dreams with images I could not shake, so sleep offered no escape.

Since I was fed nothing and given only enough water to survive, I was convinced my life was on countdown. The seconds were ticking faster and faster toward an inevitable end.

I was writhing on the floor when someone entered. I didn't know what day it was or how long I'd been there. I listened to the visitor move around, pulling a desk and chair close and humming while they sipped some sort of beverage with a sweet smell. I lacked the will to even open my eyes to see who it was. The mystery was gone when she spoke.

"Hello, dear. I'm Mrs. Bowery. I'm going to be conducting your satisfaction survey. How are you holding up, Roxanne?"

I opened my eyes, trying to focus on the Bowery in the middle of my vision. "Are you serious?"

"Of course," she said with a sentimental smile, as if we were sitting around a cozy fire eating cookies. "We make sure all our guests are treated fairly while they are here. The Regal Manager is a rather compassionate woman. I can't imagine why some of her people regard her as cruel."

"Yeah, where in the world would we get that idea?" I tried to roll my eyes, but they gave up and closed.

"No need for sarcasm. Now, do you understand why you are being detained?"

"Because Leona knows that one day I'm going to shove her in her own portal, burn down her nauseating citadel and set this city free?"

There was a long silence and an awkward shift of her chair. "You poor thing. How delusional you are! She is not a dictator, Miss Eisen, she is a governor. She welcomes all feedback and wants everyone to have a voice. In fact, I consider New York City to be the one bright spot in a world that has fallen to pieces."

I squinted at the blinding white ceiling. "You really believe that, don't you?"

She frowned. "Tell me why you feel your leader is evil. I want you to be honest. I am a safe space." She made the same motion around herself she had done with Meora. I tried to mimic her with an unsteady hand.

"You ... are a crazy space."

"Young lady, if you are going to become uncontrollable I will have to call an orderly. Don't force me to do that."

"As if I could force anyone to do anything since I've been starved and tortured and now I'm laying here on your pretty white floor trying to stay alive."

She stood up and repacked her case. "I feel sorry for you. You are obviously in quite a psychotic state. Any discomfort you have experienced has been your own doing. I hope you come to your senses before it's too late."

"I doubt that will happen, Bowery, but all aces for your pretend concern."

She left in a huff.

Time dragged on while I yearned for Levi. The fact I was being tortured in his home and hadn't seen him for days made me doubt everything I hoped was true. If he cared, why would he allow it?

The monotony of my existence was interrupted when the door disappeared and there were no guards standing on the other side. Only Levi.

He glanced up at the corner of the white ceiling where the security feed was located. With several taps on his WristCom, the eye disengaged and withdrew behind the star panels. He unlocked and removed the collar from my neck without looking at me or saying anything, although his jaw was tense. Guilt possessed his mind.

Can you hear me?

I nodded, giving all my strength to the task of rising to a sitting position. I didn't want him to know how weak I was. It made me angry that I could barely hold myself up.

You look sick.

I snarled. "I look how a person looks when they've been starved and tortured. What did you expect?"

He winced, but didn't reply. So I continued.

"This is what your precious Leona does to her enemies."

He shook his head. "I didn't know she was doing this. I was under the impression you'd been left alone."

I wished I could believe him, but it didn't make sense. Why would he not know? He was the general of the Imposer army. How could he expect me to believe he was innocent?

He looked away, and I realized he had heard my thoughts. An uncomfortable silence followed as I listened to his indecision. He felt torn in two directions. But why? What was this unseen cord that kept him tethered to Leona?

I tried to speak in a softer tone. "You aren't evil, Levi."

He refocused his attention on me. It was deliberate, as if he sensed I was reading more than he wanted me to know from his

113

scattered thoughts.

"Leona knows you killed a soldier."

I heard the words he didn't say. I had earned myself a one-way ticket to the portal.

I shrugged. "That's the price of being a rebel. If I'm portaled, then I'm portaled."

His eyebrows drew together in a miserable expression. He stared down the long hall of priceless relics. All the art meant to be shared with the world, to help people see obscure truths through the creative lens—she'd stolen it from them.

Was that his thought or mine?

"I can't do anything about these treasures," Levi said softly. "But to let her silence you?"

I shrugged. "I'm not that special. I'm sure not what my parents or Morris hoped. The bunker would probably do better without me. My death will inspire someone to help you."

He shook his head the entire time I spoke, but I hurried on before he could deny facts.

"Don't make this harder. I'm dead. Don't care about me. Let me go, or we'll both just end up in the portal and then who will save them?"

He was quiet. In his mind, in the swirl of emotions, one became solid. It was time to choose a side.

He came to me and put his hands on my arms. I could only watch him, overwhelmed by the odd sensations in his warm grasp.

"Trust me." He took out SmartCuffs and put them on my wrists, but he overrode the automatic function and left them loose enough for me to remove. He tapped his WristCom and turned on the security feed, then pushed his laser pistol into my side.

We're getting out of here.

SIXTEEN

Apparently no one in the citadel willing to go up against Levi Koenig. He marched me to the lift, down the hall past the throne room and into the portico without anyone giving us a second glance.

But as he opened the heavy bronze doors with several taps of his WristCom, he saw the guard outposts on either side of the immense marble stairway on the street and thought better of it. He took me back through the citadel to the service entrance near the kitchens. He was hoping the servants wouldn't question him. I was breathing hard and fighting to stay conscious, but I was amazed I could even stand. Was it pure adrenaline, or some strange power at work?

He got behind a maglev van transporting flowers inside. A servant was standing beside it, studying an invoice uploaded on her WristCom.

"I'm afraid I need to steal your ML, Lacey."

She looked up and blushed, her eyes darting from his face to mine. "General Koenig, what are you doing back here?"

He stepped closer to her and intimidation and admiration

spilled from her features. She was clay, and she'd be molded by anything he said to her.

"Are you questioning me?"

His voice held a hint of teasing, but enough warning to cause her to panic. She stepped back and lowered her head as if Leona was passing by. "No, sir."

He nodded and trailed a finger down her cheek. "Good girl."

He lifted me into the sparse vehicle and set me on the floor. As soon as he climbed in, he programmed the destination into the computer and used his citadel override to use the fly function.

"You're just showing off now," I said, closing my eyes.

"Guilty."

"Where are we going?" My voice was slurred. "Not the bunker. I don't want them in more danger."

"How about the subway tunnels near the bunker? We'll be hard to find if I disable my WristCom. Once I get you settled I can find food and water."

"It's not a solution."

He nodded. "It will buy some time until I think of one."

It was futility to hide beneath the city. I'd been doing it long enough to know. I heard his silent words, staining the air around us with the invisible color of blood, a color I usually associated with anger. Rage.

I won't let her kill you. I'll die first.

I reached a shaking hand to touch his cheek. I didn't want Levi to die.

"First things first." He cleared his throat and held up my knife and the chain of BioTrack spheres I had removed from the bunker kids. "Got these back."

I managed a small smile. But what he did next made my eyes sting with tears. In the mirror at the front of the van, he took the knife and made a slit over the tiny scar in his neck. He dug out his tracker without even wincing and added it to my chain. It gave a satisfying tiny clank and deactivated.

"All yours," he whispered as he put the chain over my head.

Neither of us said it, but we knew it was more. He was telling the citadel—and Leona—that he had made his choice.

A tiny part of me also wondered if this was all an elaborate method of lulling me into a false sense of security. There was no way to be sure. A spy was always a spy, wasn't he?

We abandoned the van at Canal and Bowery in timeworn Chinatown, and Levi mostly carried me the rest of the way through the tunnels. We came upon City Hall Loop station, abandoned over a hundred and fifty years earlier. I studied the architecture from the turn of the twentieth century. So impractical and beautiful all at once.

Levi led me to an office that seemed to have been overlooked by vagrants. The subway tunnels were a common place for them to seek unmonitored shelter. The dusty console looking out over shadows caused me to shiver. Hopefully the specters would stay away while Levi was getting supplies.

Since I hadn't eaten in so long and was frantic for water, he hurried. He was back in under an hour with a canister of water smelling like sulfur, and a few cans of rations he had found in a store that sold emergency items just before the quarantine. He started a fire outside the office on the tracks so he could boil the water and questionable meat product that came out of the can.

"I wish I could get you caramel bread from the citadel gardens."

I leaned back against the wall of the tunnel, holding up my hands to feel the fire's warmth. "Me, too."

But when he handed me the hot meal in a can and a spoon, I found that hunger made it seem like the finest gourmet meal I'd ever eaten. Not that I'd ever eaten a gourmet meal.

"Take it slow, Roxy. Your stomach will be weak."

I burned my mouth drinking the water. Then I slept. When I woke up I was wrapped in an old blanket that smelled stale. I was enveloped by something much warmer.

Levi's arms were around me, and I felt the electric buzz I noticed sometimes when he touched me. I felt better. After a week of constant pain and hunger, could it only take a little food, rest and a warm embrace to start feeling somewhat normal?

Levi seemed tired, so I let him sleep and wondered how we would escape. I ran through the options, but the conclusion always led to one place. I couldn't keep my bunker family safe and avoid the portal.

I think Levi knew it as well. Neither of us was surprised when we heard footfalls echoing through the tunnel. We lunged for the old office and traded laser fire with Posers for a few minutes. We had reduced their number to two, and I thought we'd have a chance of escaping, but reinforcements arrived.

"It must have been your nanos." I kicked the wall in frustration as we cowered under the console. He shook his head.

"It could have been anything. Do we agree we have no way out but to surrender?"

I almost said I'd rather die. But the images of my parents, of Morris, of the bunker kids floated through my brain as a reminder of everyone counting on me. I couldn't give up. Not till the last second. It was my duty.

Before Levi could stop me, I stood up and waved my arms in the air. Levi stood next to me and allowed the Posers to swarm our shelter and take us as prisoners.

SEVENTEEN

Leona had been staring at the two of us for a long time. Mostly glaring at Levi. I guessed she didn't like betrayal any more than I did. We had been taken straight to the portal chamber by the Posers who arrested us. I felt the static heat of the portal stretch across the long room. It wanted me.

"Am I to assume that Miss Eisen captured you and removed your tracker, General Koenig?"

He answered with a defiant stare.

"That's exactly what happened," I said, but neither of them seemed to remember I was standing there.

"If it weren't for the traces of blood you left in the service van and our ability to isolate your nanos, I may never have found you." Her voice carried the same melodic tone, beautiful and cold.

I glanced at Levi. *Told you.*

"Let her go," Levi said, ignoring my silent jab. "You have no reason to hold her."

His mind screamed though his voice was quiet. I sensed strong emotion on either side. His rage and her injury. She wanted him to pay for his betrayal.

119

Her chilling eyes suddenly found mine. The corners of her painted mouth turned up, but she wasn't smiling. "You murdered a security guard, Roxanne. Do you see how far you've fallen? What you've resorted to in your ill-advised little rebellion? What choice have you left me? You're a killer who has endangered hundreds of children."

She came close to me. I smelled her perfume. Her silk and lace brushed against my skin. I watched a strand of red hair fall across her forehead as she leaned toward me.

"You made my decision for me. Just like your mother. The guilty pay for their crimes."

I scoffed in her face. "What about your crimes? What about how you murdered my parents? Shouldn't you pay for that?"

She was disdainful, but if I hadn't imagined it, a tremor of weakness burrowed somewhere within her being. I decided to push it. What did I have to lose?

"I've heard the whole story. How you hated my mom because she got everything you thought you deserved. I heard how you killed my father because he didn't love you, and you pushed my mom in the portal." I sneered at her. "Did she beg for her life?"

Leona's expression darkened by volumes. I was treading in perilous waters. I didn't care anymore.

"She didn't, did she? I bet she gave her life for me. You wanted to kill me to hurt her. That sounds like the Regal Manager we know."

Fury engulfed her mind. "Brand her!"

All my bravado failed as Posers held me down. Levi rushed toward me, but with one motion of Leona's wrist he was captured by two more soldiers and held back. I twisted my neck so I could see him. His eyes were wide with anguish as he struggled against them. In that moment it seemed silly to have ever doubted how he felt about me.

The searing heat of the branding iron cut into my flesh. My chest was on fire, and I heard my voice scream, although it sounded distant because Levi's tormented cry inside my mind was louder. I opened my eyes and saw the veins protruding from his forehead as his face turned purple. He fought frantically to free himself.

"You're crazy! You're evil! I promise I will kill you if you don't let her go NOW!" The words tore from his throat as if he had no control over them.

She turned to him, hurt. His voice was threaded with all the emotion we endured together. Since the moment I'd told him I could feel his emotions, he'd always taken care to distill his. Dice them up and put them in manageable portions around me.

But now he was raw and unfiltered. The mad swirl of words that erupted from his mind to mine was saturated with disillusionment. It was the feeling of a little boy who'd been turned out of his own house. I watched him, the last dregs of my strength focused on him alone as I tried to reach him with a message of support.

Levi, she's not worth this pedestal you have her on.

His eyes found mine and he couldn't stop the thought fast enough.

She should be. A mother should be.

It was as if the branding iron had burned me again. The pieces of the puzzle that had stumped me began to assemble.

This whole time … he was Leona's *son*?

I heard my own moan. The soldiers held me—kept me from collapsing to the floor, really—and dragged me toward the access doors as they opened. I cried out, closing my eyes against the incredibly bright light and the black heaviness beyond it. Had I ever thought I knew what fear was before that moment?

Leona tried to soothe Levi in a musical voice. The sound was a contradiction; I felt her emotions and there was nothing compassionate or nurturing in them, only hate. She wanted me dead. She wanted to watch my atoms ripped to nothing as I was caught in the deadly swirl of the portal's thirsty drain.

"You know I love you," she murmured over him. "Everything I do is for you. She's manipulating you, baby. Can't you see that?"

He backed away from her reaching hands and scowled.

"You're unbelievable. You make this city believe you are their savior, and take everything from them in order to give yourself more. You're a coward. You hide behind your portal and kill anyone who dares to stand up to you." He stood taller. "People like you never win in the end. The heroes are always the ones like Roxy."

The guards paused, unsure of their orders. They shifted and pretended not to be witness to the scene.

Levi took a step toward Leona. "I'm standing up to you now. I've tried to believe the best about you, but you make it impossible. Are you going to portal me, too?"

She glared, barely maintaining her composure. Fury colored the space around her. "You need to be very careful, Levi."

Levi shook off the hold of the guards and came to me.

"If you send Roxy into the portal, I'm going with her."

As they stared each other down, a strange thought occurred to me. I closed my eyes and remembered my nightmares.

The mark.

Why did Leona mark victims before she threw them in? She had done it to Greer. Morris. Me. And the specter in the old theater across from the bunker had the same mark.

Somehow, I was able to find a thread of hope in the randomness of the facts. If Levi and I were destined to perish this way, I could hold on to the possibility until my life was gone.

"So be it!" Leona whispered, her face contorted. "Go with your sorceress. You are *nothing* to me. No true son of mine would choose her over me. Throw her in!"

The guards, looking terrified, moved quickly to obey. I started to panic, breathing fast and calling Levi's name in little gasps as the magnetic pull of the swirl reached for me with hungry, powerful fingers.

"Hold on, Roxy!" Levi called. He sounded far off in the distance.

The words made no sense as I felt myself torn apart. Shifted and replaced. Stretched into what seemed like unfiltered heat and light and thrown out into complete darkness. I could feel nothing, hear nothing, see nothing, yet my mind screamed with horror at the experience of being eaten alive by a giant dead star light years away.

I waited for blackness. I waited for soul reckoning.

There was only gravity.

EIGHTEEN

After the first agonizing minutes, my brain went slow and I knew nothing for what felt like years. Time seemed stuck and irrelevant as I floated. Sinking. Swirling.

Drowning.

When I made sense of my surroundings, I struggled for air and instead breathed a mouthful of water. I flailed and tried to scream, but only made a vague, impotent sound against the power of the water that held me. My lungs burned, my brain struggled for oxygen. My limbs did not work. Moving them caused me unbearable pain.

An arm grabbed me around the waist. I thought it was the water trying to pull me down, so I fought it. The arm did not let go until I knew my body had given up the fight. All faded.

I opened my eyes to a dimly lit room. The light flickered as if it came from a candle. I closed my eyes again and reopened them, hoping the setting might make sense.

I tested my voice. "Why is it so dark?"

My voice was raspy. It hardly sounded like me. Maybe I wasn't me. Maybe the portal had turned me into someone else. Who knew? No one had ever returned from the portal to explain the experience. Maybe I was dead. No one had ever come back from death to confirm the details, either.

"You're still you."

It occurred to me even before I heard the voice that I had sensed I was not alone. Someone was near, and the emotions were familiar even though the voice was garbled by my waterlogged ears.

Levi's face filled my blurry vision, blocking out the flowered wallpaper and antique frames hanging on the wall behind him.

"Hey, beautiful." He forced a lighthearted tone. "It's dark because there's no solar power or electricity here."

He wasn't telling me something important. And he knew I knew it.

"Just give it to me straight, Levi. Did the portal short out and cause another blackout or something?" I forced my throat to move enough air to make the sounds.

He shook his head. I wanted to search his brain for the things he was hesitant to say, but I was afraid.

"Take a minute to breathe," he said. "Then tell me the last thing you remember."

I skipped the breathing part and tried to focus my fuzzy brain. Everything I knew aside from Levi was locked in a bright room at the end of a long, dark tunnel.

Leona. Portal. Swirling. Drowning.

"Did we drown?" I tried to sit up and felt the excruciating pain again. Every inch of my body hurt. Levi put gentle hands on my arms to keep me still. I gave a groan I had no responsibility for.

"You wouldn't think being dead would involve so much pain."

"You're not dead, Roxy. You're ... we're ..."

I gulped back dread, which also hurt. "You're afraid."

Fear was rare in Levi's brain. Anger, confusion, hope, love, genius—but not fear.

He traced a warm finger the length of my cheekbone. "I think you have broken bones in every limb, and too many cuts and bruises to count. I guess I should be surprised that you tried to fight the portal, but it kind of makes sense." He gave me a sad smile. "But you're alive. I'm so glad you're alive."

I glared at him. Why the tone? Why the sadness? Why the fear?

"Out with it, Koenig."

His hand went to my neck. *So warm.*

"Do you have a fever?"

He only stared at me.

"Please just tell me."

He gingerly took my hand and focused all his attention on it as he spoke. "We didn't die in the portal. We were … thrown back? Violently thrown back. Our clothes look like they've been through a shredder."

"Thrown back? Thrown back where?"

"Still New York City."

"Then what do you mean we were thrown back?" I would have pinched him if it wouldn't hurt too much.

"I'm not sure what I'm trying to say here, Roxy. But the newspaper downstairs says it's June 21, 1874."

"Typo?" I furrowed my brow, trying to understand the relevance.

"Rox, when was the last time you saw a newspaper?"

Pieces in my mind still struggling for order began to assimilate. "So Leona's portal chamber wasn't just a lid on a black hole?"

He set my hand down and shrugged. "I'm not sure what to tell you. A few hours ago we were in 2074. Now, unless someone is playing an elaborate trick, we're in 1874. If I had to give a guess, I'd say the portal has a wormhole. And I think Leona knew it."

His emotions sparked when he said her name, but he didn't seem as surprised as I felt. Why not?

"The mark," I managed around a moan.

He shook his head in confusion.

"She marked her portal victims. Why would she do that if they were going to die?"

He was thoughtful, but my words did not surprise him. He sighed and looked down the length of me in concern. "Don't move, Roxy. I'm trying to fix you, but you have to hold still while I set the bones."

"Fix me?"

He got that serious expression and hesitation again. I knew there was more he was going to reveal. He pressed his lips together and looked away.

"You know how you have your superpower to read emotions and, as it turns out, every thought in my head?"

I nodded. Static passed through my brain as he deliberately touched my hand again.

"You aren't the only one."

"You're a mind-reader?" Great. Then he'd known all along how I really felt about him.

He gave me a curious smile, but he shook his head. "No, I don't read anyone's thoughts but yours, Roxy. I ... heal."

"You heal?" I was incredulous, though I had no right to be, considering my story was just as weird.

He didn't answer. He lifted my arm very gently so I could see the long, bleeding gash on my hand. As he traced his finger along the edge of the injury, barely touching it, I noticed a faint bluish glow. The cut disappeared.

I gulped. "How?"

"I'm guessing the same way you do your funky mojo," he said with a defensive tone. He set my arm down and turned away.

"Why does it make you sad?" I wished I could reach for him. "It's amazing. You're amazing. More than I realized."

I knew why it made him sad. I remembered the conversation with Leona. But I wanted to hear him say what she was to him before I'd go so far as to believe it.

"I should get this done. You need to get some sleep." He turned toward my broken legs, avoiding my eyes. After a moment he looked at me. "Let's just take one crisis at a time."

He didn't wait for a response. He took hold of my leg and gave me an apologetic look. "This is going to hurt."

"It didn't hurt when you healed the cut."

"If I heal your arms and legs before I set the breaks, you'll be deformed." The corner of his mouth turned up a little though he was still trying to be solemn. I wanted to hit him but didn't think the pain was worth it.

"What are you waiting for?" I took a deep breath. "Just think of it as payback for all the times I beat you up."

"You never beat me up." He positioned his hands around the first break just above my knee. "I think I saw some whiskey downstairs. Want me to get it?"

I sneered. "You know me better than that."

While I was talking, he pulled my leg. Hard. I gasped and cried out against the shock of the pain as I felt the crack of bones being realigned.

He held his finger to his lips and glanced at the closed door. I clenched my teeth together and determined not to make another sound. By the time he reached for the last break on my wrist, I was done with being fixed. I glowered at him and wished to be mobile so I could cause him a little pain.

"Almost done. Then you can hit me all you want."

After the bones were set, he looked at my arms with intense focus. His hand warmed with unbelievable heat that didn't burn. They glowed the same way his finger had, only brighter. Gradually I felt the pain lessen until I knew the injuries were gone.

I sat up, feeling freed from a prison. I saw my tattered citadel costume and the burn mark on my chest. It didn't hurt. It was only a scar. I touched it and wondered how many times in the past Levi had healed me without letting me know.

"I'm sorry I couldn't get the scar off." He narrowed his eyes at the mark as if it was Leona's face. "I'll try again when I'm stronger."

I frowned. He did look tired and weak.

"Did you get hurt in the portal?" I caught his hand as he

reached to touch my scar.

His gaze found mine as my fingers slipped between his. My grip tightened.

"Just a little banged up," he said. He voice was thick, and his warm eyes pulled me in. "But I've noticed I seem to trade my energy for healing."

I stared at him hard. I didn't want him wasting his perfectly good vigor on me. He smiled at my disapproval and touched my scar.

"It doesn't hurt," I insisted. His dark eyes tried to hide within the frame of his curly brown hair. "You are amazing, Levi. Your gift, I mean."

His face was too close. I could see fine stubble across his chin and lip. The urge to touch him seemed overpowering. I wanted to know he was really there, that we were somehow alive together in this strange place. My fingers danced around the edges of his jaw. I wished I could heal his scrapes.

I began to be aware that his emotions were shifting into something more distinct. I knew what would happen if I didn't stop it. His mind listened to the direction of my thoughts as his gaze dropped to my lips for a split second.

He must have known what I was about to say, because he said it for me. "We better get some sleep."

I was relieved. I looked around the room and cleared my throat. "So this is 1874. Or someone wants us to think it is."

"We're at a boarding house on Beach Street." He studied the room as well, as if he hadn't taken the time to do so yet. "I was out of it when I pulled us out of the reservoir. When I saw the sign I dragged you in and asked for help."

"What did you say?" I couldn't believe I didn't remember any of it.

"I said our money was stolen and we were beaten and thrown in the reservoir. I think she felt sorry for us. She'll let us work for her and stay until we figure something out. She can use the help anyway. She's a widow—"

"Wait a second," I interrupted. "If it's 1874, why are we sharing a room? Weren't they strict about that back then?"

He was sheepish. "I told her we just got married. In fact, this was our wedding trip until we were robbed and half-drowned."

I narrowed my eyes, but his smile only widened. "You don't have to thank me for saving your life, Mrs. Koenig. After all, I am your husband."

He patted my hand and then flinched as if in preparation for my assault. I groaned in frustration and punched him in the arm.

He laughed. "Don't think about it that way. People still get married in 1874 because they want to. Marriage isn't the political circus it is in our time."

I wasn't comforted. "Don't patronize me. If we're married in 1874, I'm basically your property."

"Well yes," he smirked. "There's that."

He might own me at the end of the day, but he was going to do it with an assortment of bruises to remind him who was really in charge. He cringed as I punched him on the other arm.

It took me some time to get to sleep, as tired as I was. I crinkled my nose at the faint smell of body odor and perfume mingled in the air as I listened to the murmurs of the other boarders around us.

Levi didn't speak again. He grabbed the second pillow and the quilt from the end of the bed and stretched out on the floor. I felt bad, but I didn't stop him. If I asked him to stay with me, there would be something comforting in being together. But my fears were too strong and my principles too much of an obstacle. I said nothing as he curled up on the floor and quickly fell asleep.

NINETEEN

When my eyes opened, I thought it would all be some weird death dream in the portal. But a quick survey of the room told me we were still in the same place. Levi was still huddled on the floor, wrapped in the quilt. I felt the quiet of his mind as he slept.

I leaned on my hand and watched him. How did he manage to be so calm even in the face of the bizarre? A strand of hair fell across his eye. For a moment I could see the little boy he'd been.

Leona's little boy. Had she watched him sleep? Pushed the lock of hair from his eye? Had it bothered her that a little girl had grown up without a mother because of her?

It made me angry. I felt like a caged bird when I realized I had nowhere to go to vent it. This was not my New York. There was no zombie flu quarantine to leave a section of the city at my disposal. I was stuck in this boarding house, in this room, with Levi, for the foreseeable future.

In 1874.

I threw a pillow at his head. "Married? Really?"

He opened his eyes and squinted at me.

"I have to keep you close," he murmured, his voice still thick from sleep. "I can't have you wandering off in 1874 and getting lost."

He smiled with eyes closed and pulled the quilt around him. "I told her I brought my bride all the way from Ohio to see the big city."

"Ohio? How would we get across the electrified wall around the border?"

He opened his eyes and shot me a forbearing look. "1874, Roxy. No wall. Nor electricity."

I made a face.

"I almost told her you got drunk at the reception. It was your fault we were soaking wet and half-drowned. We'd been walking around the reservoir and you fell in because you were smashed." His mouth turned up in a lazy smile as I glared at him. "But I needed her sympathy so I told the less likely story about being robbed."

I tried not to laugh as I kicked him. He grabbed me. When he had my hands pinned he tickled me until I broke free and elbowed him in the side.

He stood up and pulled me with him. His sleepy eyes and tousled hair did something funny to my stomach. It was dangerous, so I eyed him until he took a step back. He crossed his arms over his chest.

"It's okay, Roxy, I said it wasn't your fault. You're a naïve little girl and you thought the cider was just a little tart."

I tried to hit him again but he grabbed my wrist. "Why are you so mad? You should be thanking your dear husband for taking care of you while you were wasted."

"Don't hold your breath, mudsill."

He clicked his tongue and caught my other wrist. "Such language from a lady."

I struggled, but somehow I ended up in his arms, my head against his chest. I couldn't refuse the comfort, so I relaxed and we stood there for a long time.

"They're all alone, Levi," I said quietly. "Who's going to take care of them?"

"They aren't alone," he said. "They have each other."

"We were supposed to set them free."

"We'll find a way."

I saw clothes draped across the back of the chair by the door. "Was someone in here?"

"Mrs. Watts, the lady who owns the house, brought them, since ours were ruined."

I frowned. I didn't like that someone had seen us sleeping together. He tried to hide a smile at my thought.

I went to the chair and gathered up the simple navy skirt, white shirtwaist and underclothes. I made a gagging sound at the sight of the corset.

"We get sent to a different time in history, and I'm still forced to wear this pointless thing. I don't even know how I'll get it on. Why are men's clothes comfortable no matter the time or place?"

"Men are just naturally beautiful," he said. "We don't need contraptions. And your husband is willing to help you dress."

"Not on your life. Where's the bathroom?"

He smirked and nodded under the bed. A chamber pot peeked out.

"Great. This just keeps getting better."

"Relax. I think there's one at the end of the hall."

"We have to share with strangers?"

He shrugged and turned to grab his clothes. He started changing without asking me to look away. I frowned and turned around, trying to think of something else.

"So are we going to discuss your mom?" Admittedly, there might have been better topics I could have brought up to keep my mind off his bare chest I could see out of the corner of my eye.

He stopped moving and got quiet for a long moment. "There isn't much to tell. My mom's a psychopath. End of story."

"Why didn't you tell me?" I had to ask the question. I needed to know.

I didn't have to look at him to know he was tense as he

answered. "Why do you think? I'm not proud of her. I don't tell anyone she's my mom, and I told her I'd cut off her healing treatments if she told anyone."

"Healing treatments?"

He sighed. "She gets headaches."

"So no one knows you're her son?"

"They know," he replied. "But they know not to bring it up."

"Don't you think it's weird, us being friends? Ironic, maybe?"

I turned around to see him pull up his suspenders and slide on the overcoat.

"Why?" I could tell from his voice he was still testy.

"I don't know, just considering what happened with our moms."

He was disgusted. "Do you even know what happened?"

I knew what Morris had told me, and what Leona herself had said. My mother was pushed into the portal by Leona in a fit of rage. But the look on Levi's face kept me from saying anything.

"I'm going downstairs." He grabbed his hat and the door slammed behind him.

When I was dressed, I stepped out into the hallway with the sense that I was out of place. I found the "water closet" and plumbing I understood enough to make use of, to my relief.

When I came back into the hallway, I smelled food and realized I was ravenous. It made sense, since I hadn't eaten in two hundred years. I followed the scent of bacon, eggs and coffee, relieved they smelled the same in 1874 as they did in my time.

When I looked down from the top of the stairs, I saw Levi standing beside a long table inhabited by men. They were all talking loudly. Levi's arms were folded over his chest as he listened, and the sight of him made me stop. I took in the familiarity of his features, the strength and posture of royalty paired with a heart of kindness and thought for others.

My heart sped up just looking at him. It felt risky to be so attached to a person that was so close to my enemy. I needed to be strong. I needed to resist the emotions that made me vulnerable. They were just feelings, anyway. What did feelings accomplish for the bunker kids? Love just tangled them together, made them like spider's prey, wound in her web and at her mercy.

Love wouldn't catch me without a fight.

I steeled myself as I went down the stairs. Even though I felt many curious glances, only one pair of eyes told me he'd heard everything I just thought.

Being attached to someone's mind was going to take adjustment. I wished I knew how to turn it off when I didn't want him in my brain. I wished Morris was there to tell me how to control it.

I ignored Levi's long look in my direction, giving my full attention to the men and their strange speech. The words were English, and I understood their meaning, but they had some sort of accent I'd never heard before. I hoped we wouldn't sound too different.

"Mrs. Watts, I can see you're busy," Levi said as he caught the arm of the woman rushing back and forth from the kitchen. "Thank you for the clothes. How can we help you with breakfast?"

Shock wasn't a strong enough word for her reaction. She set down a plate of eggs and wiped the sweat from her forehead with her sleeve.

Levi glanced at me. *Did I offend her?*

I shrugged. *How am I supposed to know?*

"I suppose your wife could serve coffee," she said, gesturing to the stove in the kitchen.

"Sure." I went for the pot, wishing I could pour myself a cup and eat something. Levi followed me and took the other pot on the back of the stove. I tried to hide my smile when I saw him head down the table, refilling cups and nodding in greeting. They gawked like he was an oddity in a museum. They'd be more confounded to know he was the heir to the throne of New York City two hundred years in the future.

Levi frowned at me.

When the boarders left, Mary Watts served us our breakfast and sat down with us to eat. She took dainty bites and chewed slowly. I shoveled food in so fast I almost choked a couple times. I clearly embarrassed Mrs. Watts, but I was so hungry I didn't care.

Slow down, Roxy, you're going to make yourself sick.

Maybe, if your mom hadn't starved me, I would.

He sighed and sipped his coffee.

"I can't thank you enough for your help this morning, Mr. and Mrs. Koenig. Breakfast is the busiest time of my day."

"No problem," Levi responded. Mrs. Watts gave him a strange look.

She's suspicious, I told him before I headed to the stove to refill my plate.

"Where did you say you were from?" Mrs. Watts asked Levi.

"Ohio." Levi gave his attention to his plate of food.

"What part? My cousin lives in Springfield."

Levi studied his eggs hard. I didn't know what to say, either. In our world, Ohio was a Nationalist state known for shooting down anyone who tried to climb over their very high walls.

"Um, we're maybe an hour's ride north? It's a very small settlement. Not even a town yet."

I watched her as Levi spoke. She seemed to accept it.

"Tell me again what happened when you arrived in the city for your honeymoon trip." She sat back and sipped her coffee.

"We were on our way from the train station to our hotel when we saw the reservoir," Levi said. "We decided to walk around the … top."

"The promenade?" she prompted. He nodded and flashed a smile her way.

"The promenade. Some boys jumped out and took me down, I'm embarrassed to say. They took our money and threw us both in the water."

She shook her head in dismay. "Sounds like Leslie's Gang. I'm surprised. Those boys don't usually come up so far north. This city is afflicted by gang problems. The Rabbits Riots in the fifties killed so many. I wish the boys would find better ways to spend their time. How did you get away?"

"My wife almost drowned because they tied her hands. I managed to pull her out in time."

Mrs. Watts reached for my hand. "I'm so sorry, dear. No wonder you were unconscious so long."

I shrugged. "Mr. Koenig fixed me up."

He smiled. I looked back at her. "So what is the reservoir for?"

Levi shot me a look, but Mrs. Watts didn't seem surprised. "Croton Reservoir was built to give fresh water to certain parts of the city. We had a terrible bout of sickness some time ago. The reservoir keeps fresh water flowing. Many people even have running water for bathtubs now. Can you imagine?"

"There was an empty lot behind the reservoir," Levi said. "Any plans for the space?"

"Lots of ideas. No plans. Of course, you know about the Crystal Palace that used to be there."

I almost choked on a piece of bacon.

"The Crystal Palace?" Levi repeated.

She nodded. "It was beautiful. The poet Mr. Whitman even wrote a poem about it in the paper." She concentrated, trying to remember. *"High and rising tier on tier with glass and iron facades, gladdening the sun and sky, enhued in cheerfullest hues. Bronze, lilac, robin's egg, marine and crimson. Over whose golden roof shall flaunt, beneath the banner—freedom."*

"It's like I can almost picture it, except for the freedom part," I murmured.

"It was made of iron and glass and gleamed in the sunlight. We were all sad when it burned," she said wistfully.

"What happened?"

"The strangest thing," she said. "One afternoon, sixteen years ago this October, the whole place burned to the ground in the space of a few hours. No one perished, but since it was a symbol of the American spirit and our unparalleled freedom in the world, some

137

said it was a warning of coming oppression."

Levi and I had no response. He cleared his throat and set his napkin beside his empty plate. "I think I'll get to those tasks you mentioned. Where can I find the tools?"

She fingered a locket she was wearing. I saw her emotions were contemplative.

"Those jobs will be there tomorrow. See the sights today. Whatever you would have done if you were on your trip. You'll find some change in the pot on the windowsill in the kitchen. Only stay away from Mulberry Street and Five Points."

She stared down at her locket. "Life passes too quickly as it is."

TWENTY

"I hear you thinking."

Levi shrugged at my words. "That's why I didn't say it."

We had been lost in our separate, yet united, thoughts for hours. We ended up where we always seemed to end up—in our park.

Washington Square was supposed to belong only to Levi and me and the dead. It was crowded with people talking on benches and fanning themselves. They chatted amid manicured gardens while children splashed in the fountain until a constable came at them with his stick.

"The trees are small," Levi said.

"It looks naked."

He looked at me. "You say that like it's a bad thing."

"There's no cover. No place to hide."

"People here don't need to hide."

I sensed his irritation, so I let it go. But I wished for my Washington Square.

We walked Lafayette Street and found Colonnade Row. My future home stretched, whole, in grandeur down the length of the street. The columns were strong, though already weathered by time. Some were hidden in a thick blanket of ivy.

A sudden feeling caught me off guard. I closed my eyes, surprised. Something like adrenaline rushed through me, making my heart pump faster. I felt dizzy and reached for Levi's arm.

"What's wrong?" He stepped closer and steadied me.

"I don't know. Something feels familiar. Like someone's nearby."

I turned around and saw the theater building I had entered the night I saw the specter. It was a library in this time.

"Do you know who it is?"

I didn't know. I scanned the sidewalks and streets. Horses and carts, omnibuses and pedestrians crowded next to one another, but nothing was unusual. Nobody's emotions were noticeable above the rest.

We walked on. I kept listening for something I didn't hear. It was a sound that had been ringing in my ears all my life.

I realized what was missing. The buzz. Here, there was no hum of the portal spreading out over the city like a psychedelic cloud.

It almost made the horse manure and the smell of body odor baking in the summer heat worth it all.

In Madison Square we found poor Lady Liberty's arm and torch. They stuck out awkwardly from the side of the walk like a huge, misplaced oddity.

"What an eyesore." A man stopped behind us and peered over his spectacles. "They think if they put this here in the park it will make us willing to pay to put the thing together out on the island with the old Fort. The nerve of France, to send a gift and expect us to pay for it. They won't get one nickel of my money."

"I think she could be inspiring," Levi said with a straight face. "A symbol of hope and freedom for generations to come."

"Nonsense," he snapped. "I suppose you have something to donate? We're all broke these days. Where's the hope and freedom in that?"

When the sunlight faded, the city took on a different mood.

Taverns started to fill with young men and boys. Levi had a random thought about my safety, to which I responded with a thought that I could easily take out anyone who tried anything and he should stop acting so 1874.

We came back to the quiet street of the boarding house. We sat down on the front steps under a cover of trees rustling in the late afternoon breeze, both tired and lost in our thoughts. The peace was interrupted when a cane appeared, tapping on Levi's shoulder.

"The game is up, you two. I know what you're about."

We jumped up, ready for a fight. An older man stood in front of us, his arms wrapped around a thick chest as he stared down his nose at us. He was well-dressed, and his features were imposing and stern. His appearance would have been daunting if it wasn't for his hair. He lacked it on top so he had grown it long in the back and allowed a bushy halo around his jaw. I found it funny, so I smiled.

He scowled at me. "You think it a laughing matter to parade around this city as if you belong here?"

I bunched up my fist and took a step closer. I could easily take the old snarly man. Levi put an arm in front of me to stop me.

"I can't let you talk to my wife like that," Levi said in a warning tone.

"She's not your wife," he spat back. "But goodness knows I'm hardly one to judge."

He snorted and turned on his heel, walking away from us toward a grand house that sat on the opposite corner of the intersection. We looked at each other.

That was weird.

He had almost reached the front door when he turned back and saw us still standing in front of the boarding house, watching him. He stomped his foot.

"Are you coming?"

Is it a trick? Levi asked.

I don't think so. I think he wants to help us.

He shrugged and turned to follow the man.

We entered the mansion behind him. At first it seemed like any other house on the street, though it was larger and more ornate. But on closer inspection, I saw glimpses of things out of place. Odd bits of old machinery had been left here and there. The housekeeper stepped around them and came to take Levi's hat. The man grabbed his lapels.

"The name is Ericsson. As you can see, I'm a bit of an inventor. Pardon the mess."

"I do my best," the housekeeper mumbled with an Irish lilt.

"You do, Mrs. Cassidy, and that's all one can ask." He waited until she walked out of the room. "Now if you would kindly tell me who you are."

"Uh, I'm Levi, and this is Roxy. And no, we aren't married."

He gave us a nod of approval for telling the truth. "Good. Let's head up, Levi and Roxy."

He took the stairs two at a time, spry for a man I guessed was at least seventy. We had to hurry to catch up. While we followed him, I saw papers stretched out over hall tables with detailed drawings and plans for warships and torpedo boats.

"You design naval equipment?" Levi stopped for a moment to study one of the drawings.

"Among other things. Please keep up." Ericsson went up another flight of stairs, above the bedrooms to the attic space. There he went out the window and climbed an outdoor set of steps to the roof. We were out of breath by the time we reached the top.

I wasn't prepared for what I saw. A huge metal machine glowed in the sunset, mirrors dangling from every inch, reflecting every catch of light, turning in the breeze and focusing the energy of the light onto flat discs that contained copper wires.

I noticed Levi's excitement jump as he went to investigate the machine.

"What's this?" I reached out to touch one of the gilded mirrors and had my hand smacked by Ericsson's cane. His cane he didn't seem to need for walking, I noticed. I suppressed the urge to grab it and whack him on the head.

"An experiment harnessing the energy of the sun to use as a

power source." He paused and chuckled. "At least that's what I tell the neighbors."

"I see you have solar cells." Levi tapped one of the mirrors, making the reflected light dance. I wondered why Levi got to touch it without being caned.

"I'm not sure I completely understand it, though I hate to admit it." Ericsson shook his head. "You see, I didn't build it alone."

Something about the way he said it made a chill spread over my skin.

Without further delay he poked the end of his cane between the top buttons of Levi's shirt and ripped it open. The look on his face went beyond surprised when he saw Levi's bare chest. He was visibly shaken.

"I've never been wrong before," he mumbled. He began to pace frenetically, back and forth across the rooftop patio. He whispered to himself, tapping the cane on everything he saw.

"Maybe if you explain, we can help," Levi suggested. Ericsson turned on us.

"No!" He pointed his cane with accusation. "You came from the reservoir last night. I saw you. Drenched. Clothes shredded. She was unconscious." He almost jabbed me in the stomach with the cane. I wished for my knife. In fact, my knee might work just as well. I smiled at the thought of two splintered pieces of wood flying over the side of his house.

"Open your top buttons," he demanded, taking two large steps toward me. I crossed my arms and refused to move, glaring at him.

"Are you hard of hearing, child? Shall I speak louder?"

With his words went the rest of my restraint.

"You are a crazy old mudsill! If you poke me one more time with that cane I'm going to shove it up your—"

I didn't bother to finish the sentence since I was already lunging at him. Levi held me back.

"Give me a reason, and I'll let her go," Levi said to Ericsson. "Believe me—she's stronger than she looks."

I elbowed Levi hard in the side. "Let me go! He and his stupid cane deserve it!"

Ericsson, meanwhile, donned a pair of creepy bent spectacles. Apparently, just so he could have a better view of my rant.

"Oh, for pity's sake," he sneered. "I don't have time for female fits of hysteria. Why do you think my own wife lived in England for most of our marriage? Control your woman, Mr. Koenig. I just need to see the top of her chest. The first two buttons will do."

Levi held my shoulders until I got still. I didn't have to hear his silent words to know he wanted me to cooperate. I glared, but I shut my mouth.

"There's no need to open her shirt," Levi said to him. "I know what you're looking for and you're right, it's there. But how do you know about it?"

"Why don't you have one?" Ericsson pointed at Levi with suspicion. "I must insist on seeing her mark before I discuss this any further."

Levi silently advised me to be patient as he undid two buttons and held open the sides of my shirt for Ericsson to see the insignia that was burned into my flesh. I refused to look the inventor in the eye.

"You heal quickly, child." Ericsson grunted. "I apologize for my insistence. I've never seen one of our kind with one of theirs before."

Levi shifted. "I'm not one of your kind. I'm from the same place she is."

"Every person that has come through that portal alive in the past sixteen years has had the mark on their chest, young man. Explain to me why you don't."

Levi looked toward the sunset with a dark expression. "Because my mother did the marking. I wasn't supposed to come through. She sent Roxy, and I jumped in after her."

"Interesting," Ericsson said. "Did you know you might survive?"

"I didn't know for sure. I suspected."

I turned to him, doubtful. He had always given the impression he didn't know what Leona was doing. He hadn't even told me she was his mom.

One of those seeds of doubt that lived within me grew, and he noticed it.

"Roxy," he said, reaching for my hand. I pulled it away.

"So your mother is the one who has been sending all these people back to our time? This Regal Manager?" Ericsson ignored our personal exchange.

"Leona."

"I see." He tapped his finger on the end of the cane, looking out over the city. "Sarah has spoken of her."

Something occurred to me, and I couldn't believe I hadn't yet considered it. "So every person that comes through the portal is living here?"

"Not everyone." He shrugged. "Approximately twenty-five percent perish. Sometimes as a result of the journey, other times because of mistreatment in your time, especially since they tend to be elderly or in poor health. I keep an eye on the reservoir with my telescope and send for the bodies before they are discovered. Most arrive with injuries. Sometimes the general gets to them before we do."

I shelved the other information, focused only on hope that sprung up in me like a thirsty seedling in dry ground. Levi put a warning hand on my arm.

"Is Arabella Eisen here?" Levi asked the question for me as he watched me struggle. I bit my lip so hard I tasted blood. I didn't want to hear the answer. I didn't want to hear she wasn't and have her die all over again. I didn't want to hear she was and that she had missed my entire childhood because she was living two hundred years before me.

"Why do you want to know?" Ericsson said gruffly.

"This is her daughter, Roxanne Eisen."

His demeanor changed. He was speechless for a long moment.

"Roxanne?" It was like he was looking at me again for the first time. "Yes, I see it in the color of your hair and the shade of gray in

145

your eyes. Of course you are her daughter."

"She's alive?"

My words came as a strangled gasp, and I would have collapsed if Levi wasn't holding me up. I pushed him away and grabbed Ericsson's coat.

"Take me to her!"

TWENTY-ONE

"Taking you to her will be a little tricky. First things first. Follow the direction of the light."

Ericsson adjusted the machine. Mirrors went flying into place with hundreds of clangs. A beam emerged and shot into the evening sky, caught by the blaze of the setting sun and redirected out across the city, almost like—

"It's a laser," Levi said, impressed.

"The light is caused by a giant magnet we put inside the machine which harnesses large amounts of solar power. And where does the light project?"

I strained my eyes across the dim tops of buildings, trying to make sense of the city of the past.

"The reservoir," Levi said.

"Correct."

"So you have a fancy magnet that points at stuff. It's basically just a compass. I have one on my chain." I refused to be impressed as I held out my tracker chain. I didn't know why his silly machine was more important than finding my mom.

"The magnetic beam is helping harness the power of the same

black hole that is pulling on the earth of your time. In our time it's not strong enough, but we were able to find it. We're attempting to create an alternate wormhole to arc back to your time."

"We could go home." Levi's voice was quiet, though his excitement jumped.

"Is that possible?" I asked Ericsson.

"You got here, didn't you? All it takes is a little gravity and some direction. Well, it takes a great deal of gravity, rather."

I watched the beam, amazed at the power of light and its relationship with time. Everything worked in harmony. All the powers of the physical world could be harnessed and ridden like a wild horse across the universe. It made me feel small.

"Did my mother help you build this?"

He nodded. I didn't miss the smile that pulled at the corner of his mouth.

"Sarah has shown me many wonders from the future. Ideas inconceivable to this time. I'm overwhelmed by them, yet she only shared what I needed to know to help create the arc."

"Why do you keep calling her Sarah?"

"Sarah Thorn is her name here. She lives with her people at one of my properties in Abingdon Square, though I must tell you she is rarely at home." He powered down the machine. "How old were you when your mother came here? You hardly look sixteen."

I glared. "I was almost two."

He watched me, and it jarred me when I realized he was feeling compassion. He certainly didn't express it.

"Please take me to her," I said again. I almost asked if Morris was here, too, but for some reason, I knew he wasn't. I couldn't feel him. I was sure I'd recognize him miles away.

Besides, he was dead. Wasn't he?

"I can take you to her home, but she is not there. Lucy would have sent word if she arrived. They may have room for you both to stay there. It's not a good idea to interact with the locals too long. And you'd be safer from the general."

He turned before either of us could ask who the general was, and passed back down through the levels of the house, calling to Mrs. Cassidy who hummed as she swept around the clutter in the hall.

"We're out for our constitutional."

She saluted. "Aye, Cap'n."

We walked for blocks down Hudson. The gas streetlamps had been turned on at dusk, so I used their light to observe the city. It was like my New York, only with several layers removed. Some things were the same, though much newer, but most of it was completely different. It didn't surprise me. New York was fast-paced, never stopping for the sentimental. If something wasn't useful, it was leveled and replaced with something better.

It was our way.

I felt comfort in the thought. Even if the city had changed, it was because the people were the same. We were driven, full of ideas, always growing and straining forward to try new things. Our determination could only be hindered by dictators threatening our lives.

Deep thoughts.

I ignored Levi and watched Ericsson who was nearly breaking into a run. The cane was at his side, under his arm, unused. I was sure he carried it just to hit people and tap things.

I know! Some sort of OCD or something.

I smiled. Ericsson saw it and swerved his head. "Is something amusing, Miss Eisen?"

Miss Eisen's in trouble.

You're an idiot.

I gave Ericsson a blank stare as Levi laughed.

"I do not understand the young," Ericsson mumbled.

He has a point, Roxy. You are immature.

Speak for yourself, loser.

I felt suspicion from the inventor. He turned on us.

"Are you two communicating with your thoughts?"

For a moment both of us were too surprised to speak. We stared at him. He stared at us. Levi forced a laugh. I shrugged like he was speaking Chinese.

"Before I met your people, my world was much smaller. Now, after building a time-altering machine on my rooftop so powerful I had to learn the word *tesla* to describe it, I accept just about anything as a possibility."

I wondered if it would be a good time for Levi to tell him he could heal people with blue glowing fingers. Levi snickered and then coughed to mask it. Ericsson sighed and resumed walking.

"The people at Abingdon are mostly from the future," he said, changing the subject. "The ones we save before the general gets to them."

"Who's this general mudsill?" I asked.

"Do you children know nothing?"

"You should assume that," Levi said. "Before we arrived here, we didn't know this world existed."

I glared at him. *You knew.*

"I did not know, Roxy. I only suspected."

Ericsson huffed. "Suspected what? Am I going mad or did I miss some dialogue in the conversation?"

"Who's the general?" Levi ignored his question.

Ericsson seethed, but he answered. "Your queen has an army here. They hunt down and kill every person that comes through the portal, unless we find them first. The branding is how the general identifies them. We're working on some sort of technology that could remove the scar."

"Do we know the name of the general? What he looks like?" Levi asked.

"Joseph Brant. He looks like a ruffian."

Leona having a guy in 1874, working at her beck and call, worried me. It bothered me so much I decided I didn't want to deal with the information. As Levi tried to wrap his brain around the disturbing news, I pushed all thought of it aside.

"Okay, so back to my mom. How will we find her?" I

demanded.

"Lucy will know. She's the caretaker at Abingdon. She's like a daughter to Miss Thorn."

It was silly to be jealous of this Lucy, but it didn't stop the sting. I wouldn't know my own mother's face from any others we passed in the street.

It wasn't fair.

Ericsson used his cane to ring the buzzer of the townhouse on Abingdon Square. The building extended three stories and an attic. Red brick contrasted with green shutters, and arched stonework framed the door.

A dark-skinned girl my age answered the door, surveying us with a guarded expression.

"Good evening, Mr. John. Come in."

We were led into the parlor. An oriental rug covered the wood floors and long, elegant red draperies decorated the high windows. There was an instrument resembling a piano along the far wall and a large gilded portrait of a woman.

A couple of prim old ladies sat on the settee doing needlework, children ran up and down the stairs, and a mishmash of ages in between milled through the hallway and dining room beyond the parlor.

My gaze caught on a familiar face. I squealed and launched into his arms, affectionately punching his shoulder a few times.

"Hey, Cap'n," Greer laughed and swung me around a couple times. "You weren't worked up over me, were you?"

"Nah." I flicked the cap off his head as he put me down. "Greer can take care of Greer, right?"

"That's right." He nodded as he shook hands with Levi.

Ericsson interrupted the reunion. "Have you heard from Mrs. Thorn?"

I noticed that every head turned at her mention. She must be loved. Respected.

"She's on an orphan train with Mr. Brace. They were hoping to get some of the younger kids good homes before winter," Lucy said.

"Mrs. Thorn has made it her mission to rescue the young orphans wandering the streets in the rough areas of town. She brings them home and cleans them up so she can take them on the train to find good homes," Ericsson said to Levi and me.

"I don't know when she'll be back," Lucy said with a shrug. "You know Miz Sarah. Do you have a message for her? I could send a wire to one of the stops."

Ericsson nodded. "At your earliest convenience, please. Tell her we have visitors she will want to meet as soon as possible."

I fought disappointment. It was frustrating to be in her home with people who knew and loved her. My chest ached with jealousy.

"Do you have rooms available?" Ericsson pointed his cane up the stairs.

"We're full up, but I can always find a space. The little miss can share my bed."

She glanced at me with large black eyes that seemed sad.

"We have a place for now," Levi said.

"Send a message boy if you come up with some room," Ericsson instructed. "We don't want these two mingling with the natives any longer than necessary."

"I'll do that, Mr. John."

When we arrived back at Beach Street, Ericsson pointed his cane at us as he stood at his door. "Stay low; blend in. Alert me at once if you think you see the general."

"How will we know?"

"You'll know." He turned on his heel and disappeared into his house, closing the door in our face.

It was only nine o'clock, but the street was dark and quiet. We sat down on the front steps. I stared at the dancing flicker of the street lamp. Without the whir of maglevs and the glow of the portal, the world came into better focus. It became tangible.

The natural light of the stars filtered over us like a blanket. I hadn't realized there were so many.

"They do seem bright here," Levi answered my thoughts. "It's almost like they're shining for us. Letting us know some things don't change, even across centuries."

"Maybe."

You shine like those stars.

I scoffed. "Don't be an idiot."

He sighed. "I can't be responsible for every thought in my head. You do, though. Maybe you're reflecting some greater light, but you burn more brightly than others around you. You can call it maudlin if you want."

"It's totally maudlin," I said, trying not to draw attention to the place in my mind where I was affected by his words. He moved closer.

"I don't really miss the technology and noise," he said, changing the subject. I saw right past it. He was testing the waters. Seeing how close I'd let him get.

"You could cut the test short and just tell me." He stared down at the dark street with a hint of a smile.

I knew I should push him away, but it felt good to be close. I let his arm and leg brush mine. I felt his fingertips flutter over mine, causing the familiar electric sensation. Before I could talk myself out of it, I turned my hand over and let him hold it.

"I feel it, too." He ran his thumb along mine. "That spark. Like an electric pulse. It doesn't happen with anyone else."

I found I didn't want to consider that he had tried it with anyone else.

"So you've healed your mom?" I didn't know why I brought it up again, considering how our last conversation about Leona had gone. He didn't answer.

"Did she know you could heal before you did it?"

He twisted his mouth in a wry expression. "She's the one who told me I could. And then demanded I do it."

"What did she have? Zombie flu?"

He stared at me evenly.

"I had it once, you know," he said, his face still solemn. I raised an eyebrow before I saw the faint outline of his upturned mouth. I elbowed him.

"Maybe I have it now, and I'm about to eat you alive. You never know with Zombie flu." He leaned over and caught my earlobe with his teeth.

I tried to get away, but his arm went around me and kept me in place. The night was chilly, so I leaned against him. I wished we could just be together, but inevitably his thoughts went where they always did.

"I'm a guy, Roxy. It's what we do." He didn't let me squirm away, so I gave in and stayed there. "Why are you so against the idea, anyway?"

"Of bonding?" I shrugged, twisting my skirt in my hands. "When the kids in the bunker feel it, they just do it without thinking about the cost. But none of them will deny afterwards that there are consequences. Bonding changes you. It makes you weak."

"By weak, do you mean vulnerable?"

"Same thing."

"It's not the same thing. What would anything in life mean without attachments?"

I pulled away from him and stood up. "Probably time to head in."

And find separate rooms.

He sighed, standing up and climbing ahead to open the door. "Don't worry, Captain Eisen. I can take a hint. I won't bring it up again."

TWENTY-TWO

My dreams had existed in the portal since I'd arrived in the past. Maybe my brain was trying to process it all. Most nights I stood on the brink, pushing my mother into the light as I listened to her scream.

One night Levi was there. As I fled from the portal chamber and the citadel, both eerily empty, he followed me. Broadway was abandoned, but garish lights from the pavement flashed against his feet as he walked. His clothes were tattered and his skin a greenish hue. Dark rings surrounded his sunken eyes, and his skin melted from his face, spilling maggots. He didn't move quickly, but he seemed to take huge strides and I could not increase the distance between us as hard as I tried to run.

I glanced back and saw his blank stare and unseeing eyes. He smelled my flesh and wanted to eat me alive. I listened but there was no coherent thought in his mind. Levi wasn't there.

I reached for my weapon, tears streaming down my cheeks as I realized what I would do. I pulled out the nineteenth century pistol. It felt thick and heavy in my hands. I sobbed as I pulled the trigger and sent the bullet to his brain. His body slammed on the street, oozing black blood that pooled under his head. I kneeled to touch his hand. It was burning hot. My fingers were on fire.

"Levi!"

The street faded away and I sat up. I realized I was in bed and Levi was crouched beside me, holding my arms. He smoothed back hair from my face that was damp with sweat.

"It's alright, I'm here." His voice was soothing.

It was too soon from the dream and I didn't stop myself in time. I bunched his shirt in my fists and pulled him to me. His arms went around me, and the warmth and electric thrill reminded me of the dream and the dangerous pastime of getting too close to Levi Koenig, the son of my enemy.

I pushed him away and turned toward the wall.

I didn't go back to sleep. I listened to Levi's even breathing and the occasional creaking of the floorboards or soft click of a door. Just as I wondered if dawn would ever arrive, I heard heavy footsteps on the stairs. Coming down the hall. They stopped on the other side of our door.

I reached for my weapon before I remembered Leona had sent me into the portal unarmed. Levi had his laser rifle and WristCom, but they were drained of power and broken. He'd been planning on tinkering with them and creating a solar cell to charge them.

I wasn't going to sit helplessly while we were murdered. I sprang from bed and fell to the floor beside Levi. I shook him awake. He stared at me in confusion as the door banged open.

The first thing I noticed about the man who sauntered into our room was his confidence. He wore a long black coat and shiny boots, obviously meant to intimidate. He was tall, with wavy hair that went to his shoulder and a goatee. His blue eyes reflected the early morning light from the window.

"Forgive me for the early hour, folks. Just a bit of business. Gents, please secure this fine looking couple so we can have a chat."

The two men on either side of him reached for their guns. Levi stepped in front of me. "Get out."

"Sure, sure. The thing is, I have a job to do, and I saw you come out of the reservoir."

"You're the general." I vowed I would take Ericsson's cane and make good use of it if I ever saw him again. He could have at least given us weapons to defend ourselves.

The general laughed. "Well, that's what I hear." He motioned to one of the men. "Check for scars."

Adrenaline surged. I kicked the guy in the stomach and poked him in the eyes, sending him sprawling. The general leaped over the bed and in one moment I was pinned to the ground.

"You got a lively one here, don't you?" he said to Levi, who barely contained his anger. The only reason he held it back was the gun pointed at his chest.

"Get off her. Now!" he growled.

"Like I said, I have to check. If you don't have scars, I'll be on my way and you'll be free to go."

Levi pulled his neckline down. "See? No scar."

The man sat up taller, rubbing his facial hair. "But how did you know where it would be?"

"People in this city are obsessed with scars on the chest," Levi said quickly. "Now get off her and get out of our room."

He didn't move. His grin deepened. "I have to check. But if your lady promises to be good, I'll proceed in a more gentlemanly fashion." He gestured to the groaning man who was still rubbing his eyes.

Levi took a large step toward him and pushed him off. He punched him hard in the face three times. The general fought back, sending Levi sprawling with a hard blow to the stomach.

After another round, they were both bloody and breathing hard. I saw a look of rage in their eyes and had the strange thought that they were alike. The notion was like a bad taste in my mouth.

The general's emotions were just as peculiar. He felt

157

superiority and he was interested in his agenda, but there was a vague flip-side. He was surprised by me. Attracted? It didn't make sense, but the conflicting feelings got more noticeable the longer we were in the same room.

By that time Mrs. Watts and several of the male boarders had come to the doorway and witnessed the altercation. A constable had been called. The strange man called *the general* gave me a final perusal before he and his men disappeared from the second story window.

The terrified widow tried to breathe and held her middle with shaking arms. "I don't do well with trouble like this. I regret I must ask you to leave."

Ericsson wasn't happy about having his schedule interrupted. But he'd been awake and working on the machine, so he motioned us to follow him up.

"Maybe you can help me figure out what to do with this infernal contraption. I kept waking up thinking about it."

We followed him through the clutter to the roof, where the sunrise captured the elegance of the machine, with mirrors twirling in tandem, a dance of light and reflection. Ericsson flipped the switch and the antique engine roared to life. The hum was loud enough to earn curious or irritated looks from neighbors below. He ignored them. I got the feeling he enjoyed his reputation as the eccentric inventor experimenting on his rooftop.

"I made copper plates and connected them with wires. It's potent enough to power the laser Sarah created inside the magnetic field, but it's not enough to cause any effect on the field over the reservoir."

Levi nodded, examining the rudimentary solar cells. "Solar tech from our time is highly concentrated with chemicals. It takes very little sunlight to cause the chemical reactions that produce large amounts of energy."

Levi took one of the plates off the machine and pried it away from the mirror. "I think I could tweak these to give us more power. But we could also make more. Maybe hundreds of smaller cells."

His words lit a fascinated energy in Ericsson's brain. "You may have something."

That evening we were sent to Abingdon. Ericsson claimed he couldn't possibly accommodate two more people, especially young people that required a chaperone.

Lucy seemed happy enough to welcome us in. "Miss Roxanne, you can bunk with me. There's always room for another on the floor in one of the boys' rooms, Mr. Levi." She hesitated, avoiding our eyes. "Sorry I don't have a room for you to share."

"No, Levi and I aren't together like that," I said quickly. Levi raised an eyebrow.

"All I know is lots of you future people seem awfully free with yourselves. I don't claim to understand it." Lucy led us up the stairs to show us the rooms.

Levi smiled at me as Lucy continued to mumble about the future's lack of morals. I didn't explain that anyone arriving from our time was likely happy to be free of imposed morality standards, whether they were mine or Leona's.

Levi was still grinning. I narrowed my eyes. *I don't like drama. Or babies.*

You don't like babies. What does that say about you, Roxy?

He grunted as I kicked him in the shin.

TWENTY-THREE

I might as well have been back in the bunker.

There were noisy kids. Again we had the problem of survival, of hiding in plain sight. We kept away from the neighbors and tried not to draw attention to ourselves.

Yes, it was familiar.

I spent most of my time with Lucy. As the representatives of my mother, we were the unofficial mistresses of the house. It was an important role in 1874, because it took work to run a household in nineteenth century New York.

We kept the orphans occupied so they would stay out of trouble. There were eleven when we arrived, ranging in age from four to sixteen. We had to keep enough food in the pantry, which required daily trips to the market.

Lucy kept a small garden behind the house in the tiny space they had for a backyard, along with a little chicken coop. There was also an iron bench and a stone fountain surrounded by ivy and summer flowers. I wondered if the pocket of beauty served to give Lucy a sense of peace in such an environment. As we worked the garden I told her about the bunker gardens and the animals.

"I wish we had a cow," she said with envy.

"I'll have to figure out a way to steal one for you."

She laughed and the sound, along with the rest of her, was strong and lovely. She had soulful eyes, perfectly set within her ebony complexion. I suspected she'd seen plenty of trouble, having dark skin in her time period, but she had no thought of revenge.

I ended up telling her more than I'd ever told anyone. I knew nothing would be repeated.

"You're a safe space, Lucy," I said as we gathered eggs. I laughed at my joke while she continued her task with a tolerant expression. "Growing up in the bunker, I had to stay detached. I was the leader and everyone thought that meant I had to be on my own. Morris was like a father to me, but when he died, I was alone."

"What about Mr. Levi?" Lucy blew a piece of straw from an egg and set it on the pile in the basket. I didn't answer at first. It was hard to put into words how close—and yet how distant—Levi and I were.

"I can tell Levi everything. He's always around when I need him. And I'm telling you, Lucy, if he just brushes my hand with his fingers ..."

She watched me, her silence inviting me to continue.

"I can talk to him with my mind."

She narrowed her eyes. "You do what, now?"

I glanced around to make sure we were alone. "I've always had this power to sense other people's emotions. It's almost like I see them written in colors around a person. But with Levi, I hear his voice in my mind."

"So what am I thinking now?"

"I only know your emotions. You're wondering if I'm making this up. You're determined not to believe me even if I get it right. You think less of me because I told you I had this power."

Her eyebrow rose slightly. "Well, if it's true that you can hear the boy's thoughts, I don't know why you wouldn't trust him."

"When did I say I don't trust him?" I shook my head.

"You said you don't have anybody," she said.

The hens strutted around their pen, clucking their disapproval of our invasion. I searched for the right words.

"I can't trust him," I finally said. "He's done things, said things and thought things that make me question his allegiance."

"His allegiance to you?"

"I don't know if it's to me or his mom."

She gave a thoughtful "hmm."

I didn't see Levi much. He and Greer spent their days with Ericsson working on the machine, harnessing the impossible. Levi had a theory that we would have to use the star itself. If we harnessed its energy like our mothers did in the future, we wouldn't need anything 1874 couldn't offer, like nuclear power.

But Levi's preoccupation with getting us home didn't explain the weakened connection between us. Our friendship was fraying. Maybe it couldn't stand up to the forces at work against us, or maybe it hadn't been real. Either way, I missed him.

"Miss Roxy, you are just going to have to tell that boy how you feel. Make him choose between you and his mother," Lucy said.

"I have told him."

"You told him everything? Or you just let him read all those random thoughts in your head and hoped he figured it out?"

I didn't answer, but she shook her head in disapproval at my sheepish expression.

"I don't have the luxury of friendship, much less love, Lucy. I have people who depend on me."

"Then I think you need love more than most."

It sounded like something Levi would say.

It was two weeks before Levi or I had the courage to bring it up. He was showing me diagrams they had worked up to transform the machine. I was interested, but each time his skin accidentally

162

brushed mine, the charge distracted me from the conversation. It irritated me, because there was a wall between us, placed there brick-by-brick by his refusal to be honest with me.

My thoughts forced his attention from the plans. He tossed the pencil beside the sketches and leaned back in his chair.

"What do you think I'm holding back?" He stared morosely at the table.

I had to speak over the noise of kids playing a game in the front hallway. "You haven't told me everything."

He was disgusted. "You don't think all your *I can't bond with anyone, I have too much responsibility* or *don't make me weak* crap might be a reason for the distance?"

I didn't have a good answer. So I gave him a bad one.

"Can you blame me with all your mommy issues?"

He stood, knocking the chair against the table hard and turning toward the fireplace with his arms crossed over his chest. "My *mommy issues*."

"Am I wrong?"

It was really, really quiet for a long time. When I couldn't take it anymore, I got up and walked out. Everyone in the parlor tried to pretend they hadn't just heard every word we said. Except Lucy. She glared at me over her knitting.

I stomped out the front door and down the narrow front steps. If we had been in 2074, I would have disappeared into the subway tunnels.

An omnibus lumbered down Hudson Street. People milled about the square, standing in the shade of trees or coming in and out of shops. Horses stood at posts, swishing their tails at flies. There was nowhere to go to be alone.

I headed down the walk as fast as my uncomfortable boots would allow.

"You can't run from me, Roxy." Levi wasn't far behind me.

"Leave me alone."

I didn't know where I was going. I couldn't make sense of this version of my city. The skirts bunching up around my ankles made walking a chore. I grabbed the hem with my hand, tempted to rip it away.

"I hate 1874," I said loudly, causing several people to stare.

Levi pushed the fabric out of my hand so it fell back into place. "Why are you so angry with me?"

It annoyed me that he didn't know the answer. "Don't," I snapped. "Stop looking so hurt. I never promised you anything."

"I think I at least deserve to know why you are pushing me away. More than normal."

I shrugged. "I don't want to be around you. We're too complicated. Let's just leave it at that."

"No," he insisted. "Give me something to wrap my head around. Are you afraid?"

I glared hard at the street. "I'm not afraid of you. I could beat you up right here in my corset and high tops."

He smiled, but without joy. "I don't deny that. But you're afraid of letting me in here." He pointed to my chest. His eyes caught my scar between the folds of my shirt I had left unbuttoned, and he touched it with a frown. I pushed his hand away.

"Careful. If I screamed you'd be arrested for assaulting a lady."

"You're a lady now?" He crossed his arms over his chest. "Do you want to discuss all the times you've assaulted me?"

"Doesn't matter here."

"You're avoiding the topic."

I tapped my boot on the edge of the sidewalk. Pretended to be fascinated by a caterpillar crawling around a pile of horse manure. When I looked back at him, he was still waiting for an answer.

"Fine," I said, knowing it was pointless to argue the point but seeing no alternative to telling him the truth. "I don't trust you. But that isn't a surprise."

His anxiety spiked. I gave him a guilty glance. What could I say? Surely he knew. He sat down on the bench and glared at the ground.

"Why don't you trust me?"

"Haven't we already discussed this?"

"Humor me."

I couldn't. I didn't want to say the words because they felt like betrayal. It didn't matter anyway, because my mind suddenly flooded with all the reasons.

You still love your mom, after everything. Like you think you can change her. You keep secrets from me. You knew about the portal, but you let me think it was a death trap up to the second I was thrown in.

His hard stare betrayed the regret I sensed. I couldn't stop myself.

You forced me into that electrocution chair. Tied me down. Flipped the switch.

I wished I could take back the thought. He was wounded.

Causing you pain was the hardest thing I've ever had to do. I still feel sick when I think about it. I wouldn't have done it if you hadn't told me to.

We were both quiet. People passed, glancing at us. I'm sure they could sense the tension; it felt thick and tangible. As menacing as the hum from the portal.

Finally, he sighed. "Roxy, I can't force you to be what you don't feel," he said softly. "But I also can't deny how much I … care."

I didn't respond. Not out loud, not in our minds. There was no way to talk about it without changing what we were, and change was impossible.

"I know you think I should forget it. Maybe I should. But I can't turn it off," he continued. "Part of me accepts your lack of faith in me. But don't you know by now that I'm on your side? Even if I don't have everything figured out?"

My gaze shot up. "You can't have it both ways. She wants me dead, and I want her dead. One of us will win. You have to decide which one you want to be standing over the other in the end."

He flinched. I heard the conflict of his mind like a hundred voices talking at once.

"She's evil," I said. "That doesn't mean you are. But you can't be faithful to evil and still be on the side of good."

"Not everything is so black and white, Roxy," he said, shaking his head. "She's still a person just like you are."

"Not like me."

"That's cold, Roxy. Not to mention arrogant." His frustrated, impatient sigh made me wish I was anywhere but stuck in that conversation. We were up against a wall; there was no way to fight our way out of the truth. We might as well get out our laser rifles and settle it like the soldiers we were.

"Does it surprise you that I'm cold and arrogant?" I scuffed my foot on the ground. People were staring. I should sit down next to him on the bench. But it felt like I'd be agreeing with him, and I didn't. I couldn't afford to agree with him. I stayed where I was, my arms crossed tightly against my stomach.

He looked up toward the sky. "You know the woman you claim is evil was your mom's best friend."

"So what?" I shrugged. "Leona killed my dad and portaled my mom and me. How much do you think I should forgive?"

"I didn't say you should forgive her." He ran his fingers through his hair in agitation. "But lots of people have been pushed over the edge by raw emotion. She loved your dad. She killed him because she couldn't have him. Feelings make us do stupid things."

We were discussing the things we never dared to think about. This could only end badly, but I plunged ahead.

"She's the queen of stupid, and she hasn't regretted any of it. She's so far gone in her crazy perspective, she's never coming back. You know that, right? She won't even come back for you."

His jaw clenched. "You're only saying that because you're scared of you and me."

"I don't know what you are talking about," I said as I heaved an impatient sigh. He tugged on my hand, pulling me toward the bench. I sat down, though I sat stiffly on the edge and crossed my arms again.

"You know. That force that exists here." He gestured to the space between us. "And our weird mind meld. It scares you, so you think of excuses to push me away."

"Not excuses. Facts. I'm not scared. Love doesn't mix with destiny. You can thank Leona for ruining our chances."

"Oh, yes," he said with a harsh laugh. "Don't make you weak, right? Because loving someone makes them weak."

"I don't expect you to get it. I can't do what I'm supposed to if I'm worried about people. Everyone I ever loved died. And every time I got weaker."

Levi grabbed my shoulders and turned me toward him. I felt his disagreement, almost as palpable as his grasp. His voice was edged with fierce insistence.

"Love doesn't make you weak, Roxy," he said. "Love is power."

I didn't respond, and when he let me, I pulled away. I wished he was right. I wished I knew what kind of love he meant, though I wasn't about to ask him. Did he mean the love that went with bonding? Or was he talking about something bigger than our relationship; bigger than our lives? I didn't know, and I didn't want to hope for something that was only going to disappoint me in the end.

TWENTY-FOUR

"Tell me what happened to my parents."

Morris was teaching me how to shoot a laser rifle in a quarantined section of Central Park. I had just turned ten a few days before, and I was ready to hear the story.

I knew the basics. Morris had made sure all the bunker kids understood that my mom was the hero and she died protecting me so I could set them free someday. I always had the impression that the Regal Manager was responsible for her death. But now I was ready to know the details.

He gave me a long look. "Are you sure?"

I stared into his face. I focused on the familiar slant of his nose, the warmth of his dark eyes, the shadow of his beard. I decided that I could know how they died because Morris had been there to become my father in their place. And he had been a good one.

He crouched against the smooth black rock and folded his hands in front of him. He gave me a small smile as he collected his thoughts.

"Your mother and Leona created the portal together."

I stared at him. I had been expecting anything, but his words still caught me off guard. Why would my mother help create a death trap?

"It wasn't intended to kill people. It protected people."

"How can a portal to a black hole protect anyone?"

"Because the black hole was pulling on earth," he said. "If it got any stronger, it could have pulled us out of orbit. We all would have died. Plenty of scientists all over the world were working on a solution, but it was your mother and Leona who came up with the right formula."

"So when did Leona get evil?"

Morris considered my question. "I think it was little things along the way. She stored up every bitter thought, never speaking them, never dealing with them. The pile became so big and the bitterness became stronger than her ability to ignore it."

"What was she so mad about?"

"Your mom was amazing. She did well at everything she set her mind to do. Leona was brilliant as well, but she always compared herself to Arabella. That made her want everything Arabella had. When your mom met your dad and they fell in love, Leona decided she wanted him.

"She tried to make him love her for years. Even after your parents were married. But when you were a year old, Leona realized the truth—he had never loved her; he only had eyes for your mom. So she stabbed your father through the heart, right in front of you and your mom. After that, she pushed your mom into the portal. I think that was the moment she decided not to fight the darkness inside her anymore."

"Why didn't she kill me, too?" I gulped, not sure I was ready to process the emotions that were grabbing hold of me.

"You had a guardian angel," he said as he put his hand on my shoulder. It felt warm and strong. "Someone hid you in the gardens and took care of you until I could find you. You were in the bushes by the steps, lying on a blanket. You were tired and hungry, but you were alive."

"Who saved me?"

"Someone special, Roxy. Very special. Maybe someday you'll be able to thank them," he said, pulling me to my feet. "Now we better get back to work if you are ever going to learn to shoot this thing."

"I already know how to shoot it," I said stubbornly, but I hugged him. He was surprised. I wasn't the most affectionate child. He hugged me back, and I felt safe, if only for that moment.

"Thanks for taking care of me. Of us," I said quietly.

"My duty was—and is—my joy," he said.

I stood at the bedroom window at Abingdon, staring through the cloudy panes of the long windows. The memory had caught me by surprise as I was tying back my hair and washing at the stand.

"So you haven't talked to Mr. Levi since your fight?" Lucy said as she made the bed, a four poster with a canopy and rich red linens. I shrugged and turned away from the window.

"Nothing good comes from not talking about it," she chided.

"Nothing good came from talking about it, either," I said in retort, swishing the water in the bowl with my washing cloth. "It felt like we were trying to kick down a brick wall. Pointless."

She sniffed, but didn't lecture further. "Let's go. The earlier we get to the market the less crowded and smelly it will be."

I knew it to be a fact by now and didn't waste time following her down the stairs to the narrow front hallway. I noticed a group of kids in the front parlor taking apart a laser rifle with great enthusiasm. Lucy yelled at them to get *that infernal contraption* up to the attic where it belonged before someone saw it.

"When I get back I'll show you how to shoot cans off the fence," I promised, to Lucy's chagrin.

Washington Market loomed over the gloomy street in lower Manhattan, already caustic at the early hour. Vendor wagons lined the streets that surrounded the imposing, dilapidated building. Farmers unloaded carts full of goods to sell at their stands.

Inside the building, we quickly found our needs for the day. It was staggering the amount of food they had available to them, at least from my bunker perspective. I saw odd items like bear meat, moose meat, Chinese spices, and huge blocks of ice. Lucy bought dairy, produce and meat from a few farmers that came from Brooklyn.

"I don't buy from anybody else," Lucy explained. "Food makes people sick all the time. Some people sell milk they know is spoiled to mamas with new babies."

When we left, the streets around the exchange were already clogged with bodies. We squeezed through and walked home in silence. I used the time to ponder what I was going to do about Levi. Not that I was going to do anything. If I ignored him long enough, maybe he'd stop caring.

As we turned the corner to walk down Hudson to Abingdon, an arm abruptly snaked around my neck, cutting off my air. The force of a horse in motion pulled me up. I held on to the arm to keep from choking until I was thrown facedown across the horse. Whoever it was leaned on me to keep me in place. I gasped, my lungs begging for air. I heard Lucy scream and try to pull me back.

As the horse pounded down the brick street, I tried to fight. I squirmed and pulled myself up but he only pushed me back down with relentless strength. He tied my hands and left me to struggle until I realized it was useless. I turned my attention to looking for landmarks, trying to figure out where we were going and how I could get back when I got free.

It didn't take me long to realize where we were headed.

Five Points.

It might as well have been dark outside, as dismal and gloomy as the street was where we stopped in front of a ramshackle building. I didn't appreciate being tied and thrown over a horse's back with petticoats flying in the breeze. Whoever it was, I figured they'd better be ready for a good fight.

We stopped in front of a dark shack. He pulled me off the horse and I squinted in the dim light to see his face.

"Joe Brant."

For some reason, knowing it was him changed everything. I stepped back.

"What's the matter, little girl? Didn't you know I'd be back for you? I take my job very seriously." He was smirking.

My own thoughts surprised me. Instead of spitting into his face or taking the chance to give him a swift kick where it would count, the strangest thought occurred to me.

He's hot.

I shook my head to try to free my brain of the ridiculous notion. "I'm going to make you very sorry you ever touched me."

He chuckled. "Lots of spunk. I like that. People don't tend to stand up to me. Come on, spitfire."

He dragged me into the shack and dropped me in a filthy corner. By the smell, I was glad I couldn't see anything.

Except for an occasional swallow of water that tasted of dirt and a couple visits to the outhouse that revealed a previously unknown level of disgusting, I stayed in that corner, ignored, all day and night. I eventually figured I had been brought as bait for Levi.

I almost told him not to bother. I wasn't sure Levi wanted me back.

The place was dirtier than the refuse recycling plant in future New York and it smelled worse. At night the rooms crowded with so many bodies it was stifling to try to take a breath. The boys sprawled wherever they could find space and started snoring, hats over faces and guns in their hands with fingers on the trigger. I avoided making sudden moves.

They didn't get to sleep till after four in the morning. The streets of Five Points were alive with shouting and periodic gunfire until dawn. I could hear members of at least three different gangs meeting up where the five streets connected. There were boys called Dead Rabbits and Bowery Boys that made me think of Mrs. Bowery from the dungeon. I wondered if she'd be so proud of her heritage if she saw the original Bowerys.

I slept better during the day when the house was empty and the streets quieter. I didn't know where they all went, whether to earn an honest penny or harass upscale neighborhoods. Either way, I was glad to see them saunter off around noon.

One night a few days into my captivity, just before the noise of the brothel across the street finally trailed off, I watched the boys from the support beam I was tied to in the center of the room. Joe had moved me after I tried to break a window to cut my ropes. Avoiding groping hands was trickier in my new spot. I had to kick a few sensitive areas before they got the point.

The smell was staggering. It was a simmering pot of hot, unwashed teenage boys who ate little and drank a lot, some enough to vomit in the corners. I had thought the bunker smelled bad.

I heard voices outside on the front stoop where Joe was keeping watch. A couple of the boys stumbled back from the brothel and sat next to him. I strained to hear what they were saying.

"What are you gonna do with the girl?" One of the boys managed around a mouthful of drunkenness. I sensed he was hoping Joe would offer me as entertainment, and it made me feel queasy.

"I don't know," Joe said. "I was thinking she'd draw out her man so we could off them both. Maybe he doesn't care about her as much as I thought."

Either that or Levi thought I should be smart enough to get myself out of this mess. I should, after all.

"How'd you end up here, Joe?" The other boy didn't sound quite as drunk. He'd probably only had enough to make him talk too much. "Most of us got no parents and do what we gotta do to survive. You talk real good and got the nicest gun I ever seen. Why you hanging out with swadders like us?"

"I have a job to do. Our secret mission."

"Yeah, cussed if I know why your boss doesn't just kill 'em all hisself. Why mark his targets so someone else can pick 'em off?"

"I ain't complaining so long as they pay us in whiskey." The first boy took a long chug from a bottle to prove it.

"Gents, I like to think we're doing a service," Brant said. "We're ridding our good city of imposters, just like the boss says."

I recognized an emotion behind his words. Apparently, so did his boys.

"You going soft, Joe Brant? Gonna pick a sad tune on the gee-tar?" They both howled with laughter.

"Nah," Joe said, smiling. "I just like to believe it's worth something, after losing my folks."

"We all lost our kin. Most weren't worth saving anyhow." More laughter.

"My pa was half Iroquois Indian."

"An Injun?" One of the boys hooted. "Are you gonna scalp us?"

I heard noises and grunts I assumed were caused by Joe knocking them around. I didn't blame him. I wondered why he was bothering to discuss serious subjects with two intoxicated kids. A little voice in the back of my consciousness told me he was really talking to me.

"What about your ma?"

"Pa said she was a genuine high-society lady, with red hair and a temper to match," Joe said. I found this as hard to believe as the boys did. Still, it intrigued me.

"Where is she? Dead?"

"Nope. Had to leave. She told him she'd come back for me."

The seed of an idea occurred to me, and it grew fast. Joe Brant was the most confusing puzzle I'd ever met, and the whole picture was as obscure as ever, but one part cleared up. The facts were too convenient for it to be false.

I wanted to talk to him. I scooted close to a boy who had fallen out of his chair in a drunken stupor. His beer bottle had broken and a shard of glass lay just beyond my reach. I pulled against the ropes until the pain was too much, but I got my prize.

The glass cut through the fibers of the rope. I shook them off, rubbing my sore wrists, then crept along the shadows until I came to the door. Joe still sat on the step, deep in thought as the boys on either side slept. He watched the stars and chewed on an unlit cigar.

I tiptoed up behind him and stayed there, crouched, waiting. I jumped when he spoke.

"I'm just going to tie you back up."

TWENTY-FIVE

I sat beside him. "I could have slit your throat before you knew I was there." I held up the shard of glass as proof.

He smiled as if I was an adorable child. "You don't think I heard you moving back there? I'm trained to hunt people."

"I wouldn't be alive if I didn't know how to hide," I said, wondering why he didn't look at me.

Finally, he did. I could see his face clearly for the first time in the light dawn provided. He didn't really look Indian. But I couldn't escape the recurring and maddening thought that he sure was cute.

He smirked as if he could read my thoughts. I panicked. Could he? I tried to read his. I could barely make out emotions. The ones I barely heard seemed false. A smokescreen. Was that possible?

"Your mom is your boss, isn't she?" I didn't take my eyes off his face, but his reaction revealed nothing.

"She's crazy, you know," I said, watching him for clues.

He continued chewing.

"She has red hair. She wears expensive costumes and throws huge parties while her people starve in the streets. She manipulates

176

and toys with people before she squashes them. Like bugs." I pulled back the gathers of my shirt to show him my scar. This caught his interest and he ran his finger over its edges. I gulped when I felt my face actually flush at the contact.

"Why is your scar so healed? You been here longer than I think?"

"Maybe."

He considered it, but shook his head. "I don't miss anyone. There's something different about you and your boyfriend."

"He's not my boyfriend." I wasn't sure why it was important to me that he realized it.

He raised an eyebrow at my tone. "You got it bad for him."

He didn't wait for a response. He reached into his pocket and retrieved a faded picture.

I studied the face. She was much younger, but I was almost convinced it was Leona.

"Seems weird to carry around a picture of your boss. Unless she's your mom, of course."

He said nothing and stuffed the picture back in his pocket. I pushed my skirts between my legs and hugged my knees to my chest. "It bothers you that she orders you around, but she's never come back like she promised."

He looked at me. "Why do you think she's crazy?"

"Did you hear what I just said about her? It's all true. I know her way better than I wish I did."

For a moment I was pretty sure I felt a burst of envy from his mind, but he immediately veiled it. I wasn't used to people hiding their feelings from me. If he did it on purpose, how did he know he should?

"We're all a little crazy," was all he said.

"Most of us aren't crazy enough to murder friends and take over New York City."

He laughed. "What do you think all these boys in Five Points are trying to do? Everyone in this filthy town wants to be in charge. It's the nature of the New Yorker."

"I don't want to be in charge," I scoffed.

"But you are, aren't you?" He sat up in apparent curiosity. "I'm going to be well-rewarded for disposing of you."

I had no doubt about that.

"Do you know your mom lives in the future? The year 2074?"

"That's quite a story," he said, smiling. His emotions were as even as his expression.

I was bluffing. It was a far-fetched notion based only on the fact that he somehow reminded me of Levi. Some mannerism or facial characteristic. But my polygraph brain picked up a slight spike of emotion he forgot to hide.

Score.

"Her name is Leona," I said quickly. "She prefers we call her *Regal Manager.* You have a brother."

I still wasn't sure. It made sense that Leona would have a son in the past. It would explain some things. But I was assuming she had come back in time at some point before I was even born.

He sniffed and rubbed at his nose. "My pa gave me the picture and a letter, along with some contraption she said she'd use to talk to me someday. He said she left when I was a baby. What makes you think she's from 2074?"

"Think about it, Brant. We're different. We look different, we talk different. Some of us show up here dressed weird and we have tech you've never seen in your time. You have to know we don't belong here."

"So you think it's more of a leap to think people are crazy and dangerous than that they somehow rode in on a spaceship from the future?" He laughed at me.

"Not a spaceship," I scoffed as if he were an ignorant child. "A weighted atomic nucleus in an electromagnetic field, fueled by the energy of a dying star."

"A what-now?" He snorted.

"I'm not the authority," I admitted. "Somehow, our moms stretched this tube made of magnet with super high density. It spins, and when you throw gamma rays at it everything gets pushed back on this arc that connects your world with mine."

He raised an eyebrow. "So having magnets and rays makes a time machine, like in that book that I didn't read because it sounded ridiculous?" He laughed. Again.

"If the star pulls hard enough it thrusts matter back on the deflective arc," I said with a shrug, not at all sure I was explaining it right. If Levi was there he would point out half a dozen errors, no doubt. "Quantum entanglement plays a role, obviously," I said with haughtiness, like he should know the quantum theory well.

"I guess I'll have to take your word for it," he said, shaking his head. "And you say the boss is the crazy one?"

Without another word, he cut the remainder of the ropes tied around my hands and led me through the sea of bodies and up the stairs, where he left me in a room with a bed and fireplace. It was filthy, but it was a gesture.

"If you're good and you stay put, I won't shoot you," he said before he left me alone to overthink the entire conversation we had just exchanged.

"I didn't expect you."

Joe and I were sitting on the floorboards in front of the fireplace in my room. I must have been upgraded to house guest— he even brought me some dinner and awful coffee. I wasn't sure what the food was but I was hungry enough to choke back a few bites.

"What do you mean?" I asked him. I didn't tell him I felt the same way about him.

"You're smarter than any girl I've met, and prettier. Seems a shame to kill you."

"I'd like to see you try."

"You're worried because your boy hasn't come for you yet." He took a long drink from his bottle, looking into the fire instead of at me. I didn't answer, because I was, and I didn't want him to know he was right.

179

He glanced at me. "So my mother is a crazy dictator from future New York City. And my brother is here trying to fight her regime."

I watched him. His eyes seemed alive as they reflected the dancing flames. His wild hair was like a crown, speaking of his position as the general of the street rats. In some ways, I thought I saw glimpses of Levi. In other ways, they couldn't be more different.

I wanted to trust him. It was stupid and risky, and I hated myself for thinking it. But he was sitting by the fire with me while his boys were out carousing. He wasn't the same as them. He was more serious. He was real.

I needed to be slapped. I couldn't even trust Levi, so why did I flirt with trust when it came to Joe? Was he controlling my thoughts? I eyed him suspiciously, sure that was the answer.

"I know what you're thinking," he said. I gave a short laugh, but he ignored me and continued. "You're thinking you should take your chance and kill me. You can't understand why you don't want to. Instead of attacking me, you're hoping I'll do this."

He scooted closer and touched my face. I was about to fight back when I felt it. The sensation, similar to what I felt when Levi was near. But with Levi, the feeling made me feel safe, like I was home. With Joe, it was excitement. Anticipation, like I'd had too much wine and wasn't thinking straight.

I fought against it like it was a drug and I had to pull myself out of its grip, but I couldn't. I was trapped when he caught my gaze. His eyes burned into mine, capturing them like a tractor beam. He wouldn't let go.

"I only wanted to belong," he said softly. "I didn't know I was on the wrong side."

Fight it! I screamed inside myself. I felt overwhelming sympathy, more than was rational. I clawed against the inside of my thick consciousness.

Against every measure of my better judgment, I melted into his arms, like the brainless woman in a bad romance novel. He tilted my face toward his and would have kissed me in the next breath if the door hadn't been kicked open by Levi.

As soon as I looked at Levi and lost the contact with Joe, I was able to shake myself out of the trance. I pushed him away as Levi came at him. Levi grabbed Joe by the collar and hit him in the face so hard I was sure Joe's nose was broken.

But Joe only smiled. He punched Levi in the stomach, knocking him to the ground. I looked around for a weapon as Levi kicked Joe back. Joe stumbled and hit his head on the brick in front of the fireplace.

I thought that would be the end of it, but Joe got back up. "You aren't leaving here alive," he growled at Levi.

In the middle of their standoff, gunfire erupted downstairs.

I ran. I decided it was the only way to take their attention off each other. I ran down the stairs as fast as I could manage in petticoats and boot heels. I glanced back and saw that they were following me.

When I got to the bottom of the stairs, I realized too late I had just walked into the middle of a genuine nineteenth century gun battle.

I'm not sure if it was Levi or Joe, but someone grabbed me and pulled me behind an overturned table. Since I'd never seen anyone in that shack actually eat at a table, I assumed it was there especially for the fights. My suspicion was confirmed by the bullet holes riddling the surface.

Levi threw me a gun. I stared in surprised at the makeshift laser rifle he had created. It had aspects from the future and a few features of the 1874 models. The result worked well. We turned our attention to the fight and tried to decide who to shoot at. The room was a sea of boys unloading their weapons on other boys. Whether they were Dead Rabbits or Bowery Boys or Leslie's Gang, I had no clue. I decided to shoot only if I was defending my life or Levi's.

Or Joe's. Maybe. I considered it as I waited for the bullets to stop whizzing over my head. I knew I shouldn't look at him, but I peeked. As I did, I saw him take a bullet to the chest. It sank in with a loud thud as he grunted and fell back against the wall. Levi looked on in satisfaction, but I panicked.

"Do something!"

Levi thought I was crazy. "Did he put some spell on you? You know this is the guy who kidnapped you and is planning to kill you."

I shook my head. "It's not that simple. He's not exactly what he seems."

He was doubtful. So I used my best card.

"He's your brother."

He narrowed his eyes, pausing to take a shot at a boy who was coming at us. "Can you prove it?"

"No."

He shook his head as he shot a couple more times into the mix.

"But I'm not wrong."

I glanced at Joe. He was sitting against the wall with his eyes closed, his hand covering the spot where blood spilled freely. He would die if Levi didn't prevent it.

Levi felt betrayed. I supposed it would have hurt to find me with any other guy, let alone our enemy, when I'd pushed Levi away for so long. Now I was begging him to save Joe's life. I was asking too much.

He gave one last reproachful stare before he leaned over and put his hand on the oozing chest wound. A strange look passed over Levi's face and his eyes started to close, like he was dizzy or tired. Joe opened his eyes and watched Levi curiously. Finally the hole disappeared as if it were washed away by the eerie blue light from Levi's hand. As soon as he could, Levi let go and fell to the ground next to Joe, groaning. I went to his side.

"Levi?" I felt terror. No one could heal Levi. I pulled him into my arms and willed him to be okay.

At that moment, a figure stepped into the doorway and shot toward the ceiling with a rifle in each hand. Everyone stopped to gawk.

"I'm ashamed of all of you boys."

She was an attractive woman, maybe in her late forties. She had dark hair wound in a loose bun. She wore a fitted and elegant burgundy dress. Her brown eyes had a super smart glint, and they held authority that crackled through the room. Something about her was familiar.

She looked down at me. "Are you coming, then? Help him."

I turned back to Levi and saw he was struggling to stand up, so I put his arm around my neck and we followed her out.

TWENTY-SIX

Imagining my mother without knowing her had caused me to work up a fairly detailed picture in my brain. Meeting someone I'd shamelessly fabricated my entire life was inevitably awkward, because there was no way she could turn out exactly as I had imagined. Especially since I thought she was dead. The dead tend to reside on pedestals, absolved of all the flaws in their character.

I sat next to Levi in the carriage, across from the woman who rescued us. After the wheels were in motion, I realized both of them were watching me and smiling, like they were waiting for me to get a joke.

"What?" I was going to punch Levi in the arm, but he still looked kind of sick so I held back. "Did I miss something?"

"Roxy, remember when we first met? Remember what you said to me?"

"We said a lot of things that night," I shrugged.

"You told me your secret wish. The one that would never come true."

I glared at him, angry he would bring it up in front of a stranger. My wish for my mother to come back to life was childish and it was idiotic of me to tell him that night. I was about to poke him hard in the ribs when I noticed he was smiling at her.

And I got it. I turned around and took a long, hard look at my mother. My mother who was supposed to be dead.

"Roxanne, I've been waiting so long for this," she said with tears in her eyes. I noticed she didn't let them fall, as if she knew they would make me uneasy.

I should have propelled myself across the carriage into her open arms, but I didn't. I could only stare. She reminded me of the younger woman in my picture, and something about her was comforting. I observed her elegance and quiet confidence. Her mind was peaceful and welcoming.

But she was a stranger. Not only that, she was dressed in authentic nineteenth century fashion, like I was watching a historical on the banned internet database Lon hacked into. Wouldn't my mom seem like my mom, even if I hadn't seen her since I was a baby?

I didn't know what to say. Levi nudged me, but I only glared at him. Finally, my mother spoke.

"Morris told me how you kept all the bunker kids safe."

"Morris is here, too?" My heart was racing. He couldn't be. I'd watched him die.

Twice.

"Not anymore," she said, and my hope deflated.

"I found him stabbed to death." Saying the words brought a rush of emotion. "But then I saw him alive in the palace. Leona threw him in the portal."

She watched me with an expression I couldn't discern, even with my ability. I wasn't familiar with her emotions, so I didn't know if her hesitancy stemmed from confusion or being afraid to tell me the truth about Morris.

It's not the time, Roxy. This is your time to get to know your mom. What you always wanted.

I could see how Levi might see it that way. But I wasn't good at pretending something I didn't feel.

I don't need mom advice from you, of all people.

The thought was cruel, and I regretted it. He twisted his mouth and looked out the window.

"I couldn't keep everyone safe," I said to her.

She nodded. "And you feel like losing Morris and Sophie was your fault."

I shrugged, wondering how she knew about Sophie. "I don't know what I could have done to save them. But I failed. So many times I wished you were there."

She watched me thoughtfully, before her gaze passed to Levi. A level of emotion passed between them that I didn't understand. I wanted to ask him, but he stared out the window and refused to answer me, even silently. I didn't blame him.

I turned back to her. "I don't know where to start."

"Let's start at the beginning."

"My beginning?"

"If you like," she said. "Eli and I were so excited when we found out you were on your way. We'd almost given up the thought of having children. Then you were there."

"Eli was my dad?"

She nodded and the sadness that seemed to live just beyond her features woke, distorting them. "He was a good man. I'm sorry you never knew him." She looked up and to the right, as if she was remembering. "He was protective of you. He called you his little star because your name means *bright star of the dawn*. It broke my heart when he died."

She looked out into the darkness.

"You mean when Leona murdered him."

Levi stiffened. *You don't have to sound so glad about it.*

"What would make you think I was glad about my dad being murdered by your crazy mom?"

"Roxanne," my mother said softly. "The past is the past. If you carry its sadness into the future you'll be so weighed down you won't be able to accomplish anything."

"You know you're saying that in 1874."

She smiled. "I've been here so long that it feels more like my time than the future did."

"Don't you want to go home?" I asked the question, but I thought I already knew the answer. Why would she rather be in the miserable future where no one was free and everyone lived in fear? Why not be here in the somewhat peaceful past where she could rescue orphans and live as she chose?

"You do realize your mom has lived through the Civil War," Levi answered my thoughts.

"Stay out of my head," I said, kicking his foot.

My mom watched our exchange but didn't comment on it. "I know I must go back. But this time has left an indelible mark on me, even with its heartaches."

"Is the past true to the history books that Leona won't let anyone read?" I asked.

She considered my question. "In some ways. But it is more like your time than you think. People are not that different no matter what time they live in."

"You arrived in 1858?" Levi asked after a mental calculation.

She nodded. "I arrived on October 5th, in the evening. I had never been through the portal before. Nothing could prepare me for the journey across time, but then, I suppose you both know what I mean."

She leaned forward. "I came through the reservoir when the promenade deck was swarmed with people out for a walk during a great exhibition at the Crystal Palace, which used to stand behind the reservoir.

"A couple managed to pull me out of the water. They couldn't understand how I had come out alive when no one saw me go in. But a greater distraction soon caught their attention. The palace was burning to the ground."

"You just happened to go through the portal and arrive at the moment the Crystal Palace burned?"

She frowned. "I have wrestled with that thought for sixteen years. They never knew what set it off, though accusations were made. I'm sure I somehow caused it. At least no one was killed."

Levi shrugged. "How could you cause it? It's not like the portal spits fire balls."

"I'm not sure," she said. "I have theories, but none are directly linked to physics."

"Speaking of physics, I've been helping Ericsson with the machine. I think we might be on to something," Levi said.

"Good. John and I have been stumped trying to replace the nuclear technology that Leona and I used to power the future portal. What do you think?"

"I think the answer might be in quantum entanglement," he answered.

"Interesting," she said with a nod. "But it's difficult to force things to interact on a quantum level. They either want to go together or they don't."

"Isn't that the truth?" Levi cast a sideways glance at me. "But since we are from the future, it makes sense we would be pulled back if the opportunity was there. 2074 is where we belong."

"You think the gravity of the star would be enough to give the portal a glimpse of us?" Mom asked.

"The laser you've built could be modified to be a sort of lighthouse. Since that tech shouldn't exist here, it might be a beacon to the arc in the portal."

She reached across the small space between her seat and ours and patted his hand on the seat. "Good work, Levi. You remind me of Leona at your age."

His smile was satirical. "History repeats."

"Sometimes," she agreed. "Not always. You are not the sum total of the decisions your mother has made. Remember that. You are free to choose your own path."

He nodded, but I knew he wasn't sure if he believed it.

I wasn't sure if I did, either.

When we got back Levi disappeared. I followed my mom into

the kitchen to find something to eat. I supposed we would have to tackle sixteen years of conversations a mother and daughter should have had.

I was surprised when she sat me down at the table and proceeded to make me my favorite meal of fried chicken and potatoes. I tried not to reveal how giddy I was at the thought of my mom standing there making me a meal. It was a small wonder I had never expected to experience.

"How'd you know my favorite?" I asked when she set the plate in front of me. My mouth was watering as I grabbed the fork.

"Morris. He told me all about you. He loved you so much."

"I loved him," I said. A bite of chicken stuck in my throat. "I miss him."

"I do, too." She filled her plate and sat down across from me.

"I was never clear on how you two knew each other," I said, realizing Morris had never told me. She shook her head. I saw the hesitation before she spoke.

"He always came when I needed him. He always seemed the same age, but he came from the time I was just a little girl, giving me counsel when I needed it, even helping me with the portal. It was as if he groomed me for that responsibility. Just before Leona killed Eli and pushed me into the portal, he came, telling me to send for him when the time came. He gave me a chain with a compass on it. It had a secret button that would alert him."

"This chain?" I reached inside my shirtwaist and pulled out the chain, complete with the compass and the BTDs. "I didn't know it had a button on it."

She smiled and reached for it. Her long fingers gracefully slipped underneath the old brass compass and found the tiny recessed button.

"I never had the chance to see it work. I didn't press it until just before she pushed me in. I only hoped he would find you." She let go of the compass, though she still looked at it in contemplation. "I suspect he had help."

I didn't know what she meant. I was afraid to ask.

"Do you think if I press it, Morris will come?" This seemed like the more important question at the moment. I ran a finger over the tiny red button.

"I don't think he would hear it now," she said with apology.

"Especially not if he's dead," I said quietly. She watched me for a long moment.

"My little falling star." Her voice was far away, musical, like she was reciting a mantra. "My heart tore in half watching my baby girl dangle in that electric mist. And my best friend held you there."

Her words were strange to me, but I didn't interrupt her. I wanted to hear the story. I needed it.

"Just past her, I saw my Eli, so still, in a pool of blood. Dead by the woman who claimed she loved him first.

"How could that happen?"

She sighed. "She was my Lee. We grew up in the same school and the same class. We went through the Blackout and the war together, held each other and sobbed in terror when the bombs destroyed Boston, D.C. and parts of New York.

"She was smart and beautiful, and she had a unique perspective on everything. She was a natural leader. She had poise, and she was so confident." Mom's voice caught and she continued in a whisper. "She was better than me. She could have done so much good."

"When did that change?" I tried to reconcile her version of Leona with the one I knew.

"I don't know. Maybe it was gradual. When I was standing there watching you hover near that line that couldn't be crossed, it seemed like it had only been a moment from the time we were young and inseparable."

Her warm brown eyes sought mine and found them, holding me fast in her gaze. Her fingers reached for a strand of hair near my face, pushing it back in a motherly gesture that made me angry for missing all the moments like this one.

"That was the moment I understood that loving someone can rip your heart to pieces."

"What happened?" My voice was as breathless as hers. She

looked out the window, past the Abingdon garden. To worlds far removed. To the moment in the future, next to a portal, with a baby hanging in the balance.

"I tried to speak calmly, even though I didn't feel it. I wouldn't lose control and watch you fly away to that black beyond of nothingness. I said 'Lee, I understand you are angry. It may be you have the right, though I wish you'd said something sooner. I ask one thing—in the name of friendship.'

"She stared at me as she pushed you closer. I begged her to take me instead. I said there was nothing you could do to hurt her, it was me that should go. So she handed you back to me.

"She said, 'You deserve this, Bell. You took everything from me.' I didn't argue with her. I didn't think it would help. She had a moment of indecision. I wished I could will her to do right, but I saw when her heart turned completely to stone. 'Only one of us can rule,' she told me.

"I wanted to disagree. But I had been elected governor, and it was my job to restore the city and even work on the country, so torn apart by war and disaster. Eli and I would have pursued peace. We would have raised you to do the same." Her voice caught and she reached for my hand. "We lost so much.

"She let me kiss you goodbye. I set you in a chair, pressed the button on the compass, and put it around your neck. You stared at me with your fathomless eyes. Even then, I knew you sensed my pain. I went back to her and put my arms around her. I told her goodbye. My chest ached, and I remember having the odd thought that I was glad for the pain of the branding iron. Her arm hovered in the air after she burned me. I refused to look away. What she did, she would have to do while she looked me in the eyes."

A deep sadness filled the peaceful space where I read her emotions, and I felt tears on my cheeks.

"I've wondered if I should have looked away. Maybe things would be different if I had offered myself—if I'd jumped. Maybe the last light of hope in her went dark when she put her hands on my shoulders and pushed."

TWENTY-SEVEN

Mom went to bed, sending me with a plate of food for Levi. I found him sitting on the front porch.

"What do you know? The prettiest time-traveling, mom-finding rebel leader in the universe came to bring me dinner."

I handed him the plate and fork. His joke mismatched the tone of his mind, and that scared me. Levi was the one I counted on to stay easy-going, even under pressure. If he turned dark, where would that leave us? But I had changed, too. I sighed and sat down next to him, rubbing my face with my hands.

I suppose we have to discuss Joe.

He set the plate down on the step and folded his hands, staring up at the stars. I hadn't meant for him to hear me. I waited for his response.

"I don't even know how to respond. Your make-out partners are your choice." He sighed. "I just don't get it, Roxy. I've thought about kissing you once or twice, and you've made it crystal clear it's not going to happen. What's so special about Brant? Do you only have a thing for guys trying to kill you?"

I heard the hard edge to his voice, and I was overwhelmed by the force of his emotions. "I don't know," I said quietly. "I remember it like someone else was controlling me."

He stared at me, confused, but with a small thread of hope winding through the darker feelings. He wanted to believe me. "It is what it is. You don't owe me an explanation."

"It was just one kiss that didn't even happen. I wasn't throwing my life at his feet."

"I thought those two things were the same to you."

I felt the sting of his words. "This is why I keep telling you to back off. It's too hard when we both have all these emotions. We're so knotted together, I can't tell where I end and you start."

He watched me, then looked down and nodded slowly.

I took a deep breath. "I need to be alone. I can't think. I can't ever be free of other people's minds."

He didn't answer.

I sighed. "Why is it always like this? No matter where we are, 1874 or 2074, people are always the same. Someone always wants to control or destroy everyone else. And we always get stuck in the middle."

He shrugged. "You didn't cause it. It happened in your time and place, and you have a choice."

"The *Daughter of Hope* doesn't get a vote."

"We always have a choice. You choose whether you will put others above yourself. You choose to be safe or to be the hero. It's your decision, and no one can make it for you."

I scoffed. "It doesn't matter. I don't have what it takes. I'm seriously going to get everyone killed."

He breathed a soft laugh and turned toward me. "You should see yourself from my perspective. You're strong and brave. And so kind. The only one that doesn't know it is you."

"You see what you want to see."

He didn't answer. He rested his elbows on his knees and folded his hands. We sat there for a long time, our thoughts tangling around the other's so fiercely I couldn't tell which were his and which were mine. The night grew darker as it wore on to the early hours of the morning.

Life was weird. And amazing. This night had happened almost two hundred years before we were born, and there we were staring at it. Just when I thought I had figured it out—I knew what reality was and what was impossible—everything changed. Perspective adjusted and I realized I was looking at it all wrong.

"That was deep." Levi broke the silence.

"I forgot you were listening."

"It's not hard," he said.

I looked at the outline of his features in the dim light. "Why can we read each other's minds? Why can you heal?"

"I guess time will reveal the truth," he said.

"Levi, if I don't save them, will the bunker kids all die? And all the people here—is it all riding on me?"

He watched me. "I don't know what will happen. But I don't see how evil ever wins in the end. Sometimes it wins a few battles, but when it's said and done, good is always stronger. The worst kind of evil doesn't have a chance. I think if you and I failed, whatever is holding all the atoms together that make up the biggest stars in the sky … I think it's holding us, too. I have to believe it's all for a reason."

"Just so we could be heroes?" I leaned back and stared up at millions of stars.

"Maybe it's not about us. We're just offered the chance to be part of it."

I chewed my lip. "So it would be okay if I did my best and still failed?"

He reached up and brushed my cheek with his thumb, sending the familiar pulse all the way to my toes. "It would be okay, Roxy. You won't destroy the universe by doing your best."

I nodded and felt some relief.

"But I don't think you'll fail. You were born for this. We both were."

Mom and I wanted to make up for lost time, but it was hard with her schedule. She spent so much time in Five Points and she was afraid if she let me come with her Joe would find me. I won the argument when I reminded her I'd been a fugitive and in danger my entire life.

"Things are slowly improving here," she told me as we walked to the mission she'd helped start. "It's still the roughest part of the city, but it was much worse in the sixties. I would find children as young as four wandering the streets barefoot and alone."

"Where were the parents?"

"Some we found dead of alcohol poisoning. The little ones would eventually wander out in search of food. It breaks my heart. Every time I find a lamb lost in this sea of wretches, I see you. Every torn, bleeding little foot I've bandaged was yours."

I didn't know how to answer. I didn't know what it felt like to be a mother, but I had lost people I was responsible for.

"I'm glad you were here for them," I said with a thick voice.

TWENTY-EIGHT

The worst thing about finding myself in a daily routine in a two-hundred year-old summer was knowing it had already been lived through. People had already survived the stifling temperatures. They'd already gotten up too early every morning, ate their meals, did their labor and searched for amusements, and here they were, being forced to do it all over again. And I was stuck doing it with them.

I hated the clothes and the heat. After complaining about it for days, I began tying my weapons belt (some of the weapons I'd salvaged from parts in the attic) around my chemise and doing chores with bare feet and a ponytail. Some of the 1874 folks were offended and arguments were presented to Mom behind closed doors. I could tell Mom thought it was cute, though she officially disapproved. But Lucy took it upon herself to reform me.

"Miss Roxy, why you gotta parade around here in your nightie making everyone look at your under-drawers? Doesn't the future have manners?"

"We don't wear fifty layers of clothes when it's hot," I retorted as I half-heartedly dusted the mantel. It was one of Lucy's nonnegotiable, everyday tasks. Plenty of dust blew through the open windows, and plenty would continue to blow in after I dusted it. I was sure Lucy would not approve of the state of the bunker, where everything was pretty sticky and dusty.

"You have to learn to consider others above yourself. Not everything in this world, here or in the future, is about you, Miss Roxy. Sometimes you do something, not because you agree or understand, but because it makes someone else more comfortable."

Levi spoke from the kitchen table where he was working on drawings. "If we're having a vote, I have to side with Roxy. I don't mind her parading in her nightie."

"You do not get a vote, Mr. Levi," Lucy sassed. She picked up her bucket of water and mop and left the room in a sanctimonious huff.

Levi and I snickered. But as I watched her petite figure stomp up the stairs and heard her mumbling, I started wondering what her story was. She seemed more authentically nineteenth century, and she talked about the future as if she hadn't been there.

I brought it up that night as we cleaned up after dinner.

"You aren't from the future." I took a dish and wiped it dry. Lucy kept her eyes on the dishwater. Her skin glowed, reflecting the evening tones of sunlight. Her hair was pulled into a neat bun as it always was, and her clothes were clean and smooth even after a long day of work.

"That just occurred to you?"

"I didn't really think about it until today."

She scrubbed out a frying pan with bits of beef plastered to the bottom. If I could hop back to 2074, I'd get her a laser food remover. It was a basic kitchen tool in my time.

"My daddy was a freed slave from Georgia. He took Mama out by way of the Underground Railroad during the war. They came to New York City for a new start. He worked hard and set up a freight shipping business down by the docks. I was born, and then my little brother."

I saw her eyes start to swim with tears. She bit her lower lip

197

and took a deep breath. "Mama and the baby died from sickness in the water, before the reservoir was built. Daddy and I kept going even though lots of folks hated us. We got by until that night. That terrible night."

Tears drew lines down her smooth cheeks and she scrubbed harder. I felt dread as her emotions spread around her, red and throbbing like a wound in her soul.

"It was 1863. The war was on, and folks in the city were mad because President Lincoln wanted them to fight for the cause. Most people in New York don't think Negroes should be free. They started protesting the war and the draft, and it got out of control. The whole city went mad for a couple days. Folks were scared to leave their houses. Men and boys paraded around the city, looting and killing. The Colored Orphan Asylum on 44th and 5th was burnt to the ground.

"We were trying to sleep, even though they were running and yelling like a pack of rabid wolves. They screamed about how all the colored should be killed since we started the trouble. I had just fallen asleep when the sound of the door being broken down woke me up. I hid under my bed and heard every word. Every sound."

Lucy stopped her vicious scrubbing and gathered her apron to wipe her cheeks dry. I realized Mom was standing in the doorway, listening. She crossed to Lucy, put an arm around her shoulders and smoothed back her hair in a motherly gesture.

"They dragged her father out of his bed and into the street to beat him," Mom continued the story in Lucy's place. "He was a strong man and stood up even after they tore him to shreds. They put him on a horse, hung a noose around his neck and hanged him from a tree."

Anger boiled inside me. I wanted to take a portal trip to that night and use my knife on every heart of the scum that thought they were better than an honest man trying to make a living and take care of his daughter. I would ask Levi. He'd make it happen. Justice would be served.

Mom's voice interrupted my planning. "It was an awful time.

The army didn't get there for three days. I found Lucy the day after order had been somewhat reestablished. She was living in an old shed on John Ericsson's property. I brought her here to live."

"How old were you?" I spoke in a voice far more calm than I felt.

"Seven."

"She was the same age you would have been if I'd been in the future."

"I hate them!" I slammed my fist on the counter. "I hate people who think they are better than others. They need to pay."

Mom's other arm slipped around my waist and she pulled me close.

Lucy spoke softly. "I don't know if it's the right way to feel, but I don't wish anyone harm. I couldn't keep surviving if I let bitterness take over. You have to rise above the hate. Let the wounds heal."

Mom nodded. "Hard times make us stronger if we let them."

I wanted to argue, but I kept silent.

"Besides, who am I?" Lucy shrugged. "Just a girl. There are more important people. People like you, Miss Roxy."

I grabbed her arm. "You're wrong. You are more of a person than those losers who killed your dad could ever hope to be."

She shrugged. "We all have the potential to be evil. It takes a choice to go against our nature."

"You're the hero, Lucy," I said stubbornly.

She smiled and squeezed my hand. "Somehow I think the hero is probably going to be you, Miss Roxy. You wait and see."

We woke to commotion the next morning. I ran downstairs and found Mom standing in a circle of worried residents talking in low tones.

"What's going on?"

Mom turned to me. "One of the little ones is missing."

"I'm sorry," I said as I endured her worry. Those kids were like her flesh and blood. It seemed like she'd focused all her pent up motherly energy on saving every waif in Old New York.

"It's more complicated," she said. "This is the general's way of sending a message."

"He takes kids?"

"He sees it as returning them to where they are supposed to be. But he does it every time he's about to make a strike." Mom's hand went to her forehead.

"I don't get it. Why would he warn you?"

"He doesn't do things the easy way." Lucy shook her head and crossed her arms over her chest. "He toys. He likes games."

I frowned. I didn't want to think about Joe like that. "So what do you think he'll do next?"

Lucy sighed. "Last time he took one of the orphans? Five marked people in this house were shot in the back alley. Two of them were elderly and one was a teenager."

Mom started worrying about me. Then Levi's thoughts crowded into my mind.

You're marked, Roxy.

I know I'm marked, mudsill. So are half the people in this room.

"I don't get Brant." I was careful not to think anything that would give me away to Levi. "I'm pretty good at sensing people, and he was telling the truth when he told me he didn't want to be on the wrong side. I think I could convince him to turn."

Mom was already shaking her head before I got the words out. "You don't understand. He takes people with this mark." Her fingers went to the scar on my chest. "He marches them out to the alley, puts them on their knees and shoots them in the back of the head. That's not someone who could be convinced to switch sides. He's a killer. Leona would make sure she had someone she could depend on."   •

"I've never been wrong before," I insisted.

"You were wrong about Henry and Tori," Levi said.

"I wasn't wrong about their emotions. Just their motives."

"It could be the same. You have to admit your senses aren't reliable. Even if you could read someone's thoughts word for word, you couldn't know for sure why they were thinking them."

I sighed and stared at him with reproach. It wasn't hard to miss that he was referring to us. "You're just jealous."

The room cleared out in record time after my words. Levi waited until everyone was gone and then gave me an expectant, impatient glance. "I'm jealous?"

"Your brother and I have a connection and you think that means everything changed between us."

He twisted his mouth in irritation and stared at the wall behind me. "Everything *has* changed, and not because of your creepy relationship with your assassin. It's changed, because you don't trust me. That's our problem, Roxy. Don't blame it on me."

"This is stupid. I'm not discussing this with you, and I'm not giving up on him. I can talk him out of it."

"Then you'll end up dead."

"I can handle it."

I felt his anger. I saw it around him as static light, harsh and pulsing.

"Then go ahead and handle it," he said before he turned abruptly and left the room.

TWENTY-NINE

"What's going on between you and Levi?" Mom asked as we hiked around the neighborhood looking for the missing orphan. "Things are strained. I thought you two were close."

I glanced at her. She was beautiful. Her smooth skin and thick hair made her appear ten years younger than she was. The dresses she chose were perfect for her frame, as if she had stepped out of a painting. Even without the benefit of modern cosmetics and procedures, Mom was breathtaking.

How in the world had she given birth to a child as plain and awkward as I was? I wore the dress—well, I wore it when I had to go outside the house—but anyone could tell I belonged in a nondescript gray jacket and black leggings and boots, gripping my knife and hiding in the shadows.

"Roxanne?" She reached for my hand.

I felt her love like a blast of hot air. Love was an unfamiliar emotion. I could sense that Levi felt some version of love for me, but his was confusing and uncontrolled, requiring something of me in return if it would ever be the way it should be. Morris had loved me, purely and simply, but not like a mother. I had never known anything approaching a mother's love, and now to be lavished with it after starving for it, I was overwhelmed.

"Levi and I are close. Or we were. I don't know what's wrong."

She squeezed my hand. I sensed she was waiting for me to say something else, but I didn't. I couldn't. I didn't want to think about Levi anymore. Mom nodded at me, as if she knew I needed space.

We turned down an alley behind Abingdon where the orphans liked to play ball.

"I know you can see into the minds of others," she said slowly, as if she was afraid to bring it up.

"Did you know that before today?"

She bit her lip and looked down the gravel road. Then she nodded.

"How?"

She looked me in the eyes. "Because I gave you the power."

"Gave me the power? How do you give someone the power to read emotions? That's not normal," I said.

She nodded. "Leona and I wanted to protect you and Levi from the forces we were working with. Specifically, we wanted you to be safe from radiation poisoning, so we developed a vaccine."

"A vaccine against radiation?"

"I know, it sounds crazy," she said. "But it's not as complicated as it sounds. We found a way to use radiation itself to turn off the DNA inside your body that tells your cells to respond to radiation by destroying themselves."

I was confused. "How did that give us superpowers?"

"It didn't," she said. "But I think it freed up parts of your brain, the parts that are most uniquely you. Your deepest strength of character was made immune to the laws of physics. We didn't intend for it to happen."

I was speechless.

"For some reason, only one physical law seems to have been broken in each of you. For Levi, I believe his deep care for the safety of others translated into the protective gift of healing." She held up her forefinger and smiled. "He healed a deep cut on my finger when he was very small."

I had never thought about Mom knowing Levi as a child. But he would have been old enough to remember. He was nearly five when she was sent through the portal. I wondered where he had been that day. If he'd seen anything.

"Levi wants to fix me," I said before I could stop myself. "He hates not being able to make something right."

She nodded. "When you were a baby, I didn't know what your ability would be. But I'm not surprised by it. When you were a few months old, I could tell you had a preoccupation with the feelings of others. You were curious when someone was hurt, sad or angry. I think that's what made you a mind-reader."

"I don't read minds. I sense emotions." I didn't tell her I read Levi's mind.

"No, you have the ability to read minds, but you suppress your gift. Levi embraced his. If you developed your ability by practice and concentration, you could hear every thought in anyone's mind."

I was about to argue, even though a part of me knew she was right, but something in the way Mom turned to me in the dim light of the alley caught my attention. My eyes fell to the gold leaf pin she always wore on her shawl. It seemed familiar. And then it occurred to me.

"You were the specter!"

She stared at me in surprise. "You saw me as a specter?"

"You freaked me out! I heard someone calling me and I saw you in the ruins of the public theater. You showed me your scar."

She laughed in disbelief. "I did try to contact you. During thunderstorms, several times I went to Lafayette Street and stood about where you might be and made sure my scar was showing. I wanted you to know you didn't have to be afraid of the portal."

An idea came to me, and I grabbed her hand in excitement. "We can leave a message for the future! Lon will find it, he's super smart. We'll give them a plan for the day we return, and they can be ready on the other side."

"I think it might work," she said, and my eagerness seemed to spread to her features. You are more of a leader than you think, Roxanne."

Levi was energized by the plan. It had been our dilemma, knowing that when we got back we would need to be prepared for battle, because we had to return in the middle of the citadel.

But there were still questions. Where would we leave the message? What would it say? We discussed it at length while Ericsson listened. I argued that Lon should have a stockpile of weapons near the portal. Mom said we'd need medical supplies for those coming through with injuries. Levi thought we should take measures to prevent injuries.

"That's a good point," Mom agreed. "It's rare for anyone to come through without injuries."

I glanced at Levi. I remembered him jumping in after me, without hesitation. He was probably aware of the risks, but he didn't stop to consider them. I was ashamed of the way I had been treating him. Doubting him.

His eyes found mine. I knew it had to be said.

I'm sorry.

I'm sorry, too.

His gaze was so intense I had to look away.

"We'll need weapons and supplies, but having as many people there as possible is our best defense." Levi gave his opinion as he continued to watch me.

"The portal has to be commandeered and everyone needs to be ready to fight. Leona won't hesitate to crush a rebellion, and she will have the definite advantage," I said. "We need to give Lon a detailed schedule."

"The bunker group will have to be willing to risk everything. Do you think they'll be up for it?" Levi asked.

"They can fight," I assured him. "What do you think we did

with all our time hiding in the bunker? Morris made sure we were ready."

"Leona has sent hundreds through," Mom said. "They've spread throughout the country. But everyone is required to return for training every year for a week, to a farm in Upper Manhattan."

Ericsson cleared his throat, holding his lapels. "I believe we can give them a timeline. The machine is all but built, and it seems sound on paper. I think we'll have it ready within the week."

"John, we must be certain," Mom said, touching his sleeve. "There is no room for error."

I felt emotions spark between them and stared hard at her hand on his arm. It wasn't hard to read their feelings for each other. I was disgusted. I caught Levi smiling at me.

That's probably how your mom feels about us.

Ericsson stopped making googly eyes long enough to agree. "Of course you're right, Miss Thorn. We shall give ourselves a month. Much less of a gamble."

She smiled sweetly as he caught her hand and squeezed it. She pulled her hand back when she saw my face. I guess she was afraid I'd seen.

I had. Blech.

"So what should the message say?" Levi pulled a pen and paper from the writing desk in the parlor. I snatched it and started writing.

August 27, 1874

Lon,

We are safe. But we need your help to come home. Sorry I have to ask, but it's the only way.

On September 27, 2074, beginning at midnight, we will return through the portal. We're counting on you to take it over as quietly as you can and have medical supplies and weapons on hand.

I know what I'm asking is risky. Some of you will give your lives. Maybe everyone. But there's no way around this battle, and I know you understand that.

We have what it takes. We have to depend on each other.

Your friend, no matter what,
Roxy Eisen

I set down the pen and stared at the message in doubt. Now that it was on paper, the idea seemed ridiculous. How could I ask it of them? I was sending them to their deaths.

"There's no other way, Roxy." Levi touched my hand. "We can't escape the risks. We have things Leona doesn't."

I knew he meant we had love and community, but emotions were insignificant when I remembered the violent swirl of the portal.

"We conquered the portal. Her greatest power."

I met his eyes. It was true.

"So how do we get into Colonnade Row?" I folded the letter and sealed it with wax.

"You'll have to break in." Ericsson shrugged.

"I think you and Levi should do it," Mom said, though it made her worry. "No one else would know where to hide it."

And so later that afternoon, Levi and I climbed from an omnibus and stood before Colonnade Row once again.

THIRTY

We had been to Lafayette Street before, but this time I was less impressed. It was clear the houses had already fallen into decline, though the structure was intact and in good condition. The cobblestone cul-de-sac was quickly becoming overrun by shops. In the furthest townhouse, a sign hung over the door with the words *The Churchman* in bold print.

"That looks like the best way in." Levi directed me toward the door.

We knocked, but it was abandoned. Windows were boarded up, and some of the panels had been pried off.

Levi felt for his pistol in its holster as he pushed through the open door. It creaked from disuse, opening to reveal bare floors and dusty stairs.

"No one's been here for a while," he said. His voice echoed through the empty rooms.

Though the house was only about twenty-five feet wide, it seemed to go back forever, room after room and floor after floor. We explored the echoing marble halls, seeing forgotten desks and chairs lying on their sides.

It was eerie, having the familiar sense that I was home, but seeing nothing familiar. I felt uncomfortable until we got to the basement. As soon as we stepped down to the last stair and into the expanse of space, untouched and abandoned, I could see the bunker. I could picture the halls and rooms and people that would one day call this place their entire world. I sighed in sudden peace.

"I wish I felt that good about home," Levi said.

"Where should we leave it?" I held up a small safe. We had put the letter inside. I painted the words "FOR LON ONLY." The combination that would open the safe was his birthday.

"This is your room, isn't it?" Levi asked as he stepped into an alcove under the stairs and tapped on the concrete floor. I nodded as I surveyed the familiar brick wall with storage trapdoors.

"We have to put it somewhere where it will stay hidden during the time this place becomes a theater and past the time that the bunker is built, but where it will definitely be found by someone who can give it to Lon."

"My room used to be Morris' when I was a child. If he found it, he'd get it to him." My voice echoed across the naked room.

"Didn't Morris help build the bunker?"

I tried to remember the tangle of the story when our parents "built the ark" to keep us safe. "I think so. He may have designed it."

"Maybe we should cement it into the floor. Morris would find it when he starts construction."

It felt like a longshot and it didn't feel right, but I didn't know what else to do.

He took off his jacket as I went around the perimeter, searching for an alternative that felt better.

Levi watched me. "I need to get supplies, but I want you to be sure first."

I didn't answer him. I ran my fingers along the brick near the height of my eyes. My fingers stumbled on one of the trap doors—the one that was part of my room. It had been painted over so I'd never been able to open it, but in this time it easily fell open by the movement of my hand. The door creaked as it swung toward me. Inside the dark shadow of the closet, I saw a letter.

"Who's it for?" Levi stood behind me as I pulled the letter out. "Us."

He looked down in disbelief. We read the message scrawled on the front.

Levi and Roxy—read this before you do anything.

"Do you know the writing?" he said, stunned. I nodded.

Inside, the message was brief. Levi read it aloud. "L and R, leave the safe in this storage door, as far back as you can push it. Seal the door as best you can. I'll get it to Lon. Morris."

I frowned. If my dead adopted father, who was apparently able to return to life at will, was going to leave me a message, at least he could let me know I was doing a good job or something.

Levi gave me a look and thought along the lines of *at least you had some kind of father* as he picked up the safe and followed the instructions. I grabbed the pencil I knew Levi had in his shirt pocket, being the nerd he was.

"I heard that."

I smoothed out the paper and wrote, saying the words aloud so Levi could hear my message. "Dear Morris. We appreciate the help and all, but at some point are you going to tell me why you keep returning from the dead? Roxy."

Levi smirked. As I was about to refold the letter, he grabbed my arm to stop me.

"Uh, Roxy …"

Before our eyes, Morris' neat script appeared just below mine.

Use your brain and figure it out, Roxy. ☺

"Did he really just ghost smiley-face me?"

Levi took the paper and pen from me and wrote his own message as I read over his shoulder. "Will we ever see you again?"

Of course, Levi asked the right question. There was a long pause, and I started to think the chat was over, but eventually the words shimmered into view.

We'll meet again. When the time is right.

We wrote more, but after a few minutes it was obvious Morris had signed out.

There was an omnibus waiting at the Astor Place intersection. We climbed in, and Levi asked the driver to take us to Abingdon. Hunched over and hidden behind a thick beard and Stetson, the man grunted an assent.

Being alone in the bus on a cool summer night gave Levi aspirations to how we could spend the time. He scooted closer and tentatively touched my fingers with his. My heart sped up at the contact, but I tried to ignore him and his electric sensations.

"You're getting that look." He frowned, disappointed, though he wasn't surprised.

"What look?" I shrugged.

"The look that says you won't go for it."

"For what?" I asked innocently.

He smiled. I knew what.

"Okay, lay it on me. What are your excuses this time?" He leaned back and crossed his arms as if he was going to catch a nap.

The excuses poured from me before I could tell myself to shut up. "There's the most obvious one. It's 1874 and we're on a public street in daylight. There are rules of conduct here."

He made a show of looking around. We were on a shaded street that was off the main roads and quiet. The driver couldn't see us from his position. Levi raised an eyebrow and gave me a victory smile.

"We have unresolved issues. There's the problem of Joe, not to mention ..." I realized I couldn't be flippant about not trusting him. I closed my mouth and stared hard out the window.

"Jefferson Market Library." I pointed. "Leona forgot to empty that one. We stole some great books."

He turned my face back with a finger.

"You don't think it's weird that you believe my murderous brother without a second thought, but you begrudge me conflicted emotions about my mom?"

It *was* weird. Very weird. And yet, for some reason, I wanted to argue. The silence grew thick. I tried to pull away but he caught my hand and wouldn't let go.

"I also have a problem with the fact that he got closer than me. It's not fair."

"So that's what this is about." I sighed.

"I think I have a right to be offended," he said with a sniff. "You owe me."

I scoffed and looked away.

"There's an unwritten rule. If you let one brother get a certain distance from your lips, you have to let the other one get at least that close." His gaze held a dare.

"Nice try." I rolled my eyes even as I felt my cheeks betray me by getting hot.

"I'm serious. It's in Leona's code of proper etiquette."

"I don't follow Leona's code."

"Fine," he said. He inched closer on the seat. "Leona says if one brother almost gets to kiss you, you can't let the other one come near you. It just wouldn't be proper. It's grounds for portaling."

I couldn't help a small laugh. He took that as an invitation to gain another inch.

"Okay, you can get as close as Joe did." I eyed him with challenge. "But no closer. Wouldn't be fair."

He was amused. But then—serious. I gulped, suddenly

terrified. His lips hovered close to mine. It was like we were in the portal again and everything had gone sluggish. Just as I decided I didn't care about anything except kissing Levi for the next two hundred years, he stopped. He drifted, all but touching my lips with his.

My senses came into sharp focus. I wanted him to cover the distance, but I wasn't about to do it myself. So we stayed there, locked in a battle of wills. We forgot to notice the bus had stopped.

"Don't let me interrupt."

The driver stood at the open carriage door, one hand in his pocket and a toothpick in his mouth. He had removed the hat and false beard.

"Brant," Levi said with obvious contempt.

"Howdy," Joe replied, sneering.

I wrestled with my response. Mom's words *marked* and *shot in the head* taunted me. The scar on my chest burned, evidence I was slated for elimination.

And yet, I was happy to see him. He stared at us with a hard look, and I found myself hoping he was jealous.

Levi narrowed his eyes. *I wish to be given a pass from the disgusting place your mind is.*

"I'm not here to kill you." Joe's tone was acerbic.

"Did you kidnap the orphan?" I asked.

He shrugged. "Don't know anything about that. Orphans tend to get lost."

"There is no way I'll let you do anything to her." Levi put his hand on his gun as proof.

"Hey, now," Joe said in a lazy tone. "That any way to treat your big brother?"

Levi pulled the gun out of the holster, which made Joe draw his. Joe backed up a few paces, and Levi jumped down from the bus.

"Hold up, I'm not here to hurt her. I just keep thinking about what Roxy and I talked about. I want to continue the conversation."

Levi shook his head. "Give me one reason not to blow you

away, Brant."

"You didn't kill me before," Joe shrugged. "In fact, it seemed like you were trying awful hard to heal me. You some sort of wizard?"

"I did that for Roxy, not you. For some reason she believes you. The rest of us aren't so sure."

Joe chewed on the toothpick and took a reflective glance down the street. "Maybe I'm a changed man."

"In my experience, people like you don't change," Levi said.

Joe smirked. "You got close to her, little brother. Almost as close as I did."

"Closer." Levi bristled.

"A competition, is it?" Joe chuckled. "I might have to up the stakes."

Levi took a step forward and grabbed his wrist. "Touch her and I will undo your healing," he promised through curled lips. "Painfully."

Joe's eyes turned hard.

"Both of you stop it." I pushed between them. "Joe, why did you kidnap us?"

"I didn't kidnap you," he said as though he was insulted. "You asked for a ride home and I brought you home. See?" He swept a hand toward the Abingdon house. "I just want a minute of the lady's time."

"No way," Levi said, shaking his head.

Levi, you can watch us from the window if it makes you feel better.

And give him the opportunity to shoot you in the head? He won't care if I watch him do it. He probably prefers that.

I sighed.

Joe pointed his toothpick at us. "You two always gawk at each other like that? Kinda spooky, if you ask me."

Levi pressed the pistol into Joe's chest. "I'll be right on the other side of that door. If you try anything, you're dead."

"You're not my dad, Levi. Go inside."

"You heard the lady," Joe said.

After quite a manly stare-down that almost convinced me I was an authentic Victorian damsel, Levi turned to me.

If you get yourself killed I will never forgive you.

THIRTY-ONE

I didn't get myself killed that night. I sat on the step with one brother while the other chafed by the window.

"I know little brother is skeptical, but I want to do what's right," Joe said. "I never meant for killing to be a permanent job."

There was an odd tone in his voice. Since I couldn't see his emotions well, I wasn't sure what it meant. It felt genuine. I pushed back the doubts.

"Glad to hear it."

Didn't everyone deserve another chance?

But as soon as I had the strange thought, another part of me started arguing. At least, I think it was me. There was a chance it was *little brother.*

Does Leona deserve another chance? How about the men that murdered Lucy's father?

I gave Joe a sidelong glance. I had a hard time imagining him taking people in the back alley and shooting them in the head.

"You going to ask your question or just keep staring at me?"

I was afraid he had started reading my thoughts, so I silently told him he shot like a girl to make sure I was alone in my brain. Semi-alone.

"Do you kill marked people? I mean—execute them?"

He didn't answer right away. "I'm not proud of things the boss has convinced me to do. If it helps, I was never the one that pulled the trigger. So I guess you could say she did the killing."

It bothered me that I accepted his reasoning. There was no doubt Leona did horrible things to people. I only had to remember Sophie's lifeless expression to feel the sting of that truth.

"Leona's a monster," I agreed quietly. I wanted to believe he was genuine. He'd be a valuable addition to our army, wouldn't he? Two sons were better than one.

I knew I should ask him to convince me he was going to leave his mom and help us. But every time I started to say it, I stopped.

I would ask. Eventually.

Not having a watch or phone or light, I didn't realize what time it was when I went in. I only knew it was quiet and dark. I crept to the stairs, cringing at the squeaking floorboards. The last thing I needed was to wake Levi and have him know how late I'd talked to Joe.

"Levi knows."

He was stretched out on the settee in a pair of trousers and an untucked shirt. His hands were folded across his chest and his bare feet were crossed and sticking out past the end of the small sofa covered in flowered fabric.

"I didn't tell you to wait up." I wondered if I would have to hear some kind of fatherly lecture.

"You don't have a father to do it," he said in a tight voice as he sat up and looked at me. "And it's two in the morning. Since you were wondering."

"How was I supposed to know what time it was?" I was going to stomp off to bed, but guilt started eating at me. "Does Mom know?"

"I didn't want her to have to worry. But if you keep finding reasons to hang out with an assassin who has you at the top of his list, I'm telling her."

"Joe hasn't done anything to me even though he's had plenty of chances. I'm not helpless; I can defend myself, and you know it. I don't think this is about my safety."

"Right, I forgot. I'm jealous."

He stood up and walked toward me. The tenor of his mood was obvious as he whispered furiously. "I can't help worrying about you, Roxy. You are a prisoner who has been sent through a portal to the past, you are marked to be killed, and you're the freakin' *Daughter of Hope*."

And I'm responsible to keep you alive.

Guilt choked me. "Why? Why do you have to keep me safe? You suddenly show up in my life a year ago. I didn't ask you for anything. You aren't the one trying to kill me, so it's not like it's your fault. No one bestowed on you the sacred honor of protecting my delicate little life. You can stop! Just be my friend. That's all I want."

"I don't want to be your friend."

"Great. So stay out of my life."

He caught my arm as I tried to move toward the stairs. *I want more than friendship.*

I could tell by the heat that crept to his face he hadn't meant for me to hear it. And I was willing to pretend I hadn't.

"Roxanne."

My mother was at the top of the stairs. She came down, waiting until she was close to us before she spoke in a hushed voice that wouldn't wake everyone.

"Levi has a reason to feel responsible for you because someone did ask him to keep you safe. I put that burden on him when he was a young child. I had no choice."

Levi looked at my mom, his arms folded across his chest and his eyebrows turned slightly upward as if he were that frightened little boy again.

"Do you remember that day, Levi?"

He nodded slowly. His mind was a confusing tangle of thoughts as his eyes found mine. "I followed the compass. When my mom was still watching the portal, I picked you up and went to the place the compass showed me, out in the gardens beyond the fountain. We hid in the bushes until Morris came."

"Leona never knew?" I asked.

"As far as I know, she has no idea how you got away." His gaze attached to mine and wouldn't release me. "You didn't make a sound."

Mom came closer and touched his arm. "You weren't even five, Levi, but you were so smart and brave."

I held up my hands. "Wait a minute. So a year ago when you showed up in my life, it was no accident? You didn't just feel sorry for us and bring me a cow?"

He stared at the floor and didn't answer.

"Roxanne, he was hiding under the console in the portal chamber when I went through," Mom said. "When I set you down, I saw him and showed him the compass."

"You just figured out the rest by yourself?" I turned to Levi in disbelief. And, if I was being honest, shame.

"It was risky. But I'd known Levi since he was a baby. I knew he would do anything to protect the ones he loved. And he loved you. His tender heart is his greatest strength." Mom's voice was distant in my ears.

Love doesn't make you weak. Levi's words returned to haunt me. *Love is power.*

He met my gaze. I noticed he was trying to avoid thinking about what Mom had just said about him loving me. When he spoke, his voice was low and raspy. "What else could I do? My mother would have thrown you in the portal. I didn't know everything at that age, but I knew my mom wasn't nice to people. I couldn't let her hurt you after I saw her hurt your mom and dad."

I felt like I was seeing the real Levi hidden under the easy manner and friendly smile. It bothered me. I didn't want to know how much he cared about me. I didn't want to be put in the position of needing him.

He sighed, as if resigned to a familiar fate, and it made me hate myself.

I don't deserve you, Levi.

I left before he could respond.

THIRTY-TWO

I was assaulted by a scrubbing brush the next morning when the grandfather clock in the hall downstairs chimed eight times.

"Get your lazy self out of bed, Miss Roxy. You're sleeping the day away while everyone else does your chores like you're the Queen of the North or something."

I moaned and buried my head under a pillow. "What's the point of getting up just to dust your silly mantel, Lucy?"

"Do the people in the future have servants that do every little thing for them?" she demanded, hands on hips.

I thought of Artie and Henderson. "Kind of. They're brainless, though. I have to yell at them. I hit Artie once, but it didn't make him any smarter."

She threw something else at me, this time heavier. I dodged it while I laughed.

"Don't you be hurting the people that work for you. I won't hear of it, Miss Roxy!"

"Lucy, they really are brainless. They're robots."

"I don't care if they from the moon, you don't treat people like that. It's shameful!"

I laughed again. She held up her broom like she was thinking of hitting me with it.

"Lucy, don't hurt the people that work for you!" I screeched, mimicking her voice. She shook her finger at me, getting ready to go on another tirade, when there was a knock at the door.

"Roxy, get up."

Levi was standing in the door. His tone was serious. I sat up among the blankets.

"What's wrong?"

"Ericsson," he said. "His house was broken into."

"And?" I dreaded the news I could already sense in his frustrated mind.

"The machine has been torn apart."

Lucy pulled my corset strings, and I put on a dress and pinned my hair. Ten minutes later, my mom, Levi and I took the carriage to Ericsson's house on Beach Street.

Ericsson met us at the door as disgruntled as ever. Mom took his arm and tried to calm him. She asked him to show us the damage. He led us up to the roof, murmuring the entire way about the audacity of the intruder and the foolishness of helping our kind from the future. I could see deeper than his words, though. He was concerned. Especially for Mom.

I stole a glance at Levi, whose anger continued to multiply. I considered touching his arm, but after what had happened the night before, I thought it would only make things worse. I might be at the root of all that anger.

He didn't look at me, didn't confirm or deny anything I was thinking.

When we got to the roof, we stopped short in horror. All the brilliant mirrors that rotated in the wind and reflected the sun were smashed into a million shards like glittering stars cast across the floor. The metal frame was twisted beyond recognition.

Mom's breath caught in her throat. "All our work," she

whispered. "All our years of work, John."

The tension was still building in Levi. I was afraid that he might explode from the pressure. His face was red as he bent over and picked up a small mirror that had not been smashed. He threw it as hard as he could against the chimney, causing a cascade of glass to disappear into the rest of the destruction.

I had the jolting thought that I had somehow done this. I'd made Levi into something he wasn't supposed to be. I'd taken calm, happy Levi and wound him as tight as I could, and now I was standing back to watch him self-destruct.

He stared up at the sky, strangely clear and blue. A perfect day for disaster.

"Not everything is about you, Roxy."

"I didn't ask you to read my mind."

"Shouldn't that be my line?" His voice was sharp.

Everyone was quiet for a long time. Finally, Levi looked at me, his usually neat hair falling across his forehead and sweat beading his face. He seemed more in control, but his emotions were still black. "This is what we've been given. We can feel sorry for ourselves or do the next right thing. As a team."

Ericsson and Mom moved to the other side of the roof to start the cleanup and salvage duties.

I gave Levi a small nod of agreement, but the feeling of dread persisted. He watched me for a long time.

He clenched his jaw as if he was attempting to subdue the darkness inside. "We'll figure it out."

The next days were spent trying to fix the machine, though not by me. I was given jobs such as cleaning up glass and hauling things up and down stairs so the three of them could work on the plan to rebuild. In fact, they barely spoke to me, and in my idle time I started wondering what Joe was doing. I felt like some sort of addict, sheepishly daydreaming about my next fix and feeling guilty because the object of my obsessions was likely the one who had destroyed our machine.

I listened to them as they worked. Gradually, despair morphed into a new excitement. They had ideas about how to improve the machine. I was interested, although some of the concepts were new to me. It helped that I could hear Levi's mind. His frantic thoughts churned over and over like a song repeated so many times I knew it by heart.

"This has to be the problem," Ericsson was arguing. "The power the machine gets from the sun is weak in comparison to the magnetic field needed to affect any pull on the portal. How can we know it will be strong enough?"

"It's weak in 1874, but the portal packs a huge punch of power," Levi said. "We have hundreds of people living here that were sent from the future. That's going to make a big difference, especially when we're all standing on top of the reservoir."

"You're saying *we* will become the missing power source," Mom said.

"I realize it's a leap of faith, and we won't know for sure until we are all up there. There are risks, but I think the entanglement concept will work."

The weird idea that connection and belonging could provide a source of power made me think of Levi and me. Our stories had become intertwined. The roots of our families had grown together. Would we snap back together if we were separated?

I couldn't help the other thought that occurred to me. Did Joe and I share a level of entanglement as well?

He gave me another opportunity to find out. Exactly a week from the day we planned to return to 2074, Joe showed up while I was sitting on the front steps at Ericsson's mansion.

"Hey, little girl," he said. "Come with me."

THIRTY-THREE

His emotions swam in the air around him. Anticipation. Dread. Was he nervous?

I should have asked why I was suddenly reading him after he'd been so veiled before. But I liked the feeling of not knowing what to expect. I'd never come across another person I couldn't read. It was exciting.

I didn't want to think about what Mom and Levi would say. I half expected Levi to come stomping out the door with his gun drawn.

"I'm not supposed to go anywhere with you." I leaned back on my arms and looked up at him. He stared down the street with a half-smile, his eyes squinting against the sun.

"You don't strike me as the kind of girl who does what other people tell her to do."

I shrugged.

He smirked as he leaned closer. "So what rules do you have back there in the future?"

I was suspicious about his motives, but words tumbled out of my mouth against all good sense. "The usual. No stealing food. No toddlers on the loose. No bonding with more than one person."

He raised his eyebrows. "What's bonding?"

"You have to understand Leona's little kingdom. She uses marriage to her benefit. She puts together who she wants and denies everyone else permission. There's no freedom to choose, at least not legally. So I don't use the same words. In the bunker, we call two people ... getting together ... *bonding*. And I won't let anyone do it unless they promise to stay with that person and make it work."

"Why?" He seemed amused.

I felt like a child playing the part of a leader as I answered. "Because I don't want to deal with drama. Or babies."

"What's wrong with babies?"

I snorted. "Apparently you've never been around one. They're loud, smelly, messy and require constant attention. If people are having babies, they have to be willing to take care of them as a family."

He watched as several women passed on the sidewalk and tipped his hat. "I suppose. But if you ask me, you and your queen sound alike. Making rules about what other people can and can't feel."

I remembered Levi comparing me to Leona and how mad I was at him. "I do what's best for my people. Leona does what's best for Leona."

"Fair enough," he said, though his tone wasn't exactly yielding. "So you and Levi ... *bonded* at all?"

My first impulse was to hit him. Call him a mudsill. That's what I would have done if Levi brought it up. But as I considered it, I realized Levi hadn't said anything about us lately. Had he changed his mind about me?

It was a good thing if he had, wasn't it?

I gulped back a lump in my throat.

"You're taking your time answering. That says something."

"I'm just wondering how it's your business." I pretended to be fascinated by a line of ants in search of crumbs.

"It is or it's not," he shrugged as if it made no difference to him.

"It's not," I said. "But no, Levi and I haven't bonded."

"Whose decision was that?"

"Mine."

"You don't want to be with Levi when it's dark?" Joe smirked.

"Is that some sort of nineteenth century euphemism?"

"It gets the point across."

I made a face. "Levi's my best friend. I don't want to complicate it."

He watched me. "Sometimes you can complicate it by not bonding."

Was that what had been eating at Levi lately? If so, it irritated me. I was only seventeen, and I had a lot of responsibility. I felt justified in putting off a relationship.

But I was lonely when I imagined a life without Levi.

"Anyway, if little brother hasn't managed to stake any claim, I see no reason why you and I can't take a stroll. I'll show you my favorite part of the city."

"Are you going to kill me?"

I meant it to be funny, sort of, but he didn't smile. He stood up and offered me his arm, pushing down some emotion just out of my reach. Was it fear? I wondered what Joe Brant would be afraid of. Leona?

We heard voices.

"Meet me at Abingdon in an hour," he said, before he disappeared around the corner.

Mom poked her head out the front door. "Roxanne, I'd rather you didn't sit by the street. Joe Brant could be anywhere. Please come inside."

I got up and followed her in without saying a word. But I felt like the worst daughter ever for my ill-advised secret.

Joe and I had been walking without speaking for almost an hour. It had become obvious where he was taking me. He was

227

headed north, toward Central Park.

Central Park in 1874 wasn't quite the jungle it had become in my time, but it was remote enough that if Joe was planning to kill me, he would have plenty of privacy. I sensed a certain conflict in his emotions, though it was vague. The static of his mind kept turning on and off like radio signals going in and out.

I didn't try to get away. I justified it by telling myself if I tried to escape now, I would force him to kill me.

"So we're going to the Park," I said, breaking the copious silence.

He kept moving forward without responding. Since he didn't shoot me for talking, I decided I should keep it up.

"Central Park is called *Forest of the Regal Manager* in my time. I know all the good hiding places, since I've been hiding from her my whole life."

"You go there with Levi?" He was indifferent and seething all in the same breath.

"No. I wander. To feel free, even though I'm not."

He didn't answer, but I sensed anxiety. Maybe whatever fear he felt made it hard for him to shade his emotions.

"She portaled me because I wouldn't conform. She put me in the archives for a week without food and water. Tried to torture the truth out of me. All the while she sat above in her palace pretending to be the loving and all-knowing ruler."

"Stop it," he whispered, red seeping into the space around his head like a drop of blood in water. "She wants justice."

"She wants you to think she wants justice. What she wants is control. She manipulates people and gets what she wants from them."

"People need rules or they destroy each other."

He was right on that point. Since I agreed, I grabbed for the common ground.

"Which is why no one has the right to take a life or harm anyone except to protect someone else. But don't you think Leona has broken that rule? Shouldn't she be accountable for the lives she has taken? For the choices those people were never allowed to make?"

He didn't answer, but his discomfort continued. Sweat beaded on his forehead as the park came into view. Our pace increased as fast as his agitation.

"She never gave you a choice," I said. "You come from two times. She never asked which one you wanted. She left you here to clean up her messes."

He blew air in and out of his nose. He grabbed my arm and started to drag me toward the entrance. His fingers bit into my skin so hard my arm went numb with the pressure. As I stumbled along behind him, my skirt caught on the jagged edge of a hitching post. He jerked me, making it tear.

Still, my idiotic mouth kept spilling words.

"Levi saw the truth. He saw she wanted to kill me. But he chose to help me, even if he died with me. He believes in freedom."

"You don't know what you're talking about," he growled, hauling me off the path, deep into woods where no one else walked. I tried to scuff my boot in the dirt to leave some sort of trail.

When he was satisfied we were alone, he threw me to the ground. I saw the sky as patches of blue painted by mildly swaying trees reaching toward heaven, sheltering us in ironic serenity considering I was about to die.

THIRTY-FOUR

Later I would piece together the puzzle of events from that day and be amazed at what it took to save my life. And what sacrifices were offered.

But in the moment I was held captive under the indecisive barrel of Joe Brant's gun, I only felt fear.

It had always been a worry—what it would be like to die, but when I got to the moment that bordered my death, I was more concerned about the others my death would affect. Mom. Levi. All the bunker kids. The entire future city of New York.

"Here's the thing, Roxy," Joe said, his voice gravelly and frantic. "I like you. I like you more than I should, since I'm supposed to kill you. So I'm giving you a choice. You can choose me. *Bond* with me, and I'll stop working for the boss and help you. Or—" He shrugged and cocked the gun to show me the alternative.

"You can't force someone to love you," I said in frustration. "It has to be a choice or it's just a lie."

"Deal's the same," he said stubbornly. "Levi or me. You pick, and fast. Ten seconds."

My mind scrambled for a solution. His gun would be faster

than my knife, especially since I was sprawled on the ground in stupid skirts and a corset.

It was to be death by an insane amount of clothing. Oddly, it seemed fitting.

Just when I was closing my eyes and cringing for the blast, I heard something. Something silent.

I'm coming! Hold on, Roxy, I'm almost there!

Levi's words flooded my mind. And then I knew what to do.

"Alright, Joe. I pick you. I don't want to die." I held up my hands and stood up.

He narrowed his eyes. "You gotta prove it."

"I will if you put that gun down."

He shook his head. "No way. You prove it first."

I sighed and took a slow step toward him. My fingers reached to touch the thickness of his hair. I thought of Levi's mass of dark curls. My hand traveled the length of his scratchy face and all I saw was the smooth skin of Levi.

I closed my eyes and pressed my mouth to his, pretending it was Levi I was finally kissing, not Joe Brant. I allowed him to take over and only responded as much as I thought it would take to keep him busy and vulnerable when Levi got there.

He heard Levi's steps and pushed me back. His features twisted with rage.

"You little ..." He only had time to point his gun at either Levi or me and pull the trigger.

He chose me.

Pain exploded as the bullet hit my abdomen. I fell back, paralyzed. A fountain of blood pooled around me.

Levi barreled into Joe and they both fell. I heard the sounds of fists and flesh in violent meeting, but all I could see were those treetops, their calm movements responding to the breeze.

I heard them draw their guns in the same second and made a huge effort to see them.

Levi took a deep breath and calmed his emotions. He fired, but Joe dodged and the bullet hit him in the hand that extended the gun, causing the weapon to fly off into the brush. He roared in frustration, but he had no choice without a way to fight back. He dove into the bushes and disappeared.

I felt blood drip from the corner of my mouth and make a trail down my cheek. My body was falling into some sort of pre-death. I couldn't move anything even if I had the strength to try. It was as if I had already started to cross that line; my spirit needed only to be convinced to follow.

Come across. The light beyond the shadows of the trees beckoned, and I was sleepy. But fear forced my shallow breaths to continue. I didn't know what waited on the other side. What if it was worse than this?

Levi spared no time. He dropped his gun and fell beside me, ripping open my dress and quickly removing the corset. He found the hole in my stomach just as everything started to fade. I was floating toward those trees.

"No, you don't! You're staying!" He pressed hard on my stomach, causing blinding pain that made me wish I had died instead. But the unrelenting heat from his hands radiated and a satisfying burn cleansed my body of the injury and harnessed back my spirit.

A moment later, the pain ceased.

My clothes were ripped and soaked with blood. In fact, blood was everywhere. It was caked on my skin, on the ground. Levi was up to his elbows in it. I had never seen so much blood, and the foreboding acrid smell was strong enough to make me feel queasy.

"Whoa," I said.

He fell beside me and pulled me into a tight embrace that almost stole my newly rediscovered breath away.

"You're okay, you're okay," he repeated the words as if he was trying to convince himself it was true. I couldn't say anything, so I just hugged him back and waited for the inevitable moment when he realized this was my fault.

It didn't take long. Annoyance took hold of him and he let me go. "You were kissing him. And not in a friendly way."

"I was stalling for you," I said in exasperation. I stood up and dusted myself off, which did nothing to improve my appearance. "He was the one doing the kissing."

His frown deepened. "Not to mention I told you so. Why in the world did you let him lead you into the middle of Central Park? Sometimes you amaze me with your brilliance and other times I can't believe you'd do something so stupid."

I sulked. There was no way to make him understand why I'd gone. I didn't understand it myself.

"Maybe Joe has his own power," I said, but it only sounded like a weak excuse. I didn't blame him when he scoffed.

When we were back in polite society, it became apparent by the gasps of horror that we could not roam the streets with my dress gaping open and both of us covered in blood. I also noticed Levi's pace was dragging. The healing must have exhausted him. I hailed an omnibus and it stopped next to us.

We climbed aboard. A young man, tall and lanky with a full mustache, looked up in shock.

"Evening, sir," Levi said with a nod. "Levi Koenig. My wife, Roxanne."

He nodded, his eyes wide as he stared at me. "Thomas Connery."

"The editor of the Herald?" Levi asked, and I inwardly cringed. We were rocking the "don't mingle with the locals" rule.

"Sir," he said with a gulp. "May I inquire why you and your wife are covered in blood and her clothing is torn to shreds?"

"Yes, sir, it's actually quite a tale," Levi managed an awkward chuckle while both of us scrambled for an answer. "We were walking through the park—" He looked at me, desperate.

"We visited the zoo," I said. "A tiger escaped from his cage."

Levi made a face at me. I shrugged.

Connery's eyes grew wide. "You don't say? A tiger attacked you? We should go directly to the hospital." He started to lean out the window to signal the driver, but Levi waved his hand to stop him.

"No need, sir, no need. A policeman was able to shoot the animal before it caused any real damage. I know it seems like a great deal of blood, but it's really just the tiger's blood that got all over my wife when the animal tried to attack her and was shot."

I mentally high-fived him. Connery had actually bought the story.

"You know, I have always thought that the zoo should take more precautions with the dangerous animals they keep in that park. I suspected something like this might happen."

We tried to avoid further conversation. I sat close to Levi, who fell asleep. I was unable to tear my gaze away from him, overwhelmed at the thought of how he had saved me.

THIRTY-FIVE

It was a commotion of questions and answers when we returned to Abingdon. Mom nearly had a heart attack when she saw my clothes. As Levi explained what happened, I remembered I had never asked Levi how he knew where I was in the first place. Had he read my mind from across the city? He heard my question and turned to me.

"One of the kids came running. He said Miss Roxy was in trouble and I should follow Broadway up to Central Park. I saw where you tore your dress, and after that I followed your boot prints."

"Who told you?" I was confused. Why would one of the orphans know where I was? Had they heard Joe tell someone?

Levi and I had the same thought at the same time. Foreboding crawled across my skin in the form of goose bumps.

"Where did you meet Brant?" Levi asked with dread.

"Up by the corner," I said, ashamed. "We never went into the house, though."

Levi turned to the group. "What's his name—Oscar? I'd say he's about fourteen and he usually sits on the front porch keeping an eye on things. Has anyone seen him since I went after Roxy?"

An elderly lady who spent all her time in the parlor said he hadn't been home.

"Joe's gang," I said. Mom covered her face with her hands as Ericsson reached for her arm.

Levi ran to the door. I tried to follow, but Mom grabbed my arm. "Please stay. You need to get cleaned up, and I don't think I can bear to let you go again. I thought you were dead."

She had tears in her eyes as she pulled me into her embrace. I didn't tell her I *had* been all but dead a couple hours before.

I let her help me get cleaned up, relieved that my gunshot wound was only a faded scar I could hide as we washed blood until the bowl of water was a deep crimson. I thought several times she would ask me why there was so much, but she didn't. Maybe she knew the story was more than a mother would be able to hear.

Apparently almost dying and being brought back to life made a person super hungry, because I went down to the kitchen and cleared out the bread, cheese and fruit that was sitting on the counter where Lucy must have left it when she got home from the market that morning.

"I wish 1874 had donuts," I said, trying to make Mom smile. It worked.

"You had a sweet tooth even as a baby."

"Levi used to bring me sweets from the citadel." I could almost taste them, and I sighed at the recollection.

I attempted to push away the niggling sense of unease that had been eating at me since I got back, trying to pass it off as the unsteady feeling anyone might have after the day I had experienced. Obviously, I was also worried about Oscar. But I knew what it was when Greer stuck his head into the kitchen.

"Where's Lucy?"

Mom shook her head, peering through the door to the parlor. "I haven't seen her. Maybe she's at the market."

I nodded, feeling a little better. But the unsettled feeling wouldn't leave me. "I'm going to check our room."

"I'll run down to the market and see if she's there," Greer disappeared, concern marring his features. I hadn't missed how much time they had been spending together.

I ran up to our room, but she wasn't there. I checked the other rooms with no luck. When I went back to the kitchen, I was unable to ignore the gnawing doubt. I walked through the parlor and front hall. I retraced my steps to the kitchen. I went to the window, half expecting to see her in the garden pulling weeds. It was empty. I sensed something as I took a closer look.

Back by the small fountain, hidden by bushes, I saw a still form.

"No. No, no, no, no ..." I threw open the door and sprinted across the small lawn and down the stone path.

When I got to her, lying so still in the dirt, I screamed Levi's name. As if I might scream loud enough for him to hear me in his mad dash to Ericsson's. As if he could turn around and come running back in time to save her.

"Miss Roxy," she whispered, patting my hand with great effort. I remembered the sensation of not being able to move. I knew what it meant.

"Lucy, don't you dare," I cried as my mom came rushing behind us.

"Lucy!" she cried in a stricken voice. She ran back to the kitchen for water and bandages, but I knew it was too late.

"Levi," I moaned.

Mom returned quickly and fell to her knees beside us. She realized immediately there was nothing we could do. She choked on a sob as she feebly pressed a cloth against the wound. Lucy didn't seem to notice.

"Miss Roxy, I'm glad you're okay." Her voice was sleepy; her words slurred. "I heard that Joe fella. He was talking on some fancy instrument ..."

Her voice faded and her eyes closed. I thought she had died, but then she opened her eyes again.

"Some woman told him he had to kill you. She said you would

kill him if he didn't. She told him to take you to the park and shoot you in the head." Her breathing faltered. She continued with difficulty. "I sent Oscar ... to find Mr. Levi. When I came back, the general was waiting." Lucy chuckled softly. "At least he told me he was sorry."

"You saved me, Lucy," I said, squeezing her hand as if it would keep her alive until Levi came.

"I'm so glad." Her eyes closed again. "I don't mind dying if you're okay."

Tears came in torrents, falling from my face to hers. She weakly pressed her fingers around mine. "Must be why I didn't die with my family. So I could save you. It's all worth it. I'm ... happy to take your place. You ... got a job to do."

"No, Lucy! I don't want you to die for me! If you hold on, Levi can fix you."

She shook her head slightly, a peaceful expression resting on her beautiful features. "It's my time. I was born for this. Like you were born to set your people free."

She took a ragged breath. The soft, peaceful green of her emotions that surrounded her head became orange, which I associated with urgency. She knew she didn't have much time left.

She looked me straight in the eye. "You gotta love, Roxy. You gotta forgive. It's a power your enemy don't have."

With those words, she went quiet. Seconds later, her hand went limp. The light in her dark eyes and the soft hues of her emotions around her faded.

I sobbed while Mom gathered Lucy into her arms and rocked her back and forth. Her grief mingling with mine was too much, so I ran to my room in a mad rage, overturning furniture and slamming the door behind me before I sank to the floor and cried harder than I ever had in my life—even when Morris died.

Not long after, I heard Levi return. I heard him tell the others that Oscar had also been killed.

Lucy died for nothing.

Why hadn't I thought to check the garden before Levi left? I had run off with the bad guy, forced Levi to rescue me, and then sat and stuffed my face—all while Lucy's life bled out.

What kind of leader did that?

People in 1874 were preoccupied with death, resulting in a few creepy traditions. The practice of laying out the dead in the parlor and taking pictures was more than I was prepared to handle. I stayed in my room so I wouldn't have to walk by her still form. I wouldn't have to hear the quietness of her mind and know she was gone forever.

Mom tried without success to get me to come down. She finally sent Levi just before the funeral and burial. He didn't say anything. He just sat down on the chair in my room, staring at the floor with his hands folded in front of him. But his mind spoke in a gentle tone.

You took a newborn to Washington Park and buried him. All by yourself. You are strong enough to do this.

I didn't answer him. I had done all I could to help the baby, but I sat back and let Lucy's murder happen. I huddled deeper under the blanket that still carried the sweet scent of Lucy's soap.

Levi stood and came to rest his hand on my head. He pushed back the hair that was matted to my tear-stained face.

It's not your fault. Lucy would say it wasn't.

I knew it was.

THIRTY-SIX

The night following the funeral, people came to Abingdon. They crowded into our home and ate the food set out, politely chatting in hushed voices. Most of the visitors were either kind neighbors or portaled people from 2074 who lived their own lives until they were called back. I was sitting at the top of the stairs when the final guest left, hugging my knees to my chest. Levi came up with a plate of food.

"You need to eat."

I shook my head. He sat down next to me and pushed my knees down so he could put the plate on my lap. He wound my fingers around the fork.

"We have to keep up our strength. We have less than a week before we go back into that portal and face whatever will be waiting on the other side. You know what Lucy would say."

Lucy would shake her finger in my face and demand that I eat a plate heaped much higher than what Levi had brought.

I ate as much as I could. Levi sat next to me until I was done, then he took my hand and led me down the stairs to the parlor where everyone had assembled. They chatted, but the sound was a mournful one.

The emotions of all of them pressed down on me like a thick cloud of smoke. My heart physically ached with each beat. My throat was swollen with tears that pleaded for release.

Levi's sympathy did not need words. I wished I could let him hold me. It would be a relief. But it wasn't my way of dealing with pain. I pushed others away, dealt with it alone.

Levi watched me with a helpless expression.

Mom was standing near me. She sounded loud though she spoke softly, just to Levi and me. "It didn't start out like this."

I heard the quiet rustle of her skirts as she crossed to the window. She touched the pane with her black glove.

"Leona was my best friend. I looked up to her." Her voice faltered.

"Why are you telling me this?" I held up my hand for her to stop. I didn't want to know. I didn't want to have any idea that the woman I was going to march into the Crystal Citadel and kill without a single regret—had been a friend.

Someone's pocket watch ticked off the seconds as the quiet returned. Levi's fingers lightly brushed my hand, letting me know he was there. I felt fragile. Why did they have to make me fragile? Didn't they understand what I had to do?

Eventually the group dwindled, and then it was just the three of us. Mom came and sat in front of me and gathered my hands in hers.

"Do you think the truth will make you less effective?"

I nodded, avoiding her eyes.

She squeezed my hands. "Only if you let it. Truth will always build us up and make us strong. But you have to welcome it, Roxanne. You can't fight it. You can't be afraid of it."

I glared into her beautiful hazel eyes. "Fine. Tell me truth."

She began slowly. Softly. "I met Leona when I was six and she was five. She decided we would be best friends, and I had no argument. When the Blackout and then the war came in the next couple years, she was my rock.

"When we graduated from upper school and went to Princeton

together, we vied for top position. We knew more than our profs did, and we didn't mind making them aware of it." She smiled at the memory. "We were so young. Out to rule the world."

I was impressed. Princeton was the only Ivy League school in the country that survived the civil war. It was next to impossible to be accepted.

"When it was discovered that the earth was being pulled out of orbit, the president of the Eastern Divided States came to Princeton and asked a group of us to be part of a directive started by the newly rebuilt UN to save the world. We would be given technical resources that were closely guarded in a facility in New York City. We studied the theories and began to see the solution. If we put a cap on the area where the pull was strongest, we could deflect the influence it had on earth. We could contain the gravity. It was generally what every scientist was thinking, but Leona and I took it further. We made a magnetic tube to place inside the cap. We thought it might help us go inside and study it—actual proof of a black hole, which would be revolutionary to the science world."

Levi and I exchanged glances.

She continued. "We stumbled on the formula early one morning in June of 2050, the same year Eli and I got married. We'd been up all night, and then—there it was, to our disbelief. A way to turn the portal into a tool. Not only would we save the world, we would go down in history as the inventors of time travel."

I looked at Levi again, wondering if he had heard any of this before. He shook his head.

"We were given funding. It didn't take long to prove our theory and set up the portal. Our only dilemma was finding a way back through the time arc."

I was confused. "Leona has been here before. How did she do it?"

Mom shook her head. "She was past the point of sharing secrets with me. I think she took a gamma ray gun with her and used the atomic nucleus to get back."

"Why did she kill my father?"

"Eli was a technician who helped us build the portal. Somewhere in all those long hours and sleepless nights, we fell in love. But Leona had loved him first. Then I was elected Guardian of the Portal. She didn't say much, and I should have made her talk to me. But I was pregnant with you, and she had a toddler of her own. We drifted apart."

"Do you know who my father was?" Levi asked.

"I don't, Levi. I'm sorry. All I know is that when Eli and I decided to get married, she got angry and disappeared. It hadn't been the first time she ran off, so I didn't try to find her. When she came back she was pregnant."

"So she could have gone through the portal again," I said.

"My dad could be any man on the street in this time," Levi said, his tone morose.

Mom sighed. "I don't know. I wish I could give you an answer."

He shrugged. She gave us both a motherly look. "I knew why I had been chosen over Leona, but she didn't get it. She was a genius, but she had these emotional rages. She didn't have a sense of right and wrong, and she didn't have any concept of empathy. I watched her step on everyone that got in way, mowing them down like dandelions that were popping up just to irritate her. At first it was a word here, a fit there. But it escalated. She started manipulating situations to turn people against each other, and lying to get her own way. She wanted to be important and rich. She wanted everyone to love her.

"That's when she turned on me. I was chosen as Director of Science for the Ministry of New York, and she began a strategic plan to discredit me. She spread rumors that I'd cheated on Eli and you weren't his daughter. He didn't believe it, but that just made her more desperate. She hijacked the portal and sent dozens of people through, saying it was my faulty calculations."

Mom wiped the corners of her eyes. "I loved her. Even then. Even when she grabbed my baby girl and tried to throw you in the portal."

"We know the rest," I said, my voice tight.

"It sounds like she was making plans, even as far back as her first trip through the portal." Levi ran his fingers through his hair and leaned forward.

"And Joe was just a means to an end," I added. "Why didn't she just kill them all herself?"

"I think she wanted everyone, even herself, to believe she was a good ruler," Mom said.

"She lives in a fairy tale world," Levi said dully. "She always did. She's the princess and New York is her kingdom." His words were hoarse, as if they'd stuck in his throat. "She's crazy. My mother is crazy."

"Hate and bitterness do strange things to people." Mom patted his knee. "She wasn't always that way."

He wasn't comforted. "I don't even know my father. Maybe I was another means to an end. What a reason to exist."

I hit him hard enough to make him rub his shoulder. "Don't talk like that. You're everything she isn't."

"You were born to care for others," Mom agreed. "I've never doubted that. What would I have done if you weren't there to take care of Roxanne?"

We had to put our emotions on the shelf after that night. There was so much to do and only a few days left.

It was almost time to go home.

THIRTY-SEVEN

I was too busy to get into trouble again. I spent the last week sending messages to the checkpoints throughout the United States. Each checkpoint had a citizen with a converted WristCom kept for emergencies, powered by solar panels disguised as small windows. That person would be responsible to relay the message to everyone in their district. I kept records as the confirmations came in.

The message had been simple: *Return by portal September 27, midnight. If you come, expect to fight. Meet three days early for drills and conditioning.*

One evening, four nights before we left, an older lady, Hannah, stopped me in the parlor and said she had something to show me. I followed her up to the attic, and she showed me several trunks filled with hundreds of uniforms. I felt the material and knew immediately it was not from 1874. I had never seen anything like it in 2074 either.

"Where did you get this?" I asked.

"It was dropped off years ago by Mr. Morris," she said with a smile. "It's from the future. Waterproof, flame-resistant and even somewhat bulletproof. Your mother hopes they will provide some protection in the portal as well."

I stared in surprise at the uniforms. They were silver and white with sturdy blue bindings. If anything could hold up in the portal, I imagined these could. Wherever Morris was, I hoped he knew he was awesome.

Ericsson, Mom, Levi and Greer spent every waking moment of that week rebuilding the portal to the new specifications. I found them nearly finished when I returned from the first day of battle training in Central Park.

"How did training go?"

"Good. The hardest part was staying away from the locals, but I don't think anyone was suspicious. We stayed in the most remote areas and had surveillance watch for intruders. It looks done," I said as I studied the machine.

"I think it will be ready," Mom said as she showed me the new modifications. "But we don't know for sure it will work. Three hundred people will be lined up on the reservoir deck, counting on the portal opening. We need to make sure."

As I was opening my mouth to volunteer, I heard Greer's voice speak behind me.

"I'll test it."

I started to argue with him, but he held up his hand to silence me. "Captain, you can't stop me. No, sir. Not in this. You have the more important job, and I don't envy it." He walked to the machine and touched one of the mirrors, sending it twirling in the sunlight. He was quiet for a moment as rainbows danced across the roof. "Lucy was my heart. We were going to get married someday."

"I didn't know, Greer," Mom said with sympathy. "I'm so sorry."

"How come you didn't tell me?" I crossed my arms. Did my rules mean nothing here?

"You know as well as I do that you're always the last to know, Roxy. Everyone is scared of your reaction." His smile faded as fast as it appeared. "I want to follow Lucy's example. I'll go first and make sure it's safe. It will be my honor."

Mom put a hand on his shoulder. "It's your decision. I wouldn't try to make it for you."

"Everyone tries to make my decisions for me," I mumbled.

Greer swiped the air with his fist. "That's because you don't have good sense, Captain! That Brant put some kind of spell on you, and we gotta protect you. Levi is busy enough; he can't be traipsing around 1874 trying to save you again."

"So I should be the one to test the portal. Then you won't have to worry about me," I said. I didn't want him going through the portal and ending up as Leona's entertainment. He was my responsibility.

His eyes softened and he reached for my shoulders. "Whether Joe has some kind of hold on you or not, you are our leader. You know how to lead an army, and you have the drive to finish what we've started and make us free. I wouldn't be doing my part if I didn't make sure you get back to that citadel in one piece."

I walked to the edge of the roof and leaned on the rail, staring out over the city toward the reservoir.

"We're coming," I said. "Get ready, Leona. Your reign is about to end."

After training the next day I went to Ericsson's to help with the test. Levi wasn't happy about it. He wanted me to stay at Abingdon all evening with the doors locked. But he was outvoted.

"You need someone to assist you when we are at the reservoir, anyway," Ericsson said to Levi.

"I don't need help from someone I'd just have to babysit."

I made a face. Ericsson, Greer and Mom gathered their supplies and left for the reservoir. I followed Levi to the attic roof access.

"You don't have to be a jerk," I said.

"Maybe I wouldn't if I hadn't had to run across Manhattan five days ago and save your life because you don't know how to use your brain."

I couldn't stop the rush of emotion. *I killed them. I'm so stupid. It would be better if I was dead.*

I pushed him and turned away from him as if that would keep him from hearing my thoughts. He sighed, not saying anything for a long time as he adjusted the machine. Finally, he came to me and put his hands firmly on my arms, turning me to face him. He cradled my chin in his palm so I had to look up.

"It would not be better for me if you were dead. If I thought that, I wouldn't have saved you." His words were full of conviction. I felt breathless at the proximity of his face to mine.

"I'm sorry I pushed you."

He shrugged. "History proves I can take your abuse. History and the future, for that matter."

"I'm sorry about Joe, too. I don't know why I believed him."

His features went even softer. "Maybe he does have some kind of power. It would explain some things."

His eyes darted to my mouth before returning to meet my gaze. I felt the old familiar dread, but this time, I thought maybe I was ready to face it.

That was new.

His eyes widened at my thought, and his fingers traveled down my arms and found my hands. His skin radiated warmth, like sitting in front of a roaring fire on a cold day. I reached to touch his face.

He wore suspicion, as if he was afraid I was tricking him and I might suddenly push him off the side of the house.

I hope I don't disappoint you. It was a silly thought, but there was no way to hide it from him. He laughed softly.

If you only knew how unlikely that is.

Unlikely as in—probably won't happen, but still might?

Unlikely as in—it's not going to happen, even if your breath smells and your teeth are rotting out of your head and you sneeze on me right as I lean close. You won't hear me complaining.

Oh.

Even if you turn out to be a vampire and instead of kissing me you drain the life from my body and leave me cold and dead on the floor, it would still be totally worth it.

Good to know.

Then he was in a free-fall and I was ready for him. I forgot everything else. It was just Levi and me in our own universe. And it almost happened. But at the last second the housekeeper opened the door and stepped into the room. We jumped back a good two feet and tried to act like nothing was going on.

"Well!" she huffed. "Just what is all this?"

She set down her pail, her gaze fixed on me, because apparently what we had been doing was my fault. "Young lady, you should know better. Are you trying to ruin your reputation?"

Her words were strangely fitting, and Levi and I both had a hard time holding back our smiles.

She sat down in a chair, folding her hands in her lap. "Someday you'll thank me for this. Consider me your chaperone for the evening."

I'm never going to thank her for this, Levi assured me. *Do you think she could be distracted by a small fire in the kitchen for a half-hour or so?*

I pinched him and made him yelp.

"A lady does not pinch a gentleman," our chaperone reprimanded.

You should try to act like a lady. He raised his eyebrow.

So I kicked him in the shin. Apparently that was just as unladylike.

THIRTY-EIGHT

Miss Propriety Police trailed us up the stairs as we took the final pieces of equipment to the roof. I touched a glass plate fixed on a revolving carousel that turned cheerfully in the breeze. Levi explained what they had done.

"We made the solar cells with copper, wire and salt. They are cased in glass plates for reflection."

"They don't seem like they'd be very powerful," I said. 2074 New York operated almost exclusively on high-powered solar cells made in factories. The tops of every building were lined with them. There were invisible domes of panels over the park. Their efficiency was so strong they could take an hour of sunlight and power a block of the city for a week.

He took the plate he had given me to hold and connected it into place. "They aren't powerful. That's why there are so many. We have them revolving to generate more energy. It's the magnet inside and the magnetic field around the reservoir that we hope will help generate the power to start the portal. The machine is just a connection between the two."

"But you said 2074 will do the work and pull us back."

He nodded. "If quantum entanglement is on our side—and I'm

counting on it—2074 will have no choice but to take us back."

"How can you be so sure?"

"It's a scientific fact. It's been proven. I'm not just taking a stab in the dark and hoping for the best," he said.

It hasn't just been proven by scientists, he said silently, reaching for my hand. *What do you think is always trying to pull us together?*

The housekeeper stood and cleared her throat. Levi let go of my hand.

"So it works by relativity and quantum mechanics," I said.

"All the power charging inside it will be released and hopefully send the portal into a spin fast enough to stretch the wormhole arc."

When the sun began to set, Mrs. Cassidy made us follow her down to the kitchen while she made supper. She was our valiant defender against inappropriate intimacy.

Levi liked the sound of that word. I punched him in the arm when her head was turned. After we ate, we followed her back up the flights of stairs to the observatory.

"Mr. Levi Koenig. Please come in."

Levi's WristCom crackled with the weak signal from the other repaired WristCom he had given Ericsson.

"I'm here. We're ready to go."

"As are we. At precisely ten p.m., according to our synchronized watches, we shall commence."

That meant we had another hour to wait. We chatted about mundane events, maybe in an attempt to pretend we had normal lives. After that, we sat in silence until we heard Mrs. Cassidy's soft snores where she sat on the chair by the steps. Levi pointed to the cup of tea on the floor next to her.

"Ericsson told me to give her a little something in her tea. For her own protection."

After watching the housekeeper for a moment to make sure she was asleep, Levi leaned over and slowly kissed my jaw below my ear. His lips lingered for a few seconds. My face went hot.

"9:45," he said. His voice held anticipation. He stood up and rechecked everything again. The full moon cast an eerie light against the mirrors that still rotated.

"Please stay safe, Greer," I whispered. The minutes passed like days while we stood and waited. Finally the WristCom crackled again.

"We're ready, Mr. Koenig. For better or worse."

"Understood." Levi took a deep breath and flipped the bar that caused the huge cannon to come to life. All the absorbed solar power released into a display of glittering glass turning and clinking in the night air. It vibrated until a blue laser beam began its directive course toward the portal, as if seeking it out on a determined mission.

It became brighter and stronger until the hum was so deafening the house shook.

"The water of the reservoir is whipping up as if something underneath is waking up," Mom's voice came through the WristCom. "There's a swirl starting to dent the water."

"Captain Eisen," Greer said through the static. "Whatever happens, I'm grateful to you. You have done your best and led with your heart, which was big enough to keep us all safe. Even if you don't see it, you're the one that will make us free. I have no doubt."

Levi watched me as I worked to control my emotions. "You be safe, Greer," I said in a strangled voice.

"You too. Take care of each other. "

We heard the displaced roar of water rushing. Levi adjusted the focus of the beam and put the lever as high as it would go to release all the stored power within. It sounded like a thunderstorm through the WristCom, and we could see the faint glow over the reservoir.

"He's gone," Ericsson spoke. "Now we wait for confirmation that he made it back."

Levi reached for my hand, although his mind was so focused I didn't think he did it consciously. I held my breath and waited.

Finally we heard Mom's voice. "He made it! He sent back the brander!"

I laughed out loud and jumped into Levi's arms. He lifted me up and whirled me around as the machine powered down. Mrs. Cassidy sat up groggily and tried to focus her eyes. She gave us a disapproving glare.

"I think it is time for the lady to go home."

I laughed again. "Mrs. Cassidy, I couldn't agree more!"

Knowing the portal worked energized us, coaxing our hope. We spent the final days in deliberate preparation. Ericsson charged the machine while a few portaled men took shifts protecting it.

The older women finished the uniforms. We packed them in the trunks and stored them in a large cart ready to transport them to the reservoir. The night before departure day, Levi and I made several altered laser guns and gathered pistols so we would not enter the portal chamber unarmed. Levi made special pouches from the fabric Morris left so the weapons wouldn't be destroyed in the portal.

"I've never seen fabric like this, even in the future." I felt the crisp silver edging that was like very thin metal, but soft to the touch.

There was a crackling noise. Levi lifted his WristCom. "Ericsson?"

Static popped. As he tried to adjust the settings, I got a very bad feeling in the pit of my stomach.

"Ro-xy ..." A sing-song voice came over the communicator with absolute clarity.

I closed my eyes. Why had I thought he'd leave me alone?

"What do you want, Brant?" Levi said in disgust.

There was a long pause. I could hear him breathing.

"You aren't getting out of here. I know your plan. I've been watching. Did you think I would let any of you leave? Especially you, Roxy."

"You're just going to get yourself killed, Joe." I looked at Levi, convinced that Joe had the power to manipulate emotions, because now that he wasn't in person, I loathed the sound of his voice.

"I hope you remember it's your fault when you're staring down at all your dead friends. And Roxy, before you die, I'm going to make you watch me kill your Levi. He won't be able to fix you up this time. I'm going to make sure your death is slow and painful."

"I'm going to shoot you first," I said.

He laughed, and his voice sounded maniacal. I could see the family resemblance. His voice was musical again when he spoke. Soft and seductive. "You're going to wish you hadn't betrayed me."

Static came over the WristCom, and then it was silent.

"Was he using Ericsson's communicator?" I asked.

Levi shook his head. "I don't think so. It sounded like he cut into the connection with another device. Maybe the one Lucy saw him use. I'll go over and check on Ericsson just to be sure."

I pressed my hand against the ache in my chest. I couldn't escape the worry that I had caused all of it. I fueled Joe's anger and now he was motivated to annihilate us. It wasn't about Leona anymore. He would kill Levi and me in honor of his own vengeance.

"He's not going to kill either of us," Levi said before he left.

At dusk the next evening, Levi and I left the Abingdon house, which was filled to overflowing with portaled people who were gathering from around the city and country to return home. Levi and I took a final walk down Hudson Street to say goodbye to this version of our city where we had spent the last three months. We lingered on the stairs outside until the night sky grew darker and the moon and stars shone brightly. Lights went out in windows as neighbors retired to bed. Before long there was only the sound of the breeze blowing in the trees.

"Full moon," I said. The moon shone so brightly it cast shadows around us. Levi nodded.

"Isn't it weird to think there will be an American flag on that moon someday?" he said softly.

I looked, amazed by the thought. "The flag is still there in our time, even after America has fallen."

He nodded. "I think it proves there's no telling what we can accomplish when people are free."

I considered his thought and the implications to what we were about to do. Goose bumps rose on my arms and legs.

"Time to get dressed," Mom said behind us. I turned around and did a double take. I'd never seen her in anything but beautiful nineteenth century dresses, but now she wore the uniform of the Resistance. How could a person be so lovely and soft, and yet so strong and formidable? In a strange way, she felt more like my mom when I saw her transformed. It was easy to put her in 1874 when she looked the part of Sarah Thorn. Now she looked like Arabella Eisen, the woman who saved the future. It took my breath away.

She held out our uniforms.

After I changed, and I whispered a farewell to Lucy in the dark bedroom I had shared with her, I rejoined the group. We all walked as quietly as we could down 8th Avenue. Our group was joined by others around the city as we moved closer. By the time we reached the solid stone structure, our number had increased by hundreds.

Are all these people from 2074? I directed the silent question to Levi. He shook his head.

I don't think so. Seems like we have a few volunteers from 1874.

We planned to send the strongest fighters first with laser rifles securely bound to their legs. The children would go in the middle with the older women from the Abingdon house who volunteered to get them safely away from the battle. The rest came after, and Mom, Levi and I stood at the end of the long line with other reserved soldiers, ready in case Joe and his army made good on their threat before we reached the portal.

It was eerie to be standing with so many people, all so silent. Even the ones changing into uniforms were quiet. I had told them all during training we must be quiet, but I didn't think it was as much my instruction as the fact that we were all dreading another trip through that portal. Some, like me, had barely survived the first time.

I was the one asking them to return. And then to fight for their lives on the other side. Why did they have confidence in me? Would they still follow me in the chaos that was sure to greet us?

Levi squeezed my hand in reassurance.

At midnight, Mom's WristCom popped, and we heard Ericsson's voice.

"We're ready," he said. I could hear the thickness of his tone even with the static.

"Goodbye, John," Mom said, her voice small and vulnerable. I watched her, captured by the idea that she was just a person like me. She had feelings and doubts and the ability to love. And now she must say goodbye to someone she had loved for many years.

"God speed, Arabella, my dear."

It was the first time I'd heard him use her name. And the first time I'd ever heard his voice waver with emotion.

I touched her arm, feeling her pain and wishing I could take the burden. She smiled through her tears.

"Go ahead."

At her words, spoken into her WristCom, the night sky came alive with a blue beam, and the water began to churn and splash against the sides of the reservoir. A fixed point within the water began to glow with a light that got brighter until the night lit up around us as if it were daytime. I could feel the pull of gravity start to attract us toward the light like a magnet. The air hummed with resonance and electricity.

When the swirl of water was intense enough that a path had formed toward the light, Mom motioned for the first jumpers to go. They did not hesitate, and the group followed ten at a time, carried away into the ethereal light where their bodies appeared to pause motionless in time, caught within gravity and distorted.

When I could tear my eyes away, I looked at Levi. He was watching Mom, who was frowning as she watched each of her people become lost to the swirl.

"It will hold, Mrs. Eisen," he said in a quiet voice. "I'm sure of it. The future wants us back."

She nodded. "I know. I just hope we have enough time."

THIRTY-NINE

Waiting in that line created an odd sensation of mingled terror and anticipation in my stomach. If I didn't think too much about all the possible outcomes of that night, it was almost a relief to be getting on with the task I'd been dreading my whole life. But when I looked at Mom or Levi and thought about how we could all die, I was scared.

"I'm grateful for John's idea to send messengers to all the residents in this area telling them he'd be conducting electricity experiments," Mom said over the roar of the water, watching the light display emanate off the portal.

I watched, unable to see through light to the darkness around us. But I sensed them before anyone else saw them. I strained my ears and heard the faint sound of horses, and knew what it meant.

Joe.

Levi turned to me with a soft expression I'd come to recognize by now. I panicked as the vulnerable emotions overwhelmed me. Now more than any other time, I needed to be strong. I felt the old familiar urge to push him away.

He watched me, knowing my thoughts, but he didn't react. He

You look amazing in that uniform. So confident and strong.
I nodded. *So do you.*

His thoughts burned into my mind.

I don't blame you for having trouble trusting me. But I wish there was more time to convince you that I would never hurt you. I wish I could make up for the pain she caused. I wish you knew how much I care—

"Sorry." He was embarrassed when he saw me listening.

I nervously scanned the streets again. The fear mounted within me as the light in the portal only got brighter the more of us it swallowed. We could be about to die. I looked back at him.

I do know.

His eyes searched mine. I felt Mom take a step with the shuffling line, but we stayed where we were.

I couldn't let him think he'd ever done anything to hurt me.

"Stop taking the blame for the things your mother did. You've never done anything except be my friend, even when I didn't deserve it."

It took me a moment to realize I'd said the words aloud, and they had touched the air of a chilly night two hundred years in the past. As history moved on toward our time, it would remember my confession. Levi Koenig was my friend, and I didn't deserve him.

His warm hands gripped my arms.

Under any other circumstances, I would be patient and wait for the right moment. But I'm not about to die without doing this at least once, Roxy Eisen. His brown eyes smiled. *Whether you like it or not, you're about to be kissed like you've never been kissed before.*

I didn't bother to mention I'd never been kissed before. Besides Joe, that is. The sound of horse hooves grew louder.

Joe is getting closer. And my mother is standing five feet away.

My arguments were weak. He knew it, because he didn't bother to respond. He grabbed my waist on both sides and let magnetism have its way. Every time we touched, every time we didn't fight

259

against the current, the inevitable took over. Like lining all the atoms in a magnet to face the same way. Or like gravity, we were swirling into the vortex without a hope of escaping the power.

When his lips pressed mine for the first time, he stayed there in that first touch for a few moments. If I had thought the pulse he gave me by holding my hand was jolting, I was unprepared for the storm that blew in for our first kiss.

His feelings and mine melded together and attacked every last defense still standing within me. My knees felt feeble. If he hadn't held me up I would have melted into the concrete as he continued to weaken me with kiss after kiss.

"They're crossing Madison," Mom said softly.

Time was almost up.

How can I feel so amazingly alive when I'm probably moments away from a gruesome death?

I didn't mean to think it. His arms tightened around me and he lifted me higher against him, holding me tight. I considered the fact that we must be the first couple in all of history to be able to talk while we made out. He smiled against my mouth.

I don't have tons of experience, Roxy. All I can say is that this has been my favorite thirty seconds ... ever.

Finally, inevitably, but so regrettably, he set me down and pressed a last kiss against my lips. His hands moved to shelter my face. The moment was stained only by the bitterness of knowing the first kiss might very well be the last kiss.

Whatever happens ... He didn't finish the thought. But I understood.

I know.

There was this moment right before everything fell apart, when I got that I was about to die. Time slowed down, and I felt a crazy itch to get on with it. I didn't know what to do with myself in that millisecond before.

I stood at the top of the reservoir and watched Joe and his army

260

dismount and climb the stairs up to the promenade. We had come to the moment I'd been waiting for my whole life. The moment when I discovered the truth. Was I a falling star of freedom, or the coward that ruined everything?

As they rushed at us, there were still fifty or so people waiting to jump in. The blue beam above from the machine was starting to fade and short out. We had a limited supply of power and it was almost used up.

I began to wonder if I would make it through. Because I wasn't going anywhere until every last one of the others were safely, so to speak, inside the portal's grip.

"If I die, I die," I murmured under my breath. Levi and I shared one last glance as we braced for battle and pulled our laser rifles to our shoulders.

There was only one right choice, and it wasn't running ahead of others to jump in first. I couldn't be transient Roxy Eisen, slipping in and out of shadows, staying hidden, always moving. It was time to stand still and face the opposition.

Even if I died protecting my people, we would win. I believed it with everything in me. My side was stronger, because love isn't weak.

Love is power.

The clash of gunfire and laser rifles ripped through the stillness of the night. I pushed forward with all my strength, knocking two boys into the reservoir and catching a third in the chest with a laser blast before he sent a bullet my way. Levi got several hits as well, and we used the momentum we had gained to take out an entire row.

When they pressed in closer on us, we resorted to hand-to-hand combat. I was deep into a zone as I methodically pressed back against the enemy.

But then everything went dark. The light beam was gone and the waters began to calm. I stared at the people about to jump in, and the line of people behind them fighting for their lives.

"No," I breathed, my voice catching in my throat.

Joe's gang didn't wait long to take advantage of the turn of events. They viciously attacked those left, until blood flowed red on the pavement. Red stained the air around us as emotions turned wild with fear and rage.

"No," I said again, louder. This couldn't happen. Someone had to stop this. Someone had to do something.

I saw Joe lunge at Levi, and my desperation reached its apex. I held out my hand, screaming at Joe to stop, screaming at them all to stop, and then something happened I would not have expected in a thousand lifetimes.

On the other side of my hand, stretched toward Levi, Joe fell back as if something had hit him—something that wasn't there. I stared in confusion.

But then I saw that Levi was knocked down, too. What was happening? What was I doing?

"Roxanne!" I heard my mother call, but her voice sounded too far away. I couldn't focus on it. All I could focus on was the line of light I saw extending from my hand.

Roxanne, listen to me.

Mom's voice was louder in my mind. I tried to hear her words as the thoughts of all the people surrounding me crowded into my mind.

Focus the energy on the water.

I started to tell her I couldn't, that I couldn't control it, that it wasn't me, but I couldn't take my attention off the light long enough to form the words in my mind. I felt electricity burning all the way through me, setting every part of my body on fire with energy. With more effort than I'd ever put into anything in my life, I turned toward the reservoir, and closed my eyes, imagining the portal reopened, imagining myself as the link to the wormhole. I began to violently pulse, feeling torn in two, out of control and yet in command of stars.

Steady, baby. You're doing it. You're getting them through.

Mom ... my mind whimpered to her, wanting her to know I was going to break apart. I saw her face in my mind, smiling.

You've got this. Stand strong.

"Everyone's through," Mom called.

"Mom! Levi! Go!" I screamed, pushing down the force inside me. Subduing it, even though it wanted to consume me.

"Not before you!" Her hair blew wild around her face as the spray from the massive swirl of water hit us like a tiny hail of bullets. I moved back, thinking I'd knock her in myself. The closer we got to the vortex, the more hesitant Joe's boys seemed to be about pursuing us.

When I moved to push her in, she sidestepped me. I tried to catch my footing but I was already falling. My body braced for the excruciating force that grabbed me and sucked me in.

"I love you, Roxanne! You've got this!"

Her face faded away. I was powerless to stay and protect her and Levi. Powerless to give them a way home. Before everything in my brain turned to mush, I saw Joe. He pulled his gun on Mom. She was still looking at me. I couldn't warn her.

He pulled the trigger, and she fell.

FORTY

From behind the veil of years that separated us, I heard Levi.

He was all around me. Silent within my consciousness. His voice rang in my head as soon as thoughts returned, telling me to get up. Demanding I fight with every last bit of strength I owned.

It was the moment on which everything in our world and worlds beyond had its hinge. I had no choice but to pick up my weapon and join my people in their battle against the citadel army.

Within the portal, I was locked in a time where seconds were hours, where deepest thoughts came, and questions were considered. All moved unhurried, caught in a static sequence of still images that delayed each attempt to move.

I had obsessed over one thing during long hours of a life spent hiding. Why did Leona hold everyone captive? What was the source of her power? Why did we hide? Why did they all submit?

Was it the portal? We had all feared death by portal. I looked back at the swirl and realized I wasn't afraid of it anymore. Why should I be? I had conquered it. We all had.

Leona was just a person. A person that could be defeated. *Must* be defeated. Not because I was stronger, but because of the people I loved who couldn't be free until she was dethroned.

From the place between two times, I was snatched. The force threw me on the portal chamber floor. As reality came into focus, I remembered Levi and Mom. I looked wildly for them, but the portal had gone quiet. No one else came through.

I fell back to the ground, hopeless. I didn't want to get up and fight the battle if my world no longer held the two most important people in it. I couldn't go on without them.

I felt a hand on my shoulder. Forcing myself to turn, I saw Lon's face.

I was home.

"Got your message," he said in usual Lon style, wearing only a hint of a smile. And then I saw the rest of the chamber.

Hundreds of people, some familiar, some not, packed into the chamber in silent, ready stance. All wore the same uniform. All stood ready with weapons drawn. All eyes were on me.

"These are your people, Roxy, with plenty more surrounding the citadel as we speak. Bunker kids, people from the portal ... and hundreds more who joined the cause three months ago when they watched Leona send you and her own son into the portal on live satellite feed," he said, hoisting his laser rifle higher on his shoulder. "I hacked the security monitor."

I was going to smile until I remembered. "Lon, I lost them. I think my mom is dead. And I don't know where Levi is."

He was confused. I remembered he had no way of knowing my mom had been alive. He didn't respond; he just watched me like I was a curious oddity and he would wait for the real Roxy Eisen to show up and do what she was supposed to do.

I sat on the floor for another long moment. Lon's WristCom beeped and I wondered how he had a WristCom. It wasn't Leona's brand, either. It was sleek and black. Maybe Morris had dropped them off. Everything seemed to come from him.

"We're ready in the garden."

"Ready in the front hall. Waiting for commands," another voice said.

Lon leaned over and snapped another WristCom on me. "Your call, Roxy. No one will move a muscle in this sleeping palace until you give the command."

I glanced back at the portal. Mom and Levi seemed to speak to my mind from across centuries.

You've got this, Roxanne. I love you.

Love is power, Roxy. Get up and fight.

I stood up. And when I saw the belief written on every face, and read their will to fight for our freedom, I was stronger. We would end Leona's reign of terror today. That was something tangible, something more important than my grief.

It was time to fight.

I pressed the button on my com and drew the deepest breath I ever had. "For those who went before. For freedom!"

At my shout, the armies came to life. The portal chamber emptied as they ran, shouting the battle call and spilling into the hallways and every corner of the Crystal Citadel.

By the time security realized what was happening and called in reinforcements, we had already taken a huge advantage with our ambush. I read their fear and felt their shock. And a tiny bit of me wondered why Joe hadn't warned her.

Every one of the lives I took that day stayed with me. I didn't enjoy the task any more than I had the first time I was forced to kill. As I stood across from men and women soldiers and pulled the trigger, I could feel every bit of their horror.

I knew, many times over, exactly how it felt to take a final breath.

We fought the endless reinforcements that continued to arrive until the halls were filled with splattered blood and bodies. Most of the dead I passed were citadel casualties, but a few still forms on the floor wore the blue and silver uniforms of my people. I didn't pass one that didn't catch my eyes or my heart. They all received my silent thanks for their highest sacrifice in the name of our freedom.

Lon told me over the com he had planned covering for every

exit of the citadel complex including the rooftop maglev docking station. Leona could not escape. Before it was over, I would stand face to face with my enemy. And I would have to win.

I heard a report in the early hours of the morning as the fighting raged that someone had found her in her bedroom. Later she was seen in the front hall trying to escape. She kept slipping out of our grasp. No doubt she had Invisibility Wrap and a safe room or two. I wished for Levi, who would know every corner of the palace and where she was likely to go.

Still, part of me wondered how it might play out if Levi was there. I knew he was on my side, but would he go so far as to hand over his mother?

By the time dawn's first light began to peek through the vast windows on the east side of the palace, setting rainbows spinning off the crystal, I stood, spent, in front of the portal doors. Leona had been spotted on the security feed moments before. The exhaustion I felt was a cleansing sort of discomfort. I closed my eyes as the sun touched my face and the warmth of its kiss gave me hope.

The door opened, and I saw a familiar face.

"I hear you have business in here," Greer said, taking in the sight of me in my blood splattered uniform. I smiled in spite of everything, gesturing for him to lead the way as two Posers came toward us to block our way long enough for Leona to get out. I saw her on the monitor, frantically typing in commands on the control panel. We pushed through, and the Posers fell.

I took a key card from a fallen soldier and propped him up to be scanned. The chamber door opened as my resolve went before me, ready for anything. Leona stood next to the portal, her cold eyes watching me as if she were a trapped animal.

"Going somewhere, Leona?" I stepped into the room with my rifle propped against my shoulder.

Not only did I feel it, but I clearly saw fear flash across her features. There was jealousy and hatred, but mostly, there was fear.

I saw how pointless it had been to hide from this confrontation. I'd been stuck in limbo because I thought her power was limitless.

Looking at her now, I saw only a woman who knew she was doomed and desperately wanted to escape being called to account for her actions.

And *she* was afraid of *me*.

Seeing her without the spectacle made me see the woman who had once been my mother's best friend, the woman who hadn't been able to accept second place. I saw the woman who had, for whatever reason, given life to my best friend.

I heard Lon's voice. Not on my WristCom, but on the security feed. "Citizens of New York City, what happens in the portal chamber today will determine our future. Watch your queen dethroned."

A haunting cheer echoed through the palace. My eyes returned to Leona. My fingers traveled to the scar on my chest as I remembered her holding the branding iron over me. Marking me.

"You know how this will end," I said.

Fear multiplied in the space around her like hysterical icy sparks darting into the air. But she stuck out her chin and scoffed.

"You're just a child," she said.

"You stole the freedom of this city. Today, we take it back."

It was what the city craved. The people, hollow with misery, wanted justice. They wanted a new government like the New York of old, the symbol of the American dream. They longed for the freedom to choose.

"I wanted to help them," she said in a fragile tone.

"You really believe that?" I didn't have to ask. I knew from her emotions that she believed she was telling the truth, or at least some form of it. A seed of pity took root within me.

"I've taken care of you all for sixteen years. Just like a mother caring for her children."

I shook my head with a humorless chuckle. "I've seen the way you mother your child. You suck at it."

Anger sparked around her being. She stood up straight. "You're just a girl. His latest conquest. You can never compete with his mother."

She stood taller, and her eyes narrowed into slits. I felt the pain in my head as she focused on me. She'd done the same to me the first time I stood before her.

I took a deep breath and fought the pain. *People can only have as much control over you as you allow*, Morris had always said. I should have remembered that with Joe, too.

"Cut it out, or I shoot now." I maintained possession of my voice even though I had to force back a gasp. I propped the rifle into position and put my finger on the trigger. "Now."

The pain lessened. She leaned back against the console as if the attempt to subdue me had cost her something. I read pain, and saw the flash of it in her eyes.

She gets headaches, I remembered Levi saying.

Then we heard them. Out on the streets, within the halls of the palace, a cry rose loud and strong for quick and final resolution. Justice was demanded for the tyrant who stood cowering in front of me.

I knew exactly how much pressure I could put on the trigger without the laser discharging. I held it there as I prepared myself to do what needed to be done. I would give the people what they wanted.

But a thought occurred to me. Could I take her life, knowing that Mom and Levi had loved her?

My finger slipped away from the trigger. The words were on the tip of my tongue. I was about to order that she be taken into custody and stand trial. Our new government could decide her fate.

I looked up. Levi was standing in the doorway.

He saw my gun pointed at Leona. Before I could tell him my decision, he held out his hand.

"Roxy—"

In the moment it took me to hear him, she took a leap toward the portal.

And disappeared.

I ran to the edge, to the red line that had been painted across the last place I could step and not be swept in, hoping I could grab her back, but she distorted and gravitated into the light. I was going to jump in after her, but Levi grabbed me and pulled me back. The portal chamber was quiet for a long, awkward moment.

Later that day, when the rest of the citadel soldiers had been rounded up and taken to the prison in the archives, while the dead were being cared for, while others celebrated in the streets, I was still sitting by the portal. Levi had gone to help organize the body count and oversee the takeover of the citadel. He returned, surprised to find me still there. More surprised to find me with my head in my arms.

He came and crouched beside me. "Are you okay?"

I was angry he would even ask after everything. He reached to heal several cuts on my arms, but I pulled away. I was glad for the battle wounds. They helped to process the grief.

He held up his hands in apology. Eventually I made myself ask the question.

"Is Mom dead?"

He didn't answer for a moment. I saw his jaw tighten, and his eyes were glassy. "I don't know how she could have survived."

I pushed him. "Why didn't you save her?"

He tried to speak, but the words caught in his throat.

"You could have saved her," I said.

He shook his head. "Joe knew what he was doing. He didn't want me fixing her. He wanted you to feel the worst pain, so he shot her in the head. She died instantly."

I didn't want to believe him. Neither did I want to give up the right to blame him for her death.

"Why didn't you try?"

He reached toward me and I pushed against the floor until my back hit the wall. He stayed where he was, his face twisted in regret.

"I did try," he said in a quiet, sad voice. "She was gone. There was nothing I could do but come back and help you. I've been trying to find you since I woke up here on the floor in front of the portal a few hours ago. Roxy, when I think about how you powered that portal—I don't understand it, but it was still alive a few minutes after you were in it. It was like you were protecting me even from the place between times. I'm … I can't begin to express how amazed I am at what you did."

I had no response. I had no idea how it had happened, and I didn't like thinking about it. I didn't want to consider what I was carrying around with me. What if I'd hurt someone I loved? The image of Levi falling back on the pavement wouldn't leave me.

"What about Joe?" I said in a sullen tone.

"I knocked him over the edge of the reservoir after he shot her. His men weren't as interested in fighting after that. They ran off, and I got through the portal just as it was closing."

I tried to hold on to the anger, but it was taking another form. My shoulders started to shake with sobs I hadn't allowed. He joined me next to the wall and rested his arms on his knees.

Neither of us said another word.

FORTY-ONE

The city celebrated regardless of my grief. For now, it didn't matter that Leona had escaped. To the people who watched her disappear into the portal, she was gone. The streets were full of revelers. Singers from the past age were brought to Times Square and bands began to play the old songs, full of life and rhythm. The people danced. And not Leona's formal dancing. They danced for joy. They danced for freedom.

Levi was worried the partying would turn to violence and looting, especially when they started burning their Leona-approved costumes in huge bonfires in the intersections. It escalated into effigies of Leona being burned at the stake. Levi called a meeting of officials elected before Leona took power sixteen years before. At least the few she hadn't been able to murder.

They decided to put him in charge.

Being Levi, he couldn't understand why they would accept him. He insisted on a vote. When the result was unanimous, he was elected acting governor of New York City, three days after the Battle for the Citadel.

Levi wanted me to be elected, too. They said I was too young and inexperienced to lead a whole city, but he argued that he was as well, and negotiated until they agreed to create a position for me. I knew what he was doing. He thought he could keep me with him. He could sense me pulling in the other direction.

As usual.

I went back to the bunker. I didn't know what else to do. Most of the kids had left, but Lon, Greer and a few others lingered, not ready to let the place go. I sat in my room for a long time and stared at the picture of Mom. Now I could see the missing parts of her face. Now she was the mother I knew and loved. And missed.

My eyes caught the painted-over trap door on the brick wall I had never opened. I noticed the paint had been scraped away from the crevices. I reached up to try the latch, but before I touched it, it opened.

Inside was nothing but a piece of paper. I saw Morris' short message.

See you soon

A week later, Levi came to escort me to the grand ceremony being held in the Crystal Citadel, which was now called the Eisen Freedom Center. I had agreed to go only to tell him what I had decided. For his sake, I even wore a dress and curled my hair.

To soften the blow.

As we climbed the steps, he told me they would be holding a formal election. If he was made permanent governor, he planned to work on uniting New York City with the Eastern Divided States. He would then team together with a delegation interested in seeing the entire country peacefully restored.

"You'll make a great leader," I said softly. "I have faith in you. Just like you always had in me."

He didn't smile. He was worried. His thoughts kept knocking on the door of my brain, pleading with me.

He was going to say more, but the orchestra began to play as we entered the throne room. He straightened his new modernized uniform and turned to walk the purple carpet that led to the elevated area where Leona had sat on her throne. He stood before the masses of people and smiled his honest, beautiful Levi smile.

I winced at a twinge of jealousy. That smile had once belonged just to me. Now I would share him with the city. I was sure there would be plenty of women in his life now. Maybe that was for the best.

"All of us know the price this young woman has paid for our freedom. She devoted her life to this cause and she deserves your honor tonight. May I present Miss Roxanne Eisen, daughter of Eli and Arabella Eisen, who gave their lives in the hope that this day would come."

The applause and shouts that filled every space of the glittering hall shamed me. We were free was because people loved me enough to stay by my side. I was the fearful girl who wore the unlikely face of a leader, and that was all.

I forced my feet to move and walked the path Levi had taken. I stepped up the cool marble stairs and went to stand next to him.

"Tonight I present the first ever Arabella Eisen Freedom Award to her daughter, Roxanne Eisen." He held up the ornate gold medallion threaded with purple and white ribbon. It bore an etching of the compass that led me to safety sixteen years before.

In the arms of Levi.

He saw the tears I fought as he turned to me.

Roxy, you deserve this. I'm so proud of you. Your mom would be, too.

I looked out at the crowd. So many faces. So many souls. All free.

The applause died down eventually and Levi motioned for me to say something. My voice was timid as I began.

"I wouldn't be here if not for community. For friendship. Keep that with you as you start this new chapter. There was a time when I thought love would make me weak. I learned that without love, we'd still be hiding in the shadows, afraid to come out and change our world for the better. Remember my mom, Arabella Eisen, and move on in her memory. It was her dream that you all go free."

They cheered like I'd said something profound.

When the music began to play and the wine began to flow from Leona's fountain of cherubs, I left the palace and returned to the bunker to pack my things.

"Everyone's been asking what happened to her."

Levi was standing in the doorway of my room. Misery hovered around him like a gloomy cloud.

"Who?"

"The prettiest and freest rebel leader in the universe."

His voice was sad. He'd noticed I changed into my old clothes and ponytail, and that I was carrying a large backpack. He didn't want to ask the question, but the words hung in the air between us.

Where are you going?

I couldn't answer. I looked away.

He took a cautious step toward me. "I was told you officially turned down the job."

"I told you I would."

He took another step. "I hoped you might change your mind."

There was an uncomfortable silence.

"It's not for me. You're the one who was born to be king."

"Governor," he corrected with another step. "And it *is* for you. Stars were made to shine all through the night."

"The night's over," I said. "It's dawn. I'm not needed now."

"That's not true." His voice faltered. "How am I supposed to do this without you?"

I shouldn't have, but I met his gaze. When I saw the pain, I could hardly breathe over the pressure that burned in my throat.

But it was only proof I was making the right choice.

"I've never had a day in my life where I've been completely alone," I said, my voice barely above a whisper. "I've spent my life carrying all the burdens of everyone around me. Especially you."

"I'm sorry," he said, as if an apology would make it right.

I shrugged. "It's not your fault. It's just that I've been so tuned to the emotions of others that I hardly know who *I* am."

I didn't tell him that I needed space from him in particular. I didn't want to keep getting closer to him and have my heart twist tighter every time I remembered that he had tried to stop me from bringing Leona to justice. In the moment of his reaction that allowed her to get away, the tiny seed of doubt I thought I had laid to rest had sprung up like a weed.

"She's my mother," he said, and I realized he'd heard every word. "It was just a knee-jerk reaction. Don't let her be the reason, Roxy. Don't give her that power."

"You made your choice, Levi." *And you didn't choose me.*

He breathed an ironic laugh. "You're locking us in this prison just as everyone else is going free."

Maybe it was unreasonable. But it was my only conclusion. I didn't say anything else. I pushed past him and went down the hall to the control room to find Lon. He was at his place by the computer well, as always. Some things stayed the same.

"Goodbye, Lon." I gave a small wave. He smiled and saluted me.

"Goodbye, Roxy. Be safe."

I took one last look around my bunker. There was an apple core on the floor. Artie's mindless smile leered out of the darkness at the end of the hallway. I was overwhelmed by every memory conjured up by the sight of my home.

You won't live here forever, Roxy. Try to hold on to the memories, because there will be days you will miss it, Morris had said not long before he died. How had he known?

I pushed back the heavy steel door and walked through the corridor to the street. Brisk wind blew, beckoning me away, into the next part of my story. Future instead of history. And I wasn't afraid of going forward anymore.

"Roxy," Levi was standing behind me, his warmth trying to reach around me and hold me there. I felt his breath on my ear. "Don't go."

It was a battle, but one I was determined to win. "You'll always be with me. But I can't stay. I'm free, remember? Free to choose."

He turned me around and pulled me into his embrace. Before I could think to stop him, he was kissing me. He was insistent, as if he was making a point.

I held him. I kissed him back until we were both gasping with hearts racing. It seemed out of place, like a moment reserved for the couple ready to seal their bond. Yet, as the moment became history, I pulled away, and he let me go.

It took every bit of strength to turn away. As I moved, I refused to look back. I headed for the newly reopened bridge, my brain severing every other connection. It was the only way I would keep walking.

That bridge would take me to the rest of my life. Wherever it might be.

PARADOX

ONE

Somewhere in the back of my subconscious I was aware I had been standing on the street in the dark staring into nothingness that used to contain the fading form of my heart. But I was unable to convince my body to come out of its shock, for to move would be to admit that life must go on without Roxy. And if I dared to move now, I would only follow her. Beg her to stay or go with her wherever she was headed.

But why shouldn't I follow her? New York would be okay. They could rebuild without the son of the dictator who had ruined everything in the first place. My place was with Roxy. I only needed to convince my feet to move.

Eventually, when the air had gone cold and lightning lit up the night sky, a strong hand gripped my shoulder. It gave me the momentum I needed to move, and I turned.

"You're going to have to make up your mind about whether you're dead or not," I said, though my voice lacked the humor and came out only sounding harsh.

"You can't go with her," Morris said quietly. "There is work to be done."

I nodded, but it was a gloomy gesture.

"At least you know now." His voice remained stubbornly cheerful, though I saw in his expression he felt my sorrow, and the hand on my shoulder squeezed with understanding.

"Know what? That life sucks without her?"

He smiled. "That you love her."

I didn't have any response to that. But as his words sank into my consciousness, I realized he was right. Until the moment I saw her intentionally rip my heart out of my chest and walk away from me with no promise of return, I hadn't been sure.

I knew I liked her. I knew I enjoyed looking at her beauty, watching the graceful way she commanded attention without meaning to. I saw her strength of character and principles and the fierce loyalty that made her everything a *Daughter of Hope* should be.

But until I saw her walk away, I didn't know I loved her. Not in the purest sense of the word, the only sense that really mattered when a life was said and done, when all a person has left is the ones who will stick by him no matter what because they are family.

Now I knew I loved her like that.

"I love her." I breathed the words, testing them on my tongue like a new, exotic food. I rolled the idea around in my brain, and even though my world was dark and lonely, even though the pain was aching and cold and deep, I knew joy.

Because I loved her.

I would need that assurance in the days that followed.

To Be Continued ...

ACKNOWLEDGEMENTS

Thank you to every science fiction book, television show or movie that caught my interest, ignited my imagination and fueled my passion to write. Here's to the greats that make us think and surprise us into changing our perspective, and sometimes even our minds.

Thanks to my editor, Tanya Dennis (tanyadennisbooks.com). You always know what I meant to say.

Thanks to all my great test readers. You bolstered my confidence by reading even the rough draft version of *Transient* with enthusiasm. I appreciate every one of you and I value your opinions, and you will be able to see the parts that are better because of the suggestions you made.

Thanks to you, my readers, for taking a chance on *Transient*, and being willing to join me on this journey.

ABOUT THE AUTHOR

M.K. Parsons is an asker of questions, thinker of thoughts, and a fangirl at heart. Her word-loving obsession developed early and she has always been a storyteller.

Besides her husband and children, she is also in love with questions disguised as books, goose bump-inspiring music, and of course, the crafting of worlds and far off people and places, where the only limit is the size of the imagination.

Connect with her online!

facebook.com/authormkparsons
twitter.com/MK_Parsons
pinterest.com/QuirkyAuthor/ (Check out the *Transient* board!)

Keeping in mind this is an Indie project which is dependent on word of mouth, please leave your review on Amazon for *Transient* today and spread the word!

For more info, please go to mkparsons.com.

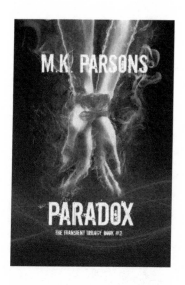

COMING FEBRUARY 2016

Levi Koenig is responsible for righting the wrongs inflicted on New York City by his mother's reign of terror. But his heart is far away, wherever Roxy is.

When he receives a threatening message from Joe, Levi goes on a risky mission to find Roxy. Meanwhile, Leona and Joe use his absence to gain access to the portal—and the delicate balance of history surrounding the birth of America.

Roxy and Levi follow and witness firsthand the beginning of their nation. With George Washington and Nathan Hale to assist, Levi finds his motivation for leading the country back to where it once was. But can Leona and Joe be stopped, and will Levi have the courage to deal justice to his family members? Can he see Roxy through the mysterious illness that seems to be weakening her by the day? Will Levi be prepared for the surprises in store when worlds touch in the ultimate paradox?

Made in the USA
San Bernardino, CA
26 January 2019